THRONE OF A THOUSAND LIES

RACHEL HIGGINSON

Copyright@ Rachel Higginson 2022

This publication is protected under the US Copyright Act of 1976 and all other applicable international, federal, state and local laws, and all rights are reserved, including resale rights: you are not allowed to give, copy, scan, distribute or sell this book to anyone else.

Any trademarks, service marks, product names or named features are assumed to be the property of their respective owners, and are used only for reference. There is no implied endorsement if we use one of these terms.

Any people or places are strictly fictional and not based on anything else, fictional or non-fictional.

This ebook is licensed for your personal enjoyment only. This ebook may not be re-sold or given away to other people. If you would like to share this book with another person, please purchase an additional copy for each recipient. If you're reading this book and did not purchase it, or it was not purchased for your use only, then please return and purchase your own copy. Thank you for respecting the hard work of this author.

Editing by Marion from Making Manuscripts, Jenny from Editing 4 Indies, and Karen from The Proof is in the Reading
Cover Design by Zach Higginson.

Also by Rachel Higginson

Other Young Adult series by Rachel Higginson

The Star-Crossed Series

The Siren Series

The Starbright Series

Love and Decay

Love and Decay: Revolution

FOLLOW RACHEL

Keep up with Rachel on her Newsletter

Connect with Rachel on her Facebook Page

Follow Rachel on Instagram

To my darling Stella

CHAPTER ONE

Moonlight streamed through the paned windows, illuminating the hallway brighter than I would have liked. Although there were still plenty of shadows to hide in, the moon seemed to taunt me. Glowing as milky white as possible just to spite my efforts.

No matter. The moon could try to ruin my plan all it wanted. I would not be unnerved. My focus was too narrow. My intent too decided. Besides, what was a little light to someone like me?

Candled sconces were placed evenly down the corridor, but this deep into the midnight hours, only every other one was lit. Giving plenty of space to slink along walls, melt into shadowy corners, and avoid detection.

Oliver was nothing but a dark cloak, camouflaged and silent, as he played the lookout ahead. I watched him while I stood still as stone, waiting for the signal. A swoop of his black cape, a flash of pale skin, and then nothing as he pressed back into soundless discretion.

Beyond him, a pair of guards tromped through the quiet hallways, sluggishly watching for all manner of evil. Neither of them would have suspected the biggest threat they faced tonight was Oliver and me. And why would they? I was their future queen. Oliver a failed monk.

Their low rumble of voices drifted toward me, but it was too mumbled to understand. A snippet of something about their suppers. A wistful sigh as the minutes ticked toward morning. And a sarcastic quip about the ghosts in residence.

Their good-humored conversation continued as they walked on, their voices and footsteps growing quieter as they got farther away. When all was silent again, Oliver still didn't move. I counted to five. I practiced stealthy breathing. I closed my eyes and imagined I wasn't just pressed against a stone wall but actually a part of it. It was cold against my back and through my own dark cloak. Pressing my palms flat against its surface, I let the coolness of it seep through me. I was surprised it still smelled faintly of dirt and the outdoors—even though it had been a wall much longer than it had been in the earth.

Or maybe that was wrong.

Maybe it had been here at the beginning of this world. A hillside or mountain. A foundational stone that was once happy to let the sun shine on it and the moon bathe it in creamy light. At some point, it had been moved here and formed into more than what it was. Now it was a decorated wall in a decorated castle. It was no longer nature, but building. No longer free, but resigned to servitude.

Even if it was for a good cause.

I couldn't help the small squeaky sigh that pushed from my lips. Was I still talking about the stone wall? Or was this some twisted version of my own troubles?

I had never been a foundational piece of stone for the earth to build and breed upon. But I had once lived a much simpler, much freer lifestyle. And through only fault of my own, I'd traded that carefree life for one trapped inside a gilded cage, destined to serve a kingdom for the rest of my royal life.

I shouldn't complain.

What was there to complain about?

I'd survived. I'd survived my childhood hidden in a tucked-away monastery. I'd survived a lengthy journey across the Nine Kingdoms with the crown secreted away in my pouch. I'd come face-to-face with the Rebel Army, somehow made allies with them, and discovered Crown Prince Taelon Westnovian's alternate identity. And I'd conquered the trial my uncle had held when I'd shown up on his doorstep uninvited. Conandra had tried to fell me, yet I prevailed. And now I was on my way to being queen. The very thing I'd wanted so badly just months ago. So why did my new, safe, stable position in the royal house feel so ... flat?

Revenge still dangled like an out-of-reach ripe fruit. Revenge for my family's murders. Revenge for the life that was snatched from me. Revenge for a lifetime of heartache and trouble.

And while I reached and stretched to touch that forbidden apple, everything else felt like ... a waste of time.

I did not expect to be so bloodthirsty. But here we were. Six months into my uncle's care, and I was merely dressed in pretty gowns, pranced around for visiting monarchs to ogle, and asked to sit still and shut up until it was my turn on the throne.

And even then, I wasn't convinced anyone would listen to what I had to say. Back at the Temple, I had been constantly stretched—both mentally and physically. Father Garius had been a relentless taskmaster when it came to my studies and training. And while there weren't many to converse with, my voice was still respected, still admired. Whether it was questions for the Brotherhood who answered in their own silent way or haggling with the village vendors who were determined to get the most coin for their wares, I felt as though my words were listened to when I spoke.

Now I was bored to tears and chomping at the bit to hold real, tangible power.

Which led us here. To this hallway.

Oliver's quick movement ahead pulled my attention back to the present. He glanced back just once, his face a flash of determination, his jerking jaw a signal for me to follow.

Real or imagined, spirits from the past followed my stealthy movements as I slinked down the corridor. This had been my family's wing once upon a time. Back when I had a family. Back when I was a child. My uncle Tyrn had renovated these rooms years ago, but since my return, he'd discouraged me from visiting them.

I had protested more than once, but there was a strong belief throughout the castle that this wing was haunted. Fascinated by the ghosts of my mother and father lingering in these rooms, I was anxious to explore. But the general tone of the haunting was malicious. Or so says the maids and guards. And so Tyrn had been reluctant to let me loose in a part of the castle where the royal bloodline could end, thanks to an incorporeal attacker.

After months of asking politely, I had decided last week to take matters into my own hands and enlisted Oliver to help execute the mission. We'd spent several days slyly observing the night watches and the comings and goings of the guards. Then we waited for an opportunity to escape my detail unnoticed.

It wasn't that I was under lock and key, at least not since the trial, but there were men to watch after me, make sure I wasn't attacked or kidnapped, and report all my comings and goings back to my uncle, etc.

So Oliver and I had been careful, bided our time, and waited until we had a decent idea of how the royal guard operated. If we were honest, the guard was not so invincible that I felt entirely safe after our assessment. But a lapse in their oversight and procedure would be a nice piece of knowledge to keep tucked away for a rainy day. One never knew when they would need to sneak in or out of a walled fortress.

But now there was to be a ball. For me. A welcome home of sorts where Tyrn invited nearly the whole of the Nine Kingdoms. Tomorrow the halls would be full of royals and their servants, dignitaries, ambassadors, politicians, and more servants. The quiet castle would burst to life with guests and ball preparations, decorations, and gossiping maids.

The same monarchs who tried to disprove my identity and throw me in a dungeon for the rest of my life were now about to parade their eligible sons in front of me as prospective husbands. The same royals who sneered at my claim over the Crown would bow and nod and do their best to catch my attention. And my good opinion.

No doubt they hated me as much today as they did six months ago, but now my position had power. Power they were desperate to grab. I was no longer the orphaned vagabond begging for their attention. Now I was heir to the Crown of Nine. And I would be their queen whether they liked it or not.

This wing especially would be packed with people. I was sure it had been many times in my absence over the past nine years. I could wait until the festivities were over and things settled once again. But . . . to be frank, I was itching for something purposeful to occupy my time. And my mind. And more than that, the need to walk where my parents once walked, to sit where my brothers once sat, and to be where my family had once been was so powerful that waiting felt like torture. So Oliver and I had decided this afternoon to sneak out of our rooms, slip our guards' watch, and snoop to our hearts' content.

I made a quiet click with my teeth and cheek, and he looked back. My head tilted toward the door I stood next to. Oliver made a great lookout, but he had no idea where he was going.

He moved back toward me while I pulled a key from my pocket. As it turned out, princess gowns didn't inherently come with pockets. But I was used to simpler styles and aprons with deep pockets from my years at the Temple. Early in my residence here, I had asked my maid to speak with the dressmaker so she could start stitching interior pockets into the sides of all dresses. The dressmaker, an elusive and longtime legend among castle residents, had been properly scandalized, but it had been well worth it. It was hard to deny the benefits of hidden pouches in every outfit. But especially in situations such as this one.

Sliding the large master key we'd pilfered from the

groundskeeping office two days ago soundlessly into the lock, I prayed no one was nearby to hear the clunk of the mechanism. When the door was unlocked and the guards successfully still at bay, we slipped inside the rooms that had been the royal family suite once upon a time.

I wasn't sure what I expected to find on the other side of the door, but the oppressive silence was almost deafening. The extreme stillness seemed to scream in my ear and steal the breath straight from my lungs.

The room was opulent, as I'd expected. It was dark of course, but the faint light from the corridor illuminated just enough for me to make out the fine furniture and expensive details.

The sitting room greeted us, perfectly styled with silk-covered chairs around a fireplace large enough that Oliver and I could step inside without touching either of the walls. A table on the other side of the room was adorned with fresh flowers and a lace covering. The maids had been here today to tidy up. The tapestry hanging on the wall boasted the Elysian kingdom, our Diamond Mountains, and rich fields. Whoever had woven it had been a master of their craft.

None of it was familiar. None of it belonged to my family.

I wasn't sure what to expect. The last time I'd been in this room, my family's bent and broken bodies had littered this now immaculate space. The floor had been coated in blood, the soles of my bare feet thick with it. My mind couldn't convince my heart that this was the same room.

Except the stillness felt oddly familiar. Something was behind it. Something . . . that tugged at the corners of my heart and swirled around the edges of my mind.

"What are we looking for again?" Oliver whispered as he soundlessly closed the door behind us.

We were enveloped in darkness quite suddenly. "I'm not sure," I admitted while my eyes slowly adjusted to the lack of light.

A bedroom, a private lady's parlor, an office, and dressing rooms were beyond this room. And their windows allowed the moonlight to penetrate the darkness, giving them the appearance of glowing. But here, in this windowless sitting room, it was all shadows and obscurity.

Oliver moved toward one of the rooms, drawn to the blueish glow and the ability to see clearly. He whistled low and softly through his teeth. "These accommodations are just a little nicer than the monastery dormitories."

"Just a little nicer," I agreed.

Oliver disappeared into the bedrooms, and I heard the creak of an ancient bedframe and subsequent depression of a plush mattress, then the rustling of silken bedcovers. Oliver groaned louder than he must have intended to. "Just a little nicer." I heard him repeat.

I was on my way to scold him when the gentle sound of fabric swirling behind me caught my attention. Less aggressive than Oliver rolling around on a bed, it was more like the swish of full skirts or the rub of a velvet jacket.

Spinning around, I squinted into the corners of the room. The fireplace waited for me, but nothing else. I took a step toward it, my heart kicking against my breastbone.

"Tessa," Oliver murmured happily, "you must try these out. It seems your uncle has been holding out on us. My bed is not half this luxe. Is yours? Is it just me that's been relegated to subpar bedding? Does my back not matter to these people? Have I been abandoned to a future of hunched-back hideousness?"

My eyes had fully adjusted by now. They keenly assessed the massive fireplace with its carved stone and embedded jewels. When the fire was lit, the large gemstones would glitter against the glow. My memory showed me a pretty image from my childhood. My family gathered around the hearth one cold winter night, my father captivating us with a story of some sea captain of old, and my mother whispering what each gemstone meant. Diamond for power. Ruby for love. Emerald for magic...

"No magic here, my love," my father had admonished.

My mother had stilled and held his gaze. "Of course not, darling. Of *course, not here. But in the old days, emerald was the power stone. The ignitor of all things magical."*

My father's smile had wobbled. "It seems it is a night for fairy tales then."

Her smile had stayed steady. "You doubt the old ways?"

"I doubt the old ways have anything to do with these new days," he'd said, not crossly, but also not kindly either.

She had dipped her head, a subtle show of his authority and her submission. "Yes, you're right. Forgotten dreams and old wives tales, nothing more."

My father had growled then, a snarling, terrifying sound that made all of us children giggle and squeal and listen closely as he spoke of shipwrecks and sea monsters. But I had been curled up in my mother's lap with my back pressed against her warmth and her arms snuggly wrapped around me. I had thought I'd imagined it. Bewitched by my father's storytelling and the lovely night, my mother's talk of magic and the old ways. Yet now I wasn't so sure. Had the emeralds glowed brighter when she'd stretched out her hand? Had the diamonds shifted from blue to yellow to blinding silver before settling back to their pure white? Had the rubies darkened to the color of blood?

I stretched out my own hand now and fingered the inlaid stones. The old magic. What a thing to think about after so much time had passed.

Myths. Fairy tales. A silly story from a mother long since dead.

The moonlight from one of the bedrooms shifted over the hearth, hitting the emerald beneath my fingertips. It glittered faintly in the dark.

I frowned, wondering at the exact timing of light and my touch. Glancing over my shoulder, I saw that there was, in fact, no moonlight. Direct light couldn't reach this far into the dark room. Nerves skittered down my spine and pulled the hair on the back of my neck into standing.

Turning back to the fireplace, I increased pressure on the

gemstone. The pigmentation increased, causing the green of the emerald to sparkle a brilliant hue. My heart beat faster. My mind spun with what this could mean.

Emerald was the power stone. My mother's words swirled around me. The past rushed to flood the present. The impossible storming the physical world as if under siege.

I wiggled the gem in its setting, wondering if I could pry it out of the stone façade and keep it. Wondering if it really did hold some ancient power that had been outlawed long ago.

To my surprise, it shifted. I tugged harder, trying to wedge my fingernail between the gem and the wall. My finger slipped instead, and I pushed instead of pulled.

There was a clacking sound, then a whirring as if gears were turning behind the stone wall. Oliver was speaking behind me from one of the bedrooms, but I was too fascinated to pay attention.

Below the emerald, a ruby suddenly glowed, burning bright red in the dark room. I reached down and pushed on it. More clicking. More whirring. And then the diamond toward the floor, flickering to life and then extinguishing so quickly I would have missed it if I hadn't been so wholly focused. This time, the sound of shifting gears lasted longer. Then spread within the stone wall to impossible to reach or see places.

The hearth was set against the wall and took up the majority of it. The suite of rooms was set into a large turret that jutted into a private courtyard. The king's bedchambers were back where Oliver was snooping. Along with the queen's. Although I remember my parents sleeping in the same bed for much of my youth. The staircase between the two chambers wound around the curve of the walls and led to the nursery. And above those, rooms for the maids and handmaids. Most rooms boasted large windows. Only this room, closest to the castle proper, had bare walls.

Instead of windows, the fireplace took up almost the entirety of this curved wall. And designed in an extravagant style, it protruded away from the castle wall by two feet and was made for a king to enjoy. To my right, toward the ground, was another click and whir. I stepped quickly to the side to watch a drawer pop out from the lowest section of the hearth.

I stooped low to inspect the hiding place. The cut into the stone was so precise, I knew the drawer would be invisible unless you knew to look for it. The decorative gemstones in that section were cut in half to further disguise such a hidey-hole would even exist.

I marveled at it. Was this Mother's doing? Father's? Tyrn's? Or someone else entirely?

Inside the velvet-lined drawer was a book. I felt disappointed at first. I wanted kingdom secrets or a severed head or *something* more interesting than an old tome. Morbid maybe. But one didn't tend to find secret drawers very often.

Instead of anything of note, it was only a book. Gold filigreed and leather bound. Well-made to be sure. But still, just a book.

"Tess," Oliver hissed from over my shoulder. "What *are* you doing? I've tried every bed and every chair, and all I've found is a sinking sense of low esteem. I am apparently too small on your uncle's purview to warrant a decent mattress. Or even a sturdy chair. I feel quite like a servant."

I'd been to Oliver's quarters. He was right to feel that way.

"I found a secret drawer," I whispered, waving my hand over the compartment.

He dropped to his haunches and nudged me to the side so he could inspect. "How?"

"The gemstones lit up at my touch" felt like a rather stupid explanation. So instead, I admitted, "Quite by accident. I meant to pull on a gemstone, and instead, I pushed. And here we are."

Oliver poked at it with his pointer finger. "What is it?"

"A book."

He pursed his lips at my dry tone. "I see that. But what kind of book? Why would anyone need to hide it away in a secret drawer? There must be something more to it."

He was right. I pulled it out, surprised at its heft. My palms buzzed as I stood again. Oliver stood as well, peering over my shoulder once more. I opened the front cover and stared at text I couldn't read.

"This . . . is familiar," I murmured, my memory searching to place it.

"I don't know that language, do you?" Oliver asked, his fingers hovering over the page but not touching it.

"Father Garius," I said, realization dawning. "He showed me a similar book before we left the Temple."

"It's a religious text then?" Oliver moved as though he was going to run his finger down the gilded edge of the page but seemed to think better of it.

"No." Less afraid than Oliver seemed to be, I thumbed through the pages until I found a match to the one Father Garius had shown me. A raven, wings stretched out, claws seeming to dig into the very pages, an ancient language neither of us could read. "Not religious."

"Tessana," Oliver shrieked. "Is that a grimoire?"

Grimoire. I knew what the word meant, but it hadn't occurred to me to use it. I also knew Father Garius had kept his hidden for a reason, but at the Temple, I had assumed it was because the witch's spell book would go against the religion of the Light. I had reasoned he'd kept it hidden from his brothers to maintain his priestly legitimacy. It hadn't crossed my mind that it was an illegal tome and to be in possession of something magical or magic-minded would mean imprisonment or death.

In fact, I was too young to remember the pagan uprisings. The pagan war had been my great grandfather's war. And before him, it had been centuries since magic had been practiced in the Nine Kingdoms.

The Marble Wall had put an end to magic. And the small pagan rebellion that happened before I was born was hardly anything to think about.

Yet here was a spell book. In what once belonged to the king and queen of Elysia. The suites of the rulers of the realm.

The door snicked open. "Wait a minute," said a deep voice from the corridor. "I heard something."

Oliver and I shared a brief glance before he toed the secret drawer closed, and we soundlessly slipped inside the massive fireplace, each pressed against an opposite wall, praying to the Light the guard didn't realize the door had been unlocked.

The burnished glow of a lantern flickered over the stone floor and across the plush rug in front of the hearth, brushing over Oliver's dark boots and the hem of my black skirt. I held my breath. And I knew Oliver did the same.

The nameless and faceless guard swung his lantern widely around the room, stoically searching for the origin of whatever he'd heard. A second set of boots entered the room.

"I wouldn't be caught in this suite alone," he announced. "These rooms be haunted."

The first guard scoffed. "Haunted by what? You're a senior officer of the Royal Guard, Leib. What is in this room that could possibly spook you?"

The lantern light flooded the hearth. Oliver and I pressed even farther back into the shadowy corners. I closed my eyes and wished they would search for their ghosts in any other room.

Leib cleared his throat. "The past is its own kind of ghost, is it not? What happened to this family . . ."

"What happened to this family was an act of malicious violence, but long since—"

A distant crash silenced both men. The sound of glass shattering and tables being overturned. Then curses by the two men who rushed to see what the problem was.

Oliver and I waited until the door closed once more before both of us breathed a sigh of relief. What would have happened to us should we have been found? Probably nothing. Although it wouldn't bode well for my uncle's trust in me.

"You should put it back," Oliver whispered, nodding toward the grimoire.

It seemed alive in my grasp, buzzing against my skin, against my chest where I held it tightly. But he was right. An ancient grimoire would only get me into trouble. It was still official kingdom policy to kill witches. Although a lifetime prison sentence was far more widely practiced.

Still . . . had it been my mother's? Had it belonged to my family? Had my father known of its existence? Was it simply a nod to the past? Or something that had been actively practiced?

I longed to open it once more, to scour the pages for signs of why it had been secretly tucked away in a suite that once belonged to my family.

Oliver gently kicked the secret drawer in an effort to open what he'd only just closed. The drawer did not move. He bent over and picked at the stone wall with his fingernails, looking for the opening.

"It was more complicated than that," I whispered. Lifting a hand, I pushed the original emerald stone in until it made a satisfying click. I paused for a few seconds, waiting, but the whirring and clicking failed to sound. I moved on to the ruby. Then the diamond. When the drawer didn't open, I repeated the same path of gemstone buttons.

The drawer remained firmly shut.

"Open it, Tess," Oliver ordered, panic lacing the command.

"I cannot." I made a show of pushing the buttons in order once again. The result remained the same—no whirring, no clicking, no drawer popping open. "It does not budge."

There was a commotion outside the door. More guards had been called to attend to the broken glass. It was time to go. Or we'd be trapped inside this room until the morn when the guards changed watch.

Oliver stared hard at the door. "We'll have to come back. After the ball."

I nodded. The book seemed to jump in my arms. Excited for the opportunity to escape its cage? Or terrified of it?

Or nothing but my imagination?

Probably that.

"You're right," I confirmed. Tucking the grimoire under my arm, I followed him to the door. We pressed our ears against the solid wood and listened until we were sure the hallway was free of guards. Then we slipped from the royal suites and slunk back to our wing, ignoring the clatter of guards discussing what could have knocked the vase off its stand.

Oliver and I split paths closer to our rooms with an additional warning to me about how dangerous the grimoire could be. I nodded politely and promised to tuck it away until the festivities ended in a fortnight.

It was the first lie I'd ever told him without remorse.

CHAPTER TWO

The following morning, I woke on my bedroom floor with the grimoire spread open as my pillow. I hadn't even bothered to undress from our midnight escapades. I'd simply sat down in the middle of the floor and opened the book.

The spine had creaked against the new pressures, having clearly been closed for quite some time. There was an inscription on the inside of the cover, but the words were written in a different language, and the only one I could make out was my mother's name at the top.

Instantly, my affection for the grimoire grew. How could it not? Pagan or not, if this book belonged to my mother, I wanted to learn every page.

Even if I couldn't understand it.

Shiksa, my pet fox I'd rescued from the Blood Woods of Tenovia when she was just a kitling, rubbed her silky white coat against my arm, rousing me from a deep sleep.

I woke disoriented, gasping for breath and struggling to untangle my mind from the dregs of unconsciousness. Something in the dreamlessness was holding me captive. Shiksa persisted, adding a mewling cry. It was enough to startle me from my sleep. And I sucked in deep, dragging breaths and rolled to my back so my fingers could dig into the decorated rug beneath me and find purchase.

I blinked, sunlight washing over my face from a crack between the drapes. Shiksa stepped over my outstretched arm and pressed her cold nose to my cheek. I could remember nothing from sleep. Not even how or when I fell asleep. Only that I had been scouring pages for clues, and now I was awake.

But something dark was between those bookends. Not simply dark in the sense of nighttime and dreams. But something evil. Something malevolent. Lying in the middle of the floor of my spacious suite, I couldn't help but feel lucky. Like I'd escaped something . . . dangerous.

Even my lungs moved quickly, gasping as if I'd run a great distance for a great length and was only just now allowed to catch my breath.

A key turned in the lock to my door, and I sprang to sitting, unable to resist the sense that I was still running from something.

My maid, Clesta, entered the room carrying a breakfast tray. She started at the sight of me in the middle of the room. I flung myself backward, relieved it was the young, unassuming servant and not some three-headed beast hunting my heart.

"I'm sorry," Clesta gasped. "You startled me, Lady. Usually, I have to wrestle you from bed at this hour. You sleep like the dead." She maneuvered around me to reach a table where she could set her tray. "I mean no harm."

She was a sweet girl from the village. She'd been serving beneath her mother, who was the head housekeeper of the castle, until I'd arrived. After the trial, Tyrn had dismissed Matilda because she'd been part of Taelon's household. Then promoted Clesta, who was obviously loyal to Elysia since she'd been born and raised in Sarasonet. Or so Tyrn thought. And honestly, I had no reason to believe otherwise, except that his reasoning seemed flawed. Clesta had been raised for housekeeping duties, though. She could sweep, mop, and dust as good as anyone I had ever encountered. She was practically militaristic about the state of my room.

But as far as handmaid capabilities went, I preferred Matilda. She had been young as well, but experienced with dressing and anticipating the needs of a royal. Clesta and I together were a bit of a disaster.

She did not know the ways of the court. Nor did I. And so more than once, we'd been caught unawares. Dressed down for regal events. Too fancy for something more casual. My hair never seemed capable of lasting the night. And I'd taken to applying rouge on my cheeks and kohl for my eyes myself, as Clesta's attempts could be ... well, frightening.

But I liked her. And honestly, I did not mind dressing wrongly for stuffy events. Although I secretly believed Clesta was Tyrn's ultimate plan to prove how unqualified for queen I was and would always be.

Still, if the realm's only fault with me was that I wore linen when I should be in silk, yet their poor were fed, their women educated, and the Ring of Shadows was stopped, I would call that a victory.

"Lady, did you fall asleep reading?" asked Clesta as she stepped over to the windows and pulled back the drapes. "Must have been something fascinating to burn your candle all the way out."

The other thing about Clesta was she had taken to calling me simply Lady. No posh titles. Or stuffy monikers. Only Lady. It was wonderful.

I realized my hair had fanned out and covered most of the grimoire. A small mercy. When Clesta's back had turned to me again, I scrambled to kneeling and closed it. I would find my place later.

She bustled around the room, opening more windows, pouring tea, doing whatever it was she usually did while I slept and was totally oblivious to her presence. While she was distracted, I took the opportunity to tuck the grimoire in the side drawer of a cabinet against the wall. It wasn't safe or secret by any means, but I would deal with that later.

"Is this breakfast?" I scooped up Shiksa and wandered over to the tray, lifting a silver dome to find quirrick eggs whipped with potatoes, spread over toast, and drizzled with lavender honey. The plate was a decadent picture of palace life.

Clesta stopped next to me and dug a polished apple from the pockets of her skirt. "Here you are, Lady," she said in a disapproving tone.

Lavish breakfasts had a time and place, but not Thursday morning. The thought of that heaviness sitting in my stomach all day made me feel ill.

I took the apple and gave Clesta a grateful smile. "You're a gem."

"Hmph."

"You eat this," I said, stepping out of the way. "It shouldn't go to waste."

"Oh, I couldn't."

"Clesta, we go through this every morning. And every morning, I eventually convince you to spare Chef's hurt feelings by cleaning this plate. Let's skip the battle this morning and get straight to the good part."

Her eyes narrowed. "Is your plan to make me fat, Lady? You must be worried my good looks will outshine yours. This is cruelty wrapped in kindness."

I laughed. I couldn't help it. Honestly, where did she come up with this stuff? "This is kindness wrapped up in more kindness. I do not need whipped potatoes and honey for breakfast, dearest. But you do. You're too skinny as it is. And you have much more work ahead of you than I do. Sit and enjoy while I bathe. And when you've had your fill, I'll allow you to try your hand at my hair. But not until you're properly fortified. I have a busy day ahead of me, and I cannot suffer loose pins and unwieldy braids."

"All right then," she conceded. "Let me have the little royal before you go. I suppose she thinks she ought to have some quirrick eggs as well."

I handed off Shiksa. Clesta's feelings for me weren't entirely clear. Some days she acted with cold indifference, others with tepidly warming affections. And while she always accepted my offer of breakfast and had taken to bringing me apples or other various fruits depending on what was available in the kitchen, she seemed to do so reluctantly.

Shiksa, on the other hand, was the light of her life. She loved the foxling as though she were her own. And Shiksa, for her part . . . tolerated Clesta. Which was as doting as Shiksa was toward anyone other than me. Even Oliver was becoming more foe than friend to her.

Now, an adult beastie fully grown and pampered more than I was, she had developed quite the sass. And a number of opinions. She was very protective of me especially. And disliked all new acquaintances.

I should probably keep her locked up, safe in my rooms. But I'd gotten into the bad habit of always keeping her with me. Or letting her roam the castle freely. The servants and other nobles roaming the halls had learned to stay out of her way. Usually, she stayed right by my side anyway, so there had only been a handful of screaming ladies and terrified newcomers when accidental and unwanted paths crossed.

Save when I slinked around the castle late at night with Oliver on a mission for forbidden magic books. Then I left her tucked in bed where she preferred.

Ahem.

"Hurry, Lady," Clesta called after me as I made my way toward the bath. "The prince has already asked for you twice this morning. But I sent word that you were not to be woke earlier than necessary lest he lose his head on the chopping block for disturbing you."

I stuck my head back in the bedroom, butterflies flapping to attention in my belly. "Prince?"

"Yes, Lady. He's been asking anyone who walks by where he can find you. I laughed outright. I said, 'Well, in bed at this hour.' But that didn't seem to deter him."

A smile lifted the corners of my mouth. Taelon. I hadn't seen him since the trial ended. We'd exchanged letters as often as possible, but nothing truly sincere was ever said in a letter. Not when you couldn't be sure it wasn't perused by multiple sets of eyes between him and me.

I breathed deeper, just knowing he was in the castle. Just knowing he was close and we could speak soon.

So much had happened since he'd left. I had so much to tell him. But more, I couldn't wait to hear what he'd been up to. I received so little news. Was the Ring of Shadows still terrorizing the Blood Woods? Had the Rebel Army reconvened? How was Eret? Dravon? Even Gunter, who had supposedly set up camp nearby, but whom I never saw. Sometimes, I smelled Cavolian spices in the air, but I had not truly seen him since the trial.

But more importantly, I wanted to know how Taelon was doing. I wanted to know everything. His victories. His failures. His burdens. His thoughts on the future of the realm. On *my* future. What did he expect from this ball and the two-week festivities to follow? On my upcoming coronation?

Going about my business as quickly as humanly possible, I washed and dressed. Clesta came into the dressing room after her breakfast to help with the corset and ties of the day dress that had been set aside by the head seamstress for today. Because of our foibles over the past six months, Tyrn had ordered the dressmakers to plan my wardrobe for the next couple weeks. They'd taken their jobs very seriously, planning each outfit down to the undergarments and slippers.

I felt it had been an overreaction to our innocent mistakes, but looking at myself now, I had to marvel at the care that had gone into this deceptively simple dress. A pale blue-gray that had seemed boring at first glance. But now that it was on, I could see that the gray was more shimmery silver than flat monotone. Delicate blue flower bouquets with emerald stems and pink string bows decorated the entirety of it, from the low-cut bodice to the short train. It was narrower than a ball gown, but still the layers of fabric had been bustled into elegant tiers. The long sleeves came to a point and looped around my middle finger on each hand. And the ties in the back were exposed, crisscrossing my back and highlighting my shape.

I looked like a princess in this dress. I *felt* like a princess in this dress.

Stepping into silver slippers, I reached for Shiksa and moved toward the bedroom. I had only had an apple for breakfast, but the riot of nerves inside me made even that settle in my belly uncomfortably.

"Lady," Clesta called after me, annoyance clear in her tone when she realized my intentions. "Your hair! You cannot go out like that."

Oh, but I could. "It's no matter," I told her. "I'll let you attempt to tame it before supper. I promise."

"At least let me keep the fox."

She didn't know Taelon at all. "Why? He'll just demand an audience the second he sees me without her."

Her face pinched. "The prince?" she gasped. "And the fox?"

If only she knew how they'd first come to meet in the dark part of the Tellekane Forest. He a rebel. She my fiercest defender. And a secret crown hidden just beneath where she lay.

"I'll be back before supper," I promised, rushing toward the door. "Thank you for your help this morning!"

The door closed behind me before she could respond, but I could just picture her standing there, staring after me with her mouth agog. We had no real bond of friendship yet, but we would. I would wear her down eventually.

Guards on either side of my door snapped to attention when I burst through into the corridor. I didn't wait for them to ask me where I was going, leaving them to chase after me.

Honestly, they were used to the pursuit by now.

Halfway toward the throne room, I realized I didn't know where to find Taelon. Where would he be waiting? Where would he go if he'd been told he couldn't see me?

There was an antechamber to the throne room where Tyrn's secretary had a desk. Maybe he would know. Or at least send a servant to track him down.

Castles were weird things in light of my childhood at the monastery. I was used to wandering the grounds unchaperoned. Save for my studies with Father Garius and chores, I was given free rein to go where I pleased, when I pleased.

But at the castle, there were procedures and restrictions for everything. I was only allowed in certain corridors. I was only allowed out of my rooms during daylight hours. I was only allowed to eat supper in the dining room with Tyrn. All other meals were to be taken in my bedroom or the library they'd given to my continuing education. The castle gardens were only accessible if I took a contingent of bodyguards. If Oliver and I wanted to practice with swords, we had to gain permission from my uncle first and then wait until the swordmaster was available to observe. Which was rare. *Of course.*

When the weather had first shown signs of summer, Oliver and I had tried to swim in the clear pond toward the back of one of the gardens and were called lunatics by the guards, my uncle, and anyone who happened to hear of the failed attempt.

The freedom and autonomy I had once enjoyed had been choked into a set of rules and royal expectations I loathed. When I was queen...

If I was ever queen...

Some of the brightness in my quest faded. There was a lot to get used to as I stepped back into my position in the Allisand line. But this would have been my life even if my parents were still alive. A princess with a crown in her future could not run off feral and unsupervised. The Nine Kingdoms were at stake. My life had value I couldn't fully understand yet.

Although I had been giving it a valiant effort.

Taelon wasn't in Master Fen's office. Nor was Master Fen. I glanced around the corridor, searching for clues on what to do next. The guards who had followed me from my rooms took a step back and moved to attention against the nearest wall. For their part, they largely tried to stay out of my way and remain invisible. But it was hard not to find their obvious attempts at blending in totally ridiculous.

"Curtis," I began, hoping the closest guard might have some clue as to where to look next. "Do you know where I could find . . . ?"

"Looking for someone? I might be able to help." The disembodied voice came from around the corner, or from the shadows behind me, or from maybe the air itself. I blinked, and a man appeared in front of me. It wasn't magic. I was just . . . expecting someone else. The man offered a low, regal bow.

He was royal. I knew it immediately. There was self-importance about him that screamed power and prestige. From the top of his head, where a thin band of black circled his head announcing his position, to his immaculate tunic that wasn't like any style I was used to, to his pointed black boots that were much shorter than the styles in Elysia and Soravale. More like slippers really. How odd.

But I didn't recognize him. Had never seen him before. Yet somehow, he seemed to know exactly who I was.

Flustered, I bit out a terse, "I am."

"The Lost Princess," he murmured. "A true miracle." He bent into a low, flourished bow, proving he did know who I was. Although there was a tension to his movement that made it seem . . . forced. When he stood straight again, he took my hand, which happened to be dangling uselessly at my side, and brought it to his lips. "My lady," he murmured, his mouth brushing my knuckles.

I stared agape, trying to make sense of what had just happened. Another man wasn't allowed to touch me without my permission. That wasn't just my personal rule but the general tenet of propriety.

"Someone was looking for me . . ." I began.

"Good news then, Your Highness, you've found him."

I stared at this man. Boy? Something in between. Older than I was, for sure. But younger than Taelon, also for sure. He had hair so dark it seemed to repel light, glimmering as the morning light tried to penetrate it but failed. His eyes were a mercurial shade of the lightest gray, as shimmering as his hair but in a different way entirely. Where his hair seemed too dark to tolerate light so it bounced off his black strands, his eyes seemed to absorb it entirely. They were so bright as he stood bathed in the morning rays stretching in through tall windows lining the far wall that they seemed to almost glow.

He was dressed in something akin to a morning suit with the style of a different realm than Elysia, gray like his eyes, *like my dress*, with a crisp white tunic beneath. He was all lithe muscle and the kind of grace that belonged only to elite breeding and a lifetime of training with masters but no actual hard work.

He was a prince. I would bet my life on it.

Had Clesta said Taelon specifically? Or had she only said a prince was asking for me?

"What is this?" I asked, retracting my hand. His boldness unnerved and irritated me. Who was this man who demanded an audience with a princess he had never been formally introduced to? I glanced around the open corridor, wondering why it was so empty. My guards moved in, their armor clanking as they closed the distance between us. But still they were slow, hesitant. "Are you unaware of kingdom customs? You cannot simply walk up to the future queen of the realm and take her hand. If we were friends or had even met before, that would be one thing. But I don't know you."

I heard how condescending I sounded and wanted to scream. Or apologize. Or bury my head in a hole in the ground. But honestly, I had never. The audacity of this man.

My interactions since I'd been here had been painfully restricted. Servants never even looked me in the eye, save for Clesta. Oliver was the only guest who was open and honest with me. The rest of the courtiers hardly spoke to me. And Tyrn simply tolerated my existence.

The daring stranger swept into another bow. "But we have met before, Your Highness. Years ago, I grant you that. But neither of us had worn more than a nappy, so surely we are as acquainted as two people can be."

"I'm sorry?" I snarled in my snottiest voice ever. "Who do you think you are talking to—"

"Caspian Bayani. Second son of King Akio Bayani. Our mothers were friends once upon a time. You visited my kingdom when you were little. Our nursemaids let us strip down to nearly nothing and climb the dunes. You were . . . unstoppable in the sand."

A long-forgotten memory surfaced with such ferocity I took an involuntary step back. Vorestra's bright sun beating down on us. The hot sand under our feet but cooler as we burrowed them deeper. Palma branches were waved over our lounging mothers by servants dressed all in white. A hand pulling me higher up the dune, sparkling gold sand shifting quickly beneath us. "Race you to the top, Tessa." Laughter as we rolled all the way down and then landed in a heap at the bottom. Only to jump to our feet and do it again. "You can call me Your *Highness*," I'd told him. "Because I can always reach the top faster than you."

My skin had turned as red as a strawberry that day. And my dark hair had lightened until streaks of gold wove through it. My brothers had gone hunting for sand dragons with Caspian's older brother Carrigan. But Caspian, Katrinka, and I had been too little. Brayn hadn't even been born yet.

I had been maybe five.

"Caspian?" The name was a whisper on my lips.

His mouth twitched. "What an incredible story," he murmured. "A forgotten princess. Raised by monks in some faraway land." He leaned forward, his voice dipping as if he were telling me a legend of old. "No one really believes you, you know? You might have fooled the council, but the rest of us can see straight through you."

He was hard to read. This man with skin the color of milky tea and eyes such a light gray they seemed almost void of color completely. "You have a scar," I said plainly. "Beneath your left shoulder blade. Your brother pushed you, and you landed on your father's shield." What I didn't say was that Carrigan had pushed him off a wall fifteen feet tall and had been disappointed when the shield hadn't killed him.

His smug expression didn't change. "Common knowledge."

I raised an eyebrow. "Oh, is it? You're often found shirtless running dunes for all the realm to see?"

"Often shirtless," he agreed. "But no longer running dunes. I'm sure several ladies can collude with your allegations. Or could have passed along the information to any interested party."

Why had he been asking after me? Was it to flaunt his bedroom prowess and belittle me? Surely, there was another reason. I restrained the urge to roll my eyes and storm off. I didn't have to prove myself to a second son from Vorestra. His opinion had no bearing on, well, anything.

"If I were an imposter," I intoned dryly, "why would the state of your shirtlessness be of any import? Surely, there is other, more vital, information to seek out about the realm. Or your kingdom. Anything at all really. Your brother's shirtlessness, for instance. The true heir to Vorestra."

He shrugged, and it was as elegant and condescending as one would expect from a spare heir. "As an imposter, I'm sure all manner of court gossip is of interest to you."

His allegations were growing tiresome. "Is this why you asked for me? To accuse me of trickery?"

He smiled, but it was all wickedness and insult. "To see for myself. I knew Tessana Allisand. She was spoiled and pampered, and generally a foolish little girl without real knowledge of the world. I guessed she would not have survived eight years in the wild. I was right. Whomever you are, you are not her."

His words cut deeper than I wanted to admit. Had I been a spoiled child? No more than he. We had grown up in palaces, our every whim pandered to.

"It is true the girl you knew all those years ago did not survive. But that does not mean she didn't become something else . . .

someone else. And not because of the wild. But because of the monks who raised me." I took a step back from Caspian and his annoying accusations. The trial was long over. The sovereigns of this realm had declared me the true heir to the Allisand bloodline. I had thought I would be done proving myself to people. But I was wrong. Were there more people out there like Caspian? More dissenters who assumed I was an imposter? Was I still on trial even now? "You didn't cry."

His gaze sharpened. "What?"

"When you fell. When . . . Carrigan pushed you. You didn't cry when the shield cut open your back. You picked it up and threw it at him. It knocked him off the wall too. He was asleep for three days because of the wound to his head. And, if memory serves me right, the fall also broke his wrist."

His face gave nothing away. "Common knowledge."

I nodded regally and turned my back on him, knowing full well it was not common knowledge.

"Never," my dad had hissed on the journey home. "I will never send a daughter of mine to marry one of those barbarians."

My mother had run her hand through my hair, holding up the fading gold strands to the light of the window. "They are wild," she agreed. "They need the taming touch of a woman, perhaps."

"They need the sharp end of a paddle. Brothers who regularly try to kill each other? What kind of life would that be for Tessana? No, there is not enough gold in the world to tempt me into a marriage deal with that family."

The memory sent a shiver down my spine, but I ignored it. The Bayani brothers had always been trouble. I shouldn't be surprised that Caspian was still trying to disrupt and unsettle as much as he could. I would just have to work hard to avoid him at all costs.

My guards, Curtis and Dover, stepped to either side of me, intuitively meeting my needs without my command. It was a clear sign that this . . . meeting with the second son of Vorestra was finished. Although I did not miss that Caspian did not have a contingent of guards with him. Was that because he was a male? And I was nothing but a delicate female who needed protection at all times?

Or was it because he was nothing but a second son. And I was the heir to the Crown of Nine?

"Till we meet again," he said to my back as I moved down the corridor toward my bedroom once again.

"*If* we meet again," I murmured more to Shiksa, who was still curled in my arms, than to Caspian Bayani. She lifted her head and touched her nose to mine, a comforting sign of affection. Which was needed since the sensation of his eyes on my retreat did not leave until well after I was back in the safety of my own rooms.

But I determined to shake off his threats, and his distrust, and the way it still felt as though he were watching me, even alone in my rooms. It was those gray eyes, I decided. They weren't natural. A beautiful terror.

No matter. We'd met. He'd delivered his threats. Now that it was over, I could move on and forget about him entirely. I'd learned to evade him when I was a child after my father had asked me to disassociate with him. It hadn't been easy then. I'd enjoyed his friendship and the way he always seemed bent toward an adventure. But I could do it easily now . . . now that we had nothing in common and no connection to bring us together. He could believe however he liked. And I would go on behaving however I liked.

And that would be that.

CHAPTER THREE

Taelon didn't arrive until much later that afternoon. I did see him, but only briefly. Tyrn asked me to stand at his side while we welcomed the arriving monarchs.

We spent the afternoon in the great hall, welcoming delegation after delegation. Unlike Conandra, when it had just been the ruling kings and queens, this affair brought out entire families. My royal peers, whom I hadn't seen since I was very young or had not yet met as they were younger than I was.

All of them had a similar reaction as Caspian. I was ogled and examined and silently assessed. And ultimately judged lacking.

When we were younger, my brothers, sister, and I had been at the top of the royal hierarchy. As children of the Seat of Power, we were looked up to and revered. But my peers had not spent the last near-decade in a rustic monastery on the edge of the realm. And so were shining diamonds of elite education and exemplary etiquette.

I, on the other hand, at least if their snobbish sneers had anything to say, was one step above a milk cow.

Of the Nine Kingdoms, Barstus, Vorestra, and Blackthorne were absent from the procession. Barstus had been delayed en route by a wobbly carriage wheel, Vorestra had already arrived, and Queen Ravanna couldn't be bothered with a tedious display of honor for a king she did not respect.

Tyrn didn't come out and say that. But he didn't say that either. Queen Ravanna had been to Elysia more than once since my trial. I hardly saw her while she was here. But I suspected neither did Tyrn.

Initially, Tyrn had told me she would be in charge of my tutoring as I stepped into being queen. But all the original plans for my education, coronation, and responsibilities were put on hold when a mysterious crisis removed Ravanna from residence. As she remained unreliable when she would come and go, Tyrn had also pushed my coronation back to my eighteenth birthday.

He'd claimed it made more sense for the health and trust of the realm. But I suspected it had more to do with what Ravanna had going on in Blackthorne than my age or maturity.

When the herald announced King Hugo and Queen Anatal, I rushed to them. Anatal swept me into a hug, and I felt warmth bubble all over me at just being in their presence. They were safe, and kind, and something absent in my life whenever they weren't around. Taelon stepped up behind them.

"Stranger," he murmured in that deep rumble that made me warm for entirely different reasons than his parents.

I pulled away from Anatal so I could offer a very proper curtsy. "Rebel."

His face broke into a tender grin. "It's good to see you, Tessa. It's been too long."

Searching his face for hints about his recent activities, I noticed bags beneath his startling blue eyes and a small cut over his left eyebrow. It was almost healed now, but I wondered what it meant. "Well, we'll have time to catch up now," I said brightly, knowing everyone in the room was listening. "Are you planning to stay for the duration of the festivities?"

"For most, yes. I hope you'll save a dance for me tomorrow evening." His gaze heated. "Or two."

"Or all of them," I said with a dreamy smile. "Since you are no doubt the only one willing to tolerate my clumsy feet."

He took a step toward me. "If memory serves, my lady, you are too hard on yourself."

I stared up into his handsome face, his hair slightly disheveled from the journey, his jaw a little darker than normal, and wondered how I could have borne these last several months without him nearby. How could either of us tolerate the distance? And how would we go back to separate kingdoms once this pomp was over?

My uncle cleared his throat. It dawned on me that Taelon and I were standing there, staring at each other, in a room full of royals and dignitaries and servants.

"If you're quite finished," Tyrn sniped. I retreated to his side. He waved a hand toward the corridors Oliver and I had explored last night. "We are glad you have arrived safely. Dinner is in an hour. A footman will arrive to escort you. The whole family is welcome, of course."

The younger Treskinats were entering the room, surrounded by an army of nursemaids and servants carrying bags. I waved at Taelon's younger siblings with a smile bright enough to cover Tyrn's annoyed tone.

It was no secret how my uncle felt about children. And Hugo and Anatal had more than most.

Except for the king and queen of Barstus, who seemed to be trying to have enough children to build an army.

We said our goodbyes, and Taelon and his family were led toward their rooms. That seemed to be the end of the curtsying and smiling. At least for now. But then Ravanna Presydia appeared from the other direction.

A chill rolled through me, chasing away all the warmth Taelon had brought with him. If Taelon was like the sun, Ravanna was an eclipse—blotting it out entirely. We were enjoying summer and plunged into dark winter at her presence.

And she looked as cold as she came off. Dressed only ever in black, today she wore a full skirt that made her waist look minuscule —as I'm sure was her intent. From her right hip, black gems made a sweeping pattern to the hem, swelling and then shrinking like a fat bird's feather. Her corset top was tightly fitted around her torso and bust and decorated with matching onyx jewels. The black stones of Blackthorne. Her kingdom was famous for them although they were not worth much. Her arms and chest were covered with a gauzy mesh overlay that gave the appearance of modesty but was somehow the opposite.

The black, whether it be her voluminous skirts or the thin, see-through material of her top, starkly contrasted her pale, porcelain skin. But it was her bright red lips that made the most shocking contradiction. She was as stunning as she was frightful.

"Tyrn," she purred, timing her entrance just right to be alone with us.

"My favorite queen," he said in response, cold, detached, careful. "Dinner is not for another hour."

Undeterred, she held out her hand for him to take and offered a short bob of her head. "I would like a word with you."

Tyrn spared me a glance. "Of course." To me, he said, "You'll be all right? You know how to present yourself tonight?"

I wrestled a smile into place. "This is for me, isn't it? Or rather for my future husband? I should be able to manage."

His eyes narrowed at my sarcastic tone, and I could tell he wasn't sure if I was baiting him or being sincere. Truthfully, I couldn't tell either.

I hated the idea of shopping for a husband for the next two weeks. I hated even more that while it had not been officially announced that that was what I was doing, I was confident the rest of the realm had been able to rightfully assume that was what was happening.

The only saving grace was getting to spend time with Taelon. And getting to know the royals whom I would soon work with.

And Katrinka.

She was set to return to the castle today. To move back in permanently with us.

Nerves, so strong and shaky, immediately threatened to knock me out entirely. I hadn't let myself dwell on Katrinka's return. I couldn't sort through my feelings to even know how to process being united again with my sister, whom I had thought was dead for so many years.

Would she hate me for abandoning her? Would she blame me for what happened? Would she be as bloodthirsty for revenge as I was?

There were no answers to my questions. Only time would tell.

And in the meantime, I only grew more nervous. More anxious. More neurotic over our eventual reunion.

The wait to be with her again had been excruciating. I had expected her immediate return to Elysia directly after Conandra had ended. But there had been delay after delay. Barstus had not been ready to release her. She had not been ready to leave. The weather over the winter had been especially bad in the Ice Mountains. Then a late spring snow in the pass between our two kingdoms further pushed her arrival. Followed by spring rains, which apparently made the journey difficult. And then there was that long month where we heard nothing.

Now in summer, without the excuse of inclement weather and a royal edict, she would finally arrive. My heart squeezed with the possibility of having family near me again. At the same time, my stomach plummeted to my toes.

"This is for you," Tyrn agreed in that flat tone he always used. "So let's hope you can manage. It is quite imperative for you to find a husband for the realm to take you seriously as future ruler."

His words grated on my already frayed nerves. "Why? You are not married." I swiveled my head but did not quite meet Ravanna's cold glare. "Queen Ravanna is not married. No one questions your authority simply because you have no spouse to share the responsibility with."

"But we are not children," Tyrn snapped in response. "You do not understand what's at stake—"

Ravanna held up a hand, silencing Tyrn's irritation. "You are right, Tessana. Neither of us is married. And neither of us has suffered for it. But neither of us are the true Seat of Power, are we? Tyrn was only an interim king. And your return has secured that the Seat of Power will never be mine. So we are not the same as you." I felt the threat in her words but could not pinpoint exactly what she meant by it. "However, your destiny is ultimately queen of this realm, and not even your uncle or I could tell you how to fully navigate that path. Use this . . . celebration to explore your options. But know your mind above all else. Never make a decision based on what someone else wants for you. Only on what you know is best for you. For the kingdom. For the realm." She assessed me with a sharp once-over. "Think of the next few days simply as an introduction to society. The husband part can come later."

Tyrn shot her an unreadable look. Either he was pleased she had put my nerves to rest. Or he was irritated she had belittled his extravagant means of finding a suitable man to watch over me.

Unwieldy and wild woman that I was.

The Crown of One Hundred Kings couldn't be handed over to a woman so easily. No, men must always ensure their legacy. Either out front and in the open or behind the puppet strings pulling and guiding and directing the way things should go.

Not that I was opposed to a husband eventually. But I was only seventeen. Hardly of marriageable age.

"Be off with you. An escort will walk you to dinner in less than an hour. You'll need to be there before everyone else so you can greet our guests as they come in," Tyrn ordered.

I nodded my obedience and turned to leave. My guards waited for me just outside the great hall and, as I approached, began to move toward my bedroom.

"We need to talk about last night," Ravanna hissed in a voice I just barely make out. "Your guards say a vase was shattered in a hallway, and one of them swore he heard something in the royal suites."

"That's impossible," Tyrn growled.

I slowed my pace without being obvious so I could eavesdrop longer.

"It's getting worse, Tyrn. Something must be done before—"

"Your Highness?" Curtis, the leader of my detail had turned around farther down the hall, his anxious gaze scanning the corridor efficiently.

"Coming," I assured him in a low voice and picked up my pace. It would do no good for me to get caught listening to Tyrn's private conversation. But what was getting worse? I knew what the sound from the royal suites was. But what about the vase?

That must have been the commotion that called the guards' attention. I had assumed clumsiness. A dark hallway, tired guards, midnight hours ... accidents were bound to happen occasionally.

So why were Ravanna and Tyrn so concerned? And why could sounds from the royal suites cause them to worry so?

I mulled over these questions while Clesta dressed me for the evening. Another special design by the master dressmaker. Tonight I would sparkle like an Elysian diamond in brilliant silver with white lace detail. My skirts were so full and long I worried I wouldn't be able to fit through doorways. And the design was much more mature than my usual attire. Lowcut necklines and tightly fitted bodices.

As I finished applying kohl to the corners of my eyes and brushed on a bit of rouge and matching lip color, I tried to make sense of the woman staring back at me in the mirror. My hair was down again—a sign of youth still rather than adulthood—but Clesta and I had decided it was best to stick to styles we could control rather than have something tall and complicated come loose halfway through the soup course.

She had pulled the front back and made a net of complicated braids over my wild curls. I had been afraid I would look like a child playing dress-up. But the overall effect was startling.

I was half feral, half tamed. Half wildling straight from the Blood Woods, half curated princess. I was the heir to the Seat of Power and an orphan raised by silent monks. I had never felt more like myself.

Not the person I was trying to be. Or the person I had been in secret. But the person I was today. New to this world and not. Fresh from a different way of life and struggling to find her place in this one. Both princess and peasant. Royal and free.

Both not yet queen and also already.

A knock on my door pulled me from my musings. I had just finished the final touches to my look and was mentally preparing for a stately dinner that would include monarchs from all Nine Kingdoms. I was already bored and tired. But such was life as a royal.

Clesta opened the door, and Oliver walked in looking as put together as I'd ever seen him. He knew it as well because he couldn't help but show off with a peacock strut around the room that ended in a playful hop and click of the heels.

"Not so monkish now, am I?" he asked with a grin.

"My uncle must truly be concerned about Elysia's image if he's willing to go so far as to erase all Heprin monk from you."

Oliver's shoulders slumped. "Not all Heprin monk, I hope."

I smiled gently and stepped over to him so I could brush a piece of lint from his blue velvet coat. His silver tunic beneath boasted ruffled cuffs and a frilly collar that reached up to his chin. Polished black boots covered matching velvety leggings. Even his buttons gleamed with silver velvet coverings.

His monkish hairstyle had grown out over the past several months. Someone, whom I highly doubted was Oliver, had slicked it straight back, exposing a rather largely proportioned forehead I had only ever seen if we'd escaped the Temple and gone swimming on especially hot days. It was longer than his normal priestly style, touching his jacket collar in the back and tucking behind his ears. The light-brown color had been darkened to almost black with whatever they'd used to keep it in place. But the look surprisingly worked for him. He somehow managed to maintain his inherited innocence from the Brotherhood while also appearing refined . . . gentlemanly.

Still, I could see the worry crinkling the corners of his eyes. He was happy to look handsome tonight but feared losing his Heprin roots. He wanted to fit in during a dinner where all Nine Kingdoms would be represented, but he was also afraid of becoming too attached to the capital.

I pressed my palm briefly against his cheek. "Not all Heprin, of course. You're a fine representative of your homeland, Oliver. And need I remind you? You could still choose to be silent whenever you wished as well. Father Garius would be so proud."

"It feels strange," he said, a melancholy tone to his voice, not even bothering to bite my taunting words, "to be so far from home that home has started to feel less like home and more like a memory."

Guilt panged through me. Oliver and I had never discussed what his future would be in Sarasonet. All those months ago, it hadn't seemed worth it when merely crossing the border into Elysia had felt so impossible. But now that we were here and I was making myself at home, did Oliver also want to? Or did he prefer to return to the Temple of Eternal Light and officially take his vow of silence? Did he want to continue his training? His life as a monk?

I held his gaze, letting him see the sincerity in mine. "Do you wish to go back? To Heprin, I mean? Do you wish to have your quiet monk life back?"

His smile wobbled, sheepishly admitting he didn't know his feelings quite as well as he'd like me to believe. "I don't know what I want, Tessana. I'm not sure my future is back there. But I'm not sure it's here either. What would I do if I stayed in this castle? I have no skills, no trade, no courtly education. I can tend chickens and milk cows and bake bread, but those positions are already occupied here. Back in Heprin, I was sure of my future, of what I would do with my life. Here, I am only your shadow."

"You are not," I insisted. "You are my friend. And if you choose to stay, you will be my chief advisor when I am queen. There will always be a place for you among my court."

If possible, he looked even more pained. "That is a too generous offer, Tess. I could not accept."

"Of course you can. Just like when we were children and you accepted Father Garius's offer to give up your silent vows. I would have been lost without you back then. And I would be lost as queen without your sage advice now. It's a lot to ask, but it's also a necessary request."

"Tess, I don't—"

"You don't have to decide anything yet. Today or even a year from now. But think about what you want. You, Oliver. Not what other people want for you. Me or Father Garius. Just what *you* want and where you want to be and if it is even possible for you to give up speaking. All evidence points to the contrary." I smiled to show him I was only teasing and patted his cheek twice.

His brows had furrowed together as he considered my proposition. "We should go to dinner," he finally said. "Lest your uncle has me beheaded for holding up the meal."

"Good idea." We stepped apart, and I kissed Shiksa goodbye. Clesta was staying with her this evening since my uncle frowned on bringing pets to royal festivities. "See what a good advisor you'd make? You're already doling out wisdom."

He made a sound in the back of his throat. "If you need me to remind you to be punctual, you're too far beyond my reach of influence. There is no hope for you after all."

We stepped into the hallway, and the guards at the door immediately flanked us. We pretended not to notice as we walked toward the dining hall, arms linked.

A strange feeling of jealousy twisted my insides. Oliver's future lay ahead of him as a blank map. He could plot the course and choose his path whichever way he wished. Mine was a map drawn for me. A map I had willingly picked up and demanded to be mine.

I shouldn't have envious feelings about Oliver's freedom or

future choices. I should be content to help him choose and glad he had stayed for as long as he had.

But friends like him were so rare. Since being in the palace, I had made no other significant relationship. Unless you counted Clesta. But even she seemed to hardly tolerate me.

If Oliver left to return to Heprin, I would be alone. Truly alone. I would have gotten everything I wanted and still have nothing.

I would do my best not to influence Oliver's decision, but I knew even I couldn't hold myself to that perfectly. Of course, I wanted Oliver to stay. Of course, I wasn't above scheming, begging, or writing royal decrees to make him stay. But hopefully, he would simply choose the right thing and let that be that.

"You meet your sister tonight," he said evenly, breaking into my thoughts.

I had quite forgotten Katrinka would be at dinner. Or rather, I had put her arrival out of my mind completely. I was equally nervous and excited with a heavy dose of fear mixed in.

Would she blame me for running away?

Would she remember me at all?

"I do," I confirmed, hoping Oliver didn't notice the way I stiffened next to him or held his arm too tightly against mine.

Which of course he did, immediately. "You're naturally nervous."

"I am."

I felt his sidelong glance on my profile. "Do you remember the time the Archbishop of Gnalghli spent a week at the Temple, and you were so anxious to make a good impression you threw yourself at his feet too forcefully? He tripped over you, then fell down the Temple stairs, broke his arm, and was in bed with a headache for a week?"

I cleared my throat. "I do."

He pressed his lips together to hold back his laughter. But just as we reached the dining hall doors, he added, "Don't do that."

CHAPTER
FOUR

Oliver and I were not the first to arrive like my uncle had wished for us to be. But we also weren't the last to arrive. And while Tyrn might not have seen the value in that, I was proud of us.

We were announced with all the pomp and circumstance I had come to expect in palace life. All my titles and future titles. And Monk Oliver of Heprin. He somehow had vastly fewer titles than I did and still managed to be delighted every time the herald mentioned his name.

Afterward, we were ushered to our seats, far away from each other. My uncle did not believe that people who knew each other should be allowed to sit by each other. It made for dull conversation. So Oliver was squeezed between a duchess from Tenovia and a portly minister of something-something from Barstus. He looked as though he had to hold his breath to fit between the two of them, and I worried his dessert eating would be cut short due to lack of room.

Although I knew him well enough to know he was resilient. Where there was a will to eat as many desserts as humanly possible before one met the great Light, there was a way.

CHAPTER 4 • 41

Meanwhile, my uncle had saved a seat for me near the head of the table. Far enough from him so that he wouldn't be forced to converse with me but close enough that I was still within earshot.

The dining hall had somehow expanded over the past few weeks of preparation. Walls had been removed to make a space larger than a ballroom. Tables had been pushed together to make a great rectangle. Elegant, high-backed chairs glittering in gold and velvet dotted the outside border all the way around. Servants stood against every wall, sharp and at the ready with carafes of wine. And the door to the kitchens was constantly being opened and shut as more servants carried in trays of spring fruits, fresh cheeses, and hunks of freshly roasted meat.

Tyrn nodded as a footman led me to my place. My skirts were so wide and so full that I worried I wouldn't need a chair at all to sit down. I could perhaps just lean back and let my skirts do the work. But the footman anticipated my dilemma and helped me sit without incident.

I turned around to offer him a genuine smile and managed to surprise him. Maybe it was that most monarchs don't make a point to meet the eyes of servants, or maybe he wasn't expecting my smile, but his eyes bugged, and he coughed in surprise. "Your Majesty," he murmured before scurrying away.

"Do you make it a point to terrify all your servants?" a cool voice to my right asked.

I turned back to my place setting, hating that I already recognized the deep timbre of the voice next to me. The seat to my left was still open. But to my right sat the second son of Vorestra himself, Caspian Bayani.

"Only once or twice a day," I responded breezily. "Honestly, I much prefer terrifying royals over servants. Their screams have a more satisfying tenor."

"She has bite," Caspian murmured, sounding surprised. "I suppose you learned this from your monks as well?"

Yes, I thought. And how to slice a man in two. But I kept those thoughts to myself. "Is your brother here? Or does Vorestra think so little of my uncle, they only sent their second son?"

My words were cutting and harsh. This wasn't who I was. I didn't offend just for the sake of offense. And I certainly didn't allow myself to get caught up in palace intrigue by snotty princes with secret agendas.

But Caspian's accusations against me ran too true to ignore. I wasn't the child who played with him on the golden dunes all those years ago. I had evolved into something that survived her worst days and fought for a better realm. He too had changed since that easy childhood. He was more cruel bully now than playful friend. More sharp-tongued serpent than promising prince.

Barbarians, my father had called him and his brother. And while he was polished tonight, as well-dressed and handsome as any of his peers in a tunic the glittering color of the golden dunes of his homeland, it was only a thin veil over the untamed savage beneath.

He was more the brother who threw a shield with the intent to wound, to kill, than the mischievous troublemaker who held my hand and helped me to higher places.

Time and circumstance had changed us both.

But he answered my question. He lifted a bored finger and gestured to a replica of himself across the room. They could be twins save for the deeper wrinkles around Carrigan's eyes and the scar that ran from his temple to his jaw on his left side. He wore a crown of pale gold with black vines wrapped around the thin band. The exact opposite of Caspian's black crown with pale gold vines. "Already entertaining the room at large."

It was true. It wasn't just that Carrigan was older that set the brothers apart. It was Carrigan's bright smile, his easy way with people, and his deep laughter that I could hear even over here. A woman watched him from a couple of seats away. She had the dark coloring of the Vorestran people. Her long black hair was separated into many braids, each wrapped in dozens of tiny gold rings. Both sides of her nose had gold rings as well, with chains that draped to her matching rings in her eyebrows and then again to the tops of her ears.

She was absolutely stunning. And she wore an even daintier crown, the feminine counterpart of Carrigan's.

Confusion rang through me. I had only just met the king and queen of Vorestra at Conandra. And while I had not spoken to them, I had memorized their faces after long days and endless hours of trial and testimony.

"Is your father—"

"Dead," Caspian answered before I could even fully form the question. "Over the winter. He grew suddenly ill and . . . died."

"So your brother—"

"King," he filled in again. I was annoyed that he kept answering my questions before I could ask them. But then again, I struggled to formulate coherent questions, so I couldn't blame him entirely. "And his queen, Lady Amalia."

"I'm so sorry," I gasped, unsure what else to say. I felt his hot gaze on my face and realized how wrong my words sounded. "A-About your father, I mean. I . . . that . . . I know what it is to lose a parent suddenly. And I wish that on no one. I am deeply sorry for your loss."

"My father wasn't . . . a man I mourn."

His sentiment was so final, so severe, I couldn't help but turn to look at him. And with my gaze fully on his face, I found his light eyes staring intently at me. What did he mean by that? Was it what my father had suspected all those years ago? That King Akio was a man who pitted his sons against each other and delighted in their warfare?

Or was it something more? Something worse?

"Tessana," my uncle's voice beckoned from behind me. "I believe I have someone you would like to meet. Or rather, be reintroduced to."

I should have taken a deep breath and prepared my mind and spirit. But Caspian's haunted look and harsh words had knocked me off balance. And so, instead, I turned quickly to face my uncle, desperate to untangle myself from the messy court life of the Vorestran palace.

But when I turned, it was not my uncle I faced, but a mirror. Or rather a poor imitation of a mirror, as though the glass were slightly distorted. My eyes were bigger but hidden behind prim spectacles. And my mouth was smaller, lips plumper. My dark hair was curlier, springy coils pulled back into a severe bun that could neither restrain nor contain their sheer volume. And those eyes. Not my mother's, but my father's. Intelligent, keen, too insightful.

My mouth dried out as I tried to form words. Katrinka.

"May I present Tessana Allisand," my uncle was saying. "Heir to the throne." His voice was a blurred buzzing in my ears as I tried to make sense of the little girl I knew once upon a time and the nearly grown woman who stood before me. "Tessana, this is Katrinka Zolotov, of the house Barstus, adopted daughter to Maksim Zolotov, king defender of the Ice Mountains."

I was surprised my uncle had memorized so many titles. And that he'd been willing to repeat them. But it gave me a short time to collect my thoughts before I attempted to stand.

My dress was too full, though. My heel caught on my skirts, and the best I could manage without making a fool of myself was a hunched-over semi-curtsy.

Kat eyed me skeptically, a knowing look bringing her eyebrows together over her nose. "Pleased to meet you," she said in a bored voice.

Meet me? I wanted to laugh, but I could tell by her very serious expression that laughing would not win me any favor with her. "Well," I said in a gentle but firm voice. "We're not exactly meeting for the first time, are we? We do know each other already, don't we, sister?"

Her chin lifted defiantly, and I realized my worst fears were coming true. "Do we? It's hard to understand what I knew since it has been so many years since I saw you last."

Well, she wasn't wrong. "It has been," I said sincerely, fudging the truth with actual truth. "I am relieved to see you healthy, Katrinka." What I really meant was I was relieved to see her alive, not dead. "But I can hardly believe you were in Barstus this whole time. Unbelievable almost. Isn't it?"

She held my gaze, a coldness shifting her expression in a way I didn't expect. Especially not from a sister I remember being beloved. "As unbelievable as a monk squirreling you away in Heprin, I suppose."

She had a point. But the flat way she delivered it made a chill scurry down my spine. Was this the sister I had left behind? Or had tragedy and time made her a total stranger?

My uncle gave me a tight smile before pulling the chair out for Katrinka and gesturing for her to sit. Her shoulders lifted in a slight shrug as though she were sighing resignedly. But her irritation only lasted a second before she plastered on a placid look and sat down next to me. Tyrn disappeared, and then it was just the two of us.

"I've missed you," I told her immediately, unable to hold back my true feelings. "By the Light, Katrinka, how I've missed you."

She did not fully look at me. Instead, her eyes stayed trained on the place setting in front of her, and she accepted my declaration with a curt nod. "I'm sure, much like myself, you believed you lost your whole family."

Finally, common ground. I reached forward and grasped her hand with mine, squeezing it tightly. "Yes, exactly. I . . . I have mourned you for so long. When I was told that you were still alive, I —" My words broke off as tears choked me. But this was a formal affair, and I desperately tried to prove myself in court. I would not let them fall here. Composing myself once again, I whispered, "I was overwhelmed with joy. After being separated from my family for so long, I am happy you are here."

She nodded again and pushed her spectacles up her nose. Her gown was much simpler than mine, in the Barstus fashion—which was all practicality and simple styles in utilitarian colors. Black. Dark blues. Simple grays. Tonight, she wore a dove dress that reminded me of the Temple and what the monks had worn. Still, she shined. Her face was the face I remembered. And even though this reuniting was as awkward as possible, she was my sister. The stilted way we spoke to each other would not last.

Could not last.

"Do you—" I began, but she turned away from me and spoke to the person on the other side of her. Someone from Barstus, but I knew not who.

Caspian made an amused sound to my left. My better judgment told me not to turn toward him. Not to engage. Not to give him the satisfaction. But the wounded heart from Katrinka's small slight, couldn't help but ask, "What?"

"I should thank you," he said, all smug tones and arrogant lilts.

"For what?"

"I've always wondered if Carrigan and I could grow colder toward each other. Didn't think it was possible. Yet your relationship with your sister has revealed how warm and heartfelt my relationship with my brother is. Last month, when he tried to have me poisoned, it was friendly banter compared to what I just witnessed."

I blinked at him. "Did he really try to have you poisoned?"

"Not with anything serious." He leaned forward, shifting the conversation back to me. "I've heard rumors about the poison masters in Barstus, though. They're said to be the best in the realm. Take it from me, don't accept drink offers from scantily-clad women who spend their time in dark corners."

I should have been able to compose myself better, but his words were so shocking. All of his words were so shocking. "I-I-I—"

Tyrn stood and clapped his hands together, saving me from a too-innocent response. No, not innocent . . . *prudish*. I turned away and hid my crimson cheeks from Caspian. But as I gave my uncle my attention, I felt my sister's eyes fixed on me, studying me.

I dropped my gaze to hers, and she quickly looked away.

"Your presence here," Tyrn began, saving me from awkward

encounters on either side, "means a great deal. After a long sabbatical of . . . celebration, we've gathered to revel in the return of not just one but both of my nieces. Saved from obscurity and . . ." Tyrn's placid gaze moved to Katrinka and then to me as he struggled to find the word he was looking for. His eyes were glossy for some reason. Maybe it was tears that made them shine like glass, but something was too far off in his stare for it to be confused with emotion. "Obstruction," he finally finished. "They are here now, in the palace of their birth. One of them was poised to take the Crown of Nine and sit on her father's throne. We are so . . ."—his dead tone dragged the word *so* out for longer than was polite—"lucky." He cleared his throat and added. "The Light be praised."

"The Light be praised," was echoed around the room.

I glanced at Katrinka to see if she noticed how strange Tyrn's address had been and found her clutching the tablecloth in her lap, her knuckles white with strain.

Tyrn raised his wine goblet and clinked it with his fork. "To our future queen," he said with a grin. "Long may she reign."

The room rumbled with shouts of, "Hear, hear!" Some of the monarchs even echoed Tyrn's sentiment. But enough of them sat still, staring at me over untouched wine. I knew not everyone felt Tyrn's sudden arousal to loyalty.

I looked around the room, desperate to catch Taelon's eyes and have at least one faithful ally in the room. Instead, my gaze caught on Ravanna Presydia's cold glare. She wasn't even sitting at the table with the rest of the party. Instead, she stood in the corner of the room, wedged between servants, a wide grin pulling her crimson lips upward.

With my attention on her, she dipped her chin, acknowledging me. Then I silently clapped for what I could only assume was my future success.

I wished I could take her dramatics as a sign of concession. That whatever rivalry had been between us before had been put away forever. She might not like me, but I would one day be her queen. There wasn't much she could do about it now.

But I knew better than that. Ravanna almost had the Seat of Power. If I hadn't shown up when I did, she would be the future queen of the realm.

Anyone who had met her knew she wasn't the kind of person to back down easily. Or gently.

Whatever this was between us was only just beginning.

Tyrn sat down, and the servants moved at once to the edges of the table where they began to serve the second course—a nest of brittle noodles with a golden selkit's egg resting in the middle. When one cracked the gilded shell with the side of a spoon, the egg split open, spilling a runny yoke made red with spice. It was quite the culinary feat, and I knew Oliver would be thrilled with it.

Next to me, Katrinka made a surprised sound at the way her shell split open and then dissolved quickly into the noodles, making them instantly soft and edible.

Turning to her, I couldn't help but smile. "Amazing, isn't it?"

"I've never seen anything like it," she admitted, her voice still tinged with awe. "Barstus is too . . . practical for anything like this."

"Not even for a holiday?" I asked. "Surely, the palace chef would make something . . ." My voice trailed off when I realized my mistake. "I had never seen anything like it either. Until I arrived here. The temple where I grew up was a slave to simple things. We were lucky to get cakes on religious holidays. Otherwise, it was porridge and stew for every other meal."

She pressed her lips together in a muted smile. "You were embarrassed because you're not sure if I was allowed to live in the palace."

"No, I was just—"

"I was," she said matter-of-factly. "I grew up as a daughter of King Maksim. I have never had to endure poor temple living or making my own porridge. That sounds dreadful."

I should have been offended. But . . . "It was."

"The Barstus court is more focused on intellectual pursuits than frivolous parties. My father would have been annoyed had Chef wasted his time on something as extravagant as this."

All I could do was blink. She'd just called King Maksim her father. And while everything in me rejected the idea that a man that pompous and uptight could be any relation to my sweet sister, I also knew that our real father might be a very distant memory to her. She had been younger than six when our parents died. And her leaving Elysia must have been rather traumatic.

Still, supper tonight was extravagant for a reason.

"It is meant to honor you, sister. To honor us. Enjoy it for what it is."

She poked at it with her spoon. "I shall try."

Her attention was pulled away by the man to her right. He was an older man with a scholarly sort of hat. It even had a tassel. Suddenly, I remembered studying the never-ending Barstus platitudes in Father Garius's library. I wished I had sat closer to Oliver. If only so I could needle him into asking the tutor or teacher or whoever he was why so many of their commands were the same instruction written only a slightly different way.

One must never withhold one's cloak should one stumble upon a cloakless widow or orphan.

If one passes a widow or orphan without a coat, one must take off one's coat and offer it to either. Widow first. Child second.

Just remembering all the foolishness of those platitudes and the many ways Father Garius would make us copy them down on parchment made my hand cramp.

"Are you confident you should share so much about your past, Princess?"

The question came from Caspian to my left. Knowing his word traps and skepticism, I should have guarded my tongue better, but he'd managed to surprise me.

"What do you mean?"

"You speak of temple life as though it were common knowledge," he noted, his voice too low for either of our neighbors to hear.

"And? What of it? It was made known at Conandra, where I have been for the past eight years."

"Yet your father's murderer has never been found. Your presence at your Heprin Temple was meant to be a secret while you were there. Maybe it should remain one still."

His words sent fear screaming through me. "What are you implying?"

"It is obvious you love your monks, your simple childhood. Yet there is someone out there"—he paused to lower his voice even more—"or in here, who wished to end the Allisand bloodline. You would be wise to bridle your tongue."

He was right. Of course, he was right. But I hadn't thought of . . . I wanted to cry in frustration. I wanted to hit something. Had I endangered Father Garius's life? Would someone really ride all the way to Heprin to punish a good man for his mercy on my life?

But to Caspian, I merely said, "And you would do well to hold yours. I am the future queen of this realm, second son. I would watch the way you speak to me from now on, lest your brother finds a staunch ally in me. As far as poisons go anyway."

His too-light eyes narrowed with distaste. "I try to warn you, and you threaten me? If I thought you knew anything of palace intrigue, I would almost feel sorry for how very bad at it you are."

I seemed to back myself into a corner whenever he was around. Why was that? The urge to punch something grew stronger. "I do not need your pity. Or your warnings. But I thank you for your very unnecessary interest in my life. You are free to now mind your own business and leave mine, palace or no, alone."

He turned back to his second course, but this time the small smile curling one side of his mouth actually made my heart pound with nerves. What did that mean?

Had I not done a good enough job to scare him away?

Why did he look more interested in my business than ever?

Despite his coy looks and insightful glances, he did leave me alone for the rest of the meal. I was left to enjoy Chef's imaginative and delicious concoctions without tasting a single thing.

All I could think about was Father Garius and the other monks at the Temple of Eternal Life. Had I unwittingly put them in danger? Would someone hunt them down because of me?

I took a deep pull from my wine and decided to right my error first thing in the morning. Oliver was questioning his future and feeling lost. Well, I had the perfect task for him. He would hopefully find the answers he was looking for. And I would find the ones I was suddenly looking for as well.

Thanks to Caspian and his plotting and scheming. He might have nefarious reasons for me to check on the Temple, but only time would tell.

CHAPTER
FIVE

The week of festivities and celebration that followed the first banquet quickly became exhausting. Used to muslin day dresses and fur-lined slippers, my body ached from too-tight corsets and heeled shoes that always seemed to end in a point and squish my poor toes to death.

All the royal men of the realm were given an opportunity to show off their skills in an archery contest. The town of Sarasonet was even invited to spectate. At first, I was excited to watch Taelon compete. I had never seen him with an arrow, but he was the kind of male who would naturally excel at anything. Only he did not enter.

Nor did Caspian, although I had been equally thrilled with the opportunity for him to fail.

Instead, it was mostly ministers and valets and a fourth son from Tenovia who took the champion's wreath on the basis that everyone else stopped trying once he stepped up to shoot. I had sat in the spring heat, bored and underwhelmed. Katrinka had actually fallen asleep next to me, and I probably should have roused her, but it had saved me from trying to make awkward small talk while old men struggled against bowstrings and failing eyesight.

The following day, the men went for a hunt in the mountains. Queen Ravanna hosted a tea for the ladies, but far from being entertaining, we were forced to sit through a musical concert based on the fifth-century Ulala tribes from across the Crystal Sea.

Katrinka was not as kind to me when I started to doze off.

The banquets lasted well past midnight every night. Feats of strength. More contests. Concerts. Teas. I woke every morning well before sunrise to primp and posture. And went to bed well into the morning hours after much drinking of wine and cider and headaches from the boisterous laughter. And more small talk than anyone should ever be subjected to.

At each event, Katrinka and I were thrust together. Whether by nefarious plan or natural instinct, my uncle orchestrated ample opportunities for us to get reacquainted. Only, that would require real conversation and authenticity—of which my sister seemed to possess neither. Maybe deep down, beneath the layer of frost as thick and impenetrable as the Ice Mountains themselves, was a genuine person who cared about our family and me. Or even our realm. But she was either unwilling or incapable of treating me with anything but cold indifference thus far. So our forced interactions were wearing on me more than the festivities.

Not once was kingdom policy discussed or debated. Kings never gathered to talk about the threat of the Ring of Shadows or even the Rebel Army. Poverty was rampant across the realm, and these monarchs reveled in rich foods and constant drinking. Whole villages in Tenovia burned while I had journeyed across the width of it, but you would not know it from the way its monarchs behaved. The same could be said of Elysia. I hadn't seen the rest of the realm for myself, but I had no doubt the tale could be told from any kingdom.

What had started off as an exciting prospect to get to know and understand the other royals I would be working with in the future had devolved into something deeply depressing. And by the fifth day, I could no longer hide my disgust.

We were at lunch in the gardens. The spring blooms were at their peak. And sheer, billowing tents that came to sharp points at each corner and in the middle had been set up to offer shade.

The gardens were my favorite part of Castle Extensia. Unlike the hall, which seemed to always be dark no matter the time of daylight and reminded me of ghosts and too many hard memories, the gardens were exquisitely untouched by my past. My uncle had renovated them after he took the throne.

He'd brought in flowering desert bushes from Kasha and Vorestra. Orange and lemon trees from the coast of western Soravale. Towering thin-limbed shrubs from the edges of the Tenovian forest. Each section of the sprawling gardens represented a different kingdom. The gardeners were trained specifically to make the glory of each kingdom shine. Which wasn't easy given the castle's mountain domain.

But when walking down the path with budding Aramore rose trees, each bloom a vibrant pink or orange or red, it was impossible not to feel transported to a wealthy kingdom with more gold than they knew what to do with. The scents from the fruit trees from Soravale were enough to make one's mouth water. And the white-barked paths of Blackthorne with its bone-colored oaks that bloomed with equally snow-white buds that turned into translucent leaves made one feel as unsettled and paranoid as I was sure their queen intended.

Clesta walked me to the table reserved for me, Katrinka, and a smattering of other delegates and royalty from around the realm. The sun was unseasonably hot this afternoon, but a delicious breeze made the heat bearable.

Thankfully, the dress designer had accounted for the weather, so my gown was made of thinner, lighter material, even if there were as many ruffles and folds as usual. I had to resist the urge to start ripping layers off, but, seeing my valiant battle not to start sweating, Clesta quickly grabbed a nearby wicker fan and waved it my way.

We were the first ones to sit down besides Katrinka. Even our uncle had yet to arrive. I relaxed into my low-backed lawn chair and smiled at her. "This weather reminds me of Heprin. It always seemed unseasonably warm there. Unless of course we were in the dregs of winter. Then it was always unseasonably too cold."

She tipped her face toward a slice of sunlight that had reached her chair. It was then that I noticed she'd inched away from the table in order to be more completely doused with it. "It is always cold in Barstus," she said, sounding annoyed with her adopted country for the first time since we'd been reunited. "Cold and wet. We have no snow. Not like I remember in these mountains. But it never stops raining. I feel as though I have not seen the sun shine since I was a child."

I let the smile sound in my voice when I teased, "You *are* dreadfully pale for an Allisand."

Her sharp eyes found mine, and I could tell she was ready to strike. I grinned wider, showing her I wasn't serious. She looked away, biting back whatever retort sat on her tongue.

Not for the first time, I wondered about her upbringing. Did they not have fun in Barstus? Was there no joking or play? Did they simply read tomes all day and practice their intellectual serenity?

I yawned on instinct. I would have been driven mad there. The silent temple had been hard enough for me to endure, and I was given free rein to wander the grounds, explore the nearby village, and laugh as often as I liked with Oliver. How the monks must have hated our devilries. But oh, how my wild spirit needed them.

"What else was Barstus like?" I asked after a long stretch of silence. Katrinka had been reluctant to talk to me about herself. I'd asked countless questions about the palace, her education, her adopted siblings, and what she'd been up to for the past nine years. But she had always avoided answering with anything of substance. I'd been left to sort through clues that provided no real answer. My concern for her only grew.

But maybe she would be willing to talk about the country itself. The weather. The terrain. Dragon's blood, I would even talk about religious holiday traditions if it got her to say more than two sentences to me.

"I just told you," she said with that same knife-edge glare. "Wet. The kind of wet that sinks into your bones and makes you live with a constant shiver. My maids would put hot stones in my blankets before bed so I didn't freeze to death through the night. I remember winters here, but I also remember hot summers. The rain in Barstus is relentless."

"Gray," I conjectured. "It must be very gray."

She nodded, but then a small smile pulled at the corner of her mouth. The first I'd seen from her. "And green. The land is . . . lush. Muddy as well, but so very fertile. And in contrast, with the rolling thunderheads in the sky and the vibrant tall grass below, the landscape is not as gloomy as one might imagine."

"I have never been to Barstus, but that sounds surprisingly lovely."

She turned her face away from me as her smile spread. "It is."

"Did you miss—"

"Good afternoon, Your Highness," Taelon's strong voice interrupted our small moment of connection. And for once, I didn't mind. Busy with our family responsibilities, we'd hardly seen each other over the past several days. He looked at Katrinka, then me and added, "Highnesses."

I smiled at him, just pleased to gaze upon his masculine figure dressed in all his Soravalian finery. "Hello, Prince Taelon. So good to see you."

He swept into a curt bow, then collapsed into the chair next to me, tugging at the high buttons of his collar. "What a week your uncle has prepared for us. I'm afraid I'm not fit enough to survive all these celebrations."

I yawned again. "Agreed. It appears as though he wants to revel us to death."

Taelon shared a sly look with me. "If that is true, he's smarter than I give him credit for."

Aware of Katrinka's listening ears, I laughed. "Truly, if I have to sit here much longer in this heat, I'm afraid I'll fall asleep before the food arrives. The whole of the Nine Kingdoms will be treated to my snoring. And I will never be taken seriously as queen."

Taelon's gaze sharpened. "Are you even hungry?"

I understood his question at once. We'd been so stuffed with rich meats and sugary desserts for the past five days that the seamstress had to let my corset out this morning. "I haven't been hungry in days."

"Agreed." He jumped to his feet. "I say a walk is in order. Let us move our bodies and shake off this drowsy afternoon."

My mouth unhinged. "You can't be serious. What will my uncle say if we abandon his elaborate lunch for exercise?" What would the kingdom say if we were known to have wandered off together?

"I think it shows ... diplomacy." He held out his hand for me.

"We cannot go alone," I reminded him, hating how prim I sounded.

His eyes twinkled with amusement. "And why not?"

Dragon's blood, how I wanted to go alone with him. How I wanted to get lost in the recesses of this magnificent garden and ask him a thousand questions about his life over these past several months. And then give him a thousand kisses to make up for all this time apart.

But I also wanted to be queen someday. And seducing the Crown Prince of Soravale whilst my uncle hosted a luncheon in the royal gardens didn't exactly seem to be a wise idea.

"Taelon," I whispered, eyes bugging out. The dark mystery in his gaze made my heart trip over itself.

His knowing smile was too beautiful. It put the gardens to shame. "Of course, you're right. But surely the princess would like to accompany us and explore as well." He turned to my sister and held out his hand to her. "What thinks you, Princess Katrinka? We would love for you to join this rebellious escapade with us."

Her porcelain cheeks heated with a pretty blush. "Oh, I don't—"

"And what about me?" a dark voice insisted from the only shadowy corner in the tent. Caspian stepped into the light, and I couldn't help but wonder how long he'd been there. "Am I invited as well?"

Taelon met Caspian's cruel smile with a short bob of his head. "Only a prince from Vorestra could manage to surprise so many of us."

Caspian smiled. "Are you calling me sneaky, Taelon, Prince of Soravale?"

"Sly," Taelon corrected. "Sneaky is something a child does. Your spymaster would hardly take credit for turning out children in the royal court."

Caspian's gaze danced with a fight I was reluctant to see play out in my pretty garden tent. I stood to my feet and reached for Katrinka's hand. "I wasn't aware the two of you knew each other."

"We were rivals for the same bride at one point," Caspian explained, his voice as flat as I'd ever heard it. "Of course we know each other."

His words stole my breath. Did he mean me? I hadn't thought my father had considered Caspian seriously.

Taelon cleared his throat. "A bride neither of us won in the end."

"Are you so certain?" Caspian sneered.

Katrinka's gaze flattened once again, and her blush disappeared almost as quickly as it rose. "I think I shall remain," she intoned. "I'm not used to this climate. The sunlight has already taken much of my energy."

I could tell she was lying. And not just because she was still positioned in a way to be mostly in the sun. It was a sister's intuition, something brought to life by our proximity.

"Please come," I begged her. Then on the hill walking toward us, I saw my greatest hope. "You can meet my friend, Oliver. He'll join us too. And he is *so* much fun."

Katrinka glanced over her shoulder in a bored way and then did a quick double take as the sight of Oliver, with his shaggy grown-out monk's haircut and gentry-style suit, caught her attention.

"He is your friend?"

My one and only. But to her, I said, "Yes, we grew up together. He helped me walk the long distance from Heprin to here."

"He did?" she demanded, underestimating him like everyone else. "He helped you survive all the way from Heprin?"

He tripped over a hole in the ground and flailed his arms to regain his balance, unaware that the four of us were watching him. "Yes, he's wonderful."

"Let us be off then," Taelon commanded. "Before our elders arrive and demand our company."

"You're sure we won't get into trouble?" Katrinka asked, sounding more open to the idea, now that Oliver was included but still not quite sure.

"I'm sure," I lied. "Clesta will tell everyone where we've gone. And we'll be back before desserts."

Clesta looked as though she were about to have apoplexy. I smiled at her reassuringly. She turned the fan on herself and tugged at her tight bodice.

"It will be fine," I reassured her and everyone. "Just mention to my uncle that Katrinka and I went to explore the gardens. But he shouldn't worry because we have"—I looked around at the rather large party—"so many capable escorts."

Oliver swatted at a fly buzzing around his head rather dramatically and nearly tripped over his tangled feet again.

Clesta narrowed her eyes at him. "Yes, very capable."

I smiled brightly at her. "We'll be back before you can miss us."

At her look of grim disapproval, I waved at the rest of the party to follow. We were in a courtyard of sorts. The larger sections of the gardens were connected by stone paths and lined with tall hedges of varying plants, displaying whatever kingdom they were meant to represent.

But I knew that the manicured garden paths and foliage eventually gave way to a wilder section of palace grounds. When I had first been free to be on my own, I had spent much of my time there. It vexed my uncle like nothing else, but I preferred the feral solitude of the gardens to the cultured courtesy of the palace.

Eventually, Tyrn had tired of my rebellious escapes for peace and quiet and threatened to mow the whole lot of trees down if I continued to wander off alone. I had submitted to his will to save the land. I did not doubt he would follow through with his harsh promises. But I also knew he wasn't asking too much of me.

I was, after all, heir to the throne. Heir to the realm. I could learn to behave. Even if I thought it might kill me.

Besides, I had reasoned, I would be queen one day. And then I could do whatever I wished.

See him try to stop me then.

Oliver was at my side as soon as we started off. I wasn't even sure if he had totally heard the plan, but this was who Oliver was. Loyal in every way.

A shiver of doubt ran through me at the prospect of losing him back to Heprin. But I shook it off. It was too beautiful of a day to let dark thoughts blot out the sunshine.

Behind us were my sister, Taelon, Caspian, and several guards. Not all mine.

Once we were away from the festive tents, I half turned and said, "Oliver, may I present my sister, Katrinka."

He made an awkward, mobile bow as he turned clumsily to the side so he could acknowledge her. "Charmed to meet you, Princess Katrinka."

Her expression remained blank, but she didn't sneer at his failed attempt of chivalry, so that was a partial victory. "You are my sister's suitor?"

Oliver's wide-eyed look of horror clashed with mine before we both burst into laughter. "No, never!" he exclaimed.

At the same time, I said, "Never in his wildest dreams."

Then to me, he said, "You're daft if you think I would ever dream about *that*."

More laughter from the two of us. It couldn't be helped.

"Oh," Katrinka murmured, "I just thought."

"No, you're not wrong to assume . . . that," Oliver reasoned diplomatically. "I would do anything for Tess. Die for her even. I just . . . we're not like . . ."

"Nor will we ever be . . ." I added, trying to explain what neither of us could even say.

"Simply friends," Taelon cut in, saving us from losing our breakfast on the stone path. "They are friends and nothing more. I assure you." Katrinka turned to look at him, clearly pleased he'd saved us all. "And sometimes I'm not even sure they're that."

Oliver chuckled gently. "No, you're wrong there. When we disagree or bicker, that is merely the purest version of our friendship. We care too deeply about each other to let polite excuses or false opinions taint our true feelings. We are always honest, always upfront. And that is how we know we can always trust each other."

I threaded my arm through his, beaming with his assessment. "Sometimes, we might want to pull our hair out and abandon each other to the pits of Denamon. But Oliver is right. I trust his opinion and advice above everything else. I know he will tell me the truth I need to hear. And even more, the truth I don't want to hear."

"The Light must have looked upon you favorably, Tessana," Katrinka said, a cold tone to her voice. "To find a friend like that. And in a monastery of all places."

Her words stole my happy mood and replaced it with dread. She was not happy for me. That much was clear.

But Oliver did not notice. He laughed again and echoed, "A *silent* monastery of all places."

I led them deeper into the gardens, our polished heels clicking against the weathered stone. Nearly a battalion of guards was behind us, but thankfully, they stayed far enough in our wake so as not to interrupt our conversation. I knew there were even more royal guards stationed around the grounds. Otherwise, they would not have let us wander so freely. But with so many monarchs in one place, my uncle would have taken every security measure.

"That might be the only place to find a true friend," Caspian said from further behind me. "In disguise, at a place for peasants. Royals aren't given the luxury of real friendship. Not like the two of you enjoy."

He sounded as bitter as Katrinka. I retracted my arm, feeling as though it was showing off. "That can't be true," I argued. "Maybe it is harder as a royal to make friendships. But it can't be impossible." I glanced at Taelon. "You have friends, surely. I've seen them. Met them."

He gave me that brief look he sometimes did when I confused his dual personality. "As a royal," he clarified without an obvious inflection to his voice, although I heard it nonetheless, "I do find it hard to make friends. I have those I respect more than others. And those who respect me more than others. But I would not call them friends."

"Haemon? Really?" I could not believe him. Although I did realize there was a distinction between the men he knew as Arrick the Rebel Commander and Taelon the Crown Prince of Soravale. But I had seen him interact with his captain of the guard. I had seen their easy conversation and laid-back manners with my own eyes. "I cannot believe you do not consider him your friend."

His lips twisted into a frown. "It is not that I consider him less than a friend. But Haemon would give up his life for mine without hesitation." I opened my mouth to argue victory, but he added, "Out of duty. Sure, a part of him might loyally sacrifice his life for mine because we are close, but I will never know. His position requires him to act the same whether he loves me or hates me. And that puts a divide between us that no amount of friendship can close. Caspian is right. It is the rare royal that enjoys a friendship with anyone."

I looked at Katrinka. Was that how her life had been in Barstus? Lonely and friendless? My heart ached for my abandoned sister. Had I heard a whisper about her survival during my time at the Temple, I would have left immediately to find her. To give her the friendship she so dearly missed. To be the family she needed.

We walked for several minutes in silence, each lost in our thoughts. But finally, Caspian couldn't seem to help himself.

"How is it that Barstus managed to keep the sole living heir to the Allisand bloodline a secret for eight years? You would think someone would notice a princess wandering around a palace that did not belong to them."

"I grew up in a temple, not a palace," I reminded him tersely.

His voice held the hint of a smile even though I refused to turn around and acknowledge it. "I wasn't talking about you, Tessana."

"O-Oh," Katrinka stuttered, caught off guard to have the prince of Vorestra's attention. "I'm not sure, actually. Everyone in residence at Bale, er the Castle Bale, knew who I was and where I had come from. But there was never talk of my taking over the throne." She thought for a moment before adding, "Maybe they knew I would not have accepted the offer."

Could that be true? Her shy demeanor did seem to speak for itself. I couldn't imagine her ever desiring to wear the Crown of Nine. But it should have at least been proposed.

"It is odd, though," Taelon agreed. "It would have comforted the realm to know an Allisand had survived. In Soravale, we knew Maksim had a daughter that did not make public appearances. Still, we couldn't have guessed he was hiding you, Katrinka."

"He wasn't hiding me," she argued immediately. "I preferred not to be in public. He was respecting my wishes."

A hitch to her tone made me ask, "The choice was given to you then, sister? You were asked whether you wanted to be in public or not?"

She took her time crafting an answer before saying, "Well, no. No, I suppose not. But ... well ... you're making this into something it's not. My father, rather, my adopted father, was not a cruel or unkind man. His charity and secrecy kept me alive. Same as Tessana's priest."

I spun toward her, stretching for the hope in her story. "Is that why you remained a secret? Because Maksim was afraid for your life?"

Her chin wobbled, but her voice did not. "It was not said like that. But I'm sure that's why. Look at what happened to you once the realm learned about your survival. Multiple attempts to kill you before the council had even decided. And my father has said the palace guards have stopped assassins every day since you were made heir to the throne." She inhaled so deeply that her shoulders rose and fell. "It will only get worse."

I craned my neck to find Taelon. "Is that true? Assassins every day?"

He narrowed his gaze on the back of Katrinka's head in a concerned way. "No, of course not." He cleared his throat. "Not every day."

Implying that there were still plenty.

The occasional assassin should be expected. But who was sending them?

Oliver choked back something that sounded surprisingly like a laugh. "You're surprised that people are trying to kill you, Tess? Only you."

"And what does that mean?" I demanded to know.

"Hmm," Caspian mused, sidling up to me and forcing Oliver to move behind us. "Only that the Allisand darling hates it when people hate her, possibly?"

My brow furrowed tightly. "No, that's not true." And that was all I was determined to say about the matter. But then he didn't immediately respond, so I couldn't help but say, "I genuinely understand that people hate the position, the ruler of the realm. I'm sure Tyrn has had his fair share of would-be assassins."

"Aha!" Caspian crowed. "You can't stand the idea of someone hating you. You have to blame the *position*."

He mimicked my voice at the end, though he sounded nothing like me.

"She has not even been in power long enough to garner true hatred," Taelon added diplomatically. "Of course they hate what she stands for."

Caspian looked at me, his long legs and wide strides taunting me to walk faster. "Do you only surround yourself with people who tell you exactly what you want to hear?"

We'd reached a part of the gardens I'd never been to before. The narrow path opened up to sprawling pastures. The grass was allowed to grow taller here. So tall that the tops turned white and waved like wheat in the gentle breeze. It reminded me of Heprin. Of the Rolling Hills of Gain. And my heart thumped in my chest so fiercely that I thought it would punch a hole straight through my skin.

Oliver glanced back at me. "Tess?"

I shook my head, shaking off Caspian's insult. "I did not know, or we would have visited much sooner."

The two of us set off down a gentle slope of the land, our hands brushing the tops of the tall grass as we went. Memories assuaged my vision as I thought of all the times Oliver and I had run through fields nearly identical to this one as children. Or when we would hide from Father Tarkus when he wanted us to scrub pots and pans larger than our entire bodies. When we were older and unafraid of hard work, we would take books, stretch out like kittens in the soft blanket of grass, and read for hours in warm sunlight.

Oliver was as silently reverent as I. No doubt remembering the scent of home. The touch of Heprin on our skin and in our souls. I had never expected to miss the Temple. Or the priests who raised me. But as the wheat grass tickled my ankles and caressed my palms, a wide, gaping hole opened inside me.

How lucky was I to have two homes? How blessed had I been to be found by Father Garius and not whisked off to a damp, cold prison like Castle Bale?

The Light had looked out for me. I could not deny my fortune.

Even now, as assassins hunted me and I learned to navigate the difficult pathways toward the throne, I knew a bigger purpose than my life was playing out. Something, something good, had orchestrated these events in my life. Even if I had faced hard things, the outcome had been blessed. And I could not speak for the gratitude stuck in my throat.

The wheatlike grass met a copse of trees but did not cease to grow. Our steps became more difficult as roots tangled in the thick grass where we could not see. Without the sunlight to feed the grass, one would think it would wither beneath the thick canopy of leaves overhead. But it did not. It seemed even denser in the shade.

Oliver and I pushed forward, both of us fascinated by the strange, familiar grass. Someone called my name from behind us, but I was too focused on moving forward to turn around.

After several minutes of walking and stumbling over tangled roots, the grass finally did give way to a shorter version of itself. In fact, the whole of this small forest seemed to make way for something else entirely.

CHAPTER
SIX

A crumbling stone temple sat in the middle of a large opening. It was a much smaller version of the Temple of Eternal Light, but I would have recognized its replica anywhere.

The roof had caved in over everywhere but the chapel. And the forest had moved in. The pale stone walls were nearly covered in pale green ivy. One of the large trees with exposed roots seemed to have sprouted up directly in the center of the building—probably why and how the roof had disappeared. Some of the stained glass windows were still intact and playing magnificently with the shafts of light poking in through the forest ceiling. And some had broken away. It was beauty and mayhem all at once. The past in the present. The decayed in the vibrant life of forest surrounding it.

And in and out of the dark trees surrounding it, fireflies blinked.

"What is this place?" Katrinka gasped, sounding out of breath. Whether it was from the difficult hike here or the serene splendor of the old chapel, I could not say.

"It is a Temple," Oliver said, taking careful steps toward it. "A . . . smaller one than is standard. But do you suppose it was intended for the king's use?"

"Are you sure?" Caspian asked, taking a closer look at the doorway that seemed in fine shape despite the disrepair of the rest of the building. "We have a Temple of Light near our home, and it does not have these markings along the archway. Nor does it have . . ." He dragged his finger over the carvings on the double doors.

I moved up the small stone staircase to inspect the doors myself. "Yes, Oliver is right. These are almost identical markings to the doors where we're from." I traced a dragon holding scrolls in its long talons. "The front door of the Temple and the doors to the library are inscribed just like this. And the stained glass. Well, the modern chapel might not have boasted stained glass such as this, but the old chapel, which the priests use for brewing beer, did."

"There's a Temple for the king's use already," Katrinka added. "Maksim took me to pray there before we arrived that first night. It was why we were late. But it is connected to the castle. Not far from the throne room."

"Maybe my father, or his father, got tired of walking this far to pray, so they had one built into the castle proper?" I guessed, testing the door handles and finding them unlocked. Although I met resistance almost immediately.

I pushed harder, hoping nothing permanent had grown up behind them. Without my asking, Caspian joined me, pushing with all his might. When neither of us was enough, Oliver and Taelon jumped in too. After several attempts and some manly grunting, we were able to push the door back just far enough to squeeze our bodies through a small gap.

The floor of the chapel was almost completely covered with overgrowth. But there was a natural path toward the center. I stepped toward the tree that took up most of the space, but a hand on my bicep stalled me.

"We're not sure what manner of wildlife could have made this its home," Caspian warned. "This place has been clearly untouched by men for some time."

He had a point. But . . . I took another step, something deep and unnamable inside urging me forward.

"Tessa," Taelon spoke up, his voice hoarse with wonder. "Let Caspian and me look around before you go farther. Our lives are less valuable than yours."

His excuse made me laugh. "The Crown Prince of Soravale? And the second and only other son to Vorestra? No, no. You are both of equal import." I smiled at them and playfully skipped forward. "Let me look around for you."

"You will not stop her," Oliver said. "Once she decides something . . ."

He went on, but something caught my eye. Fireflies buzzed and blinked all around us. But in the center of the tree was another light. One I had seen two other times now.

A small glow, almost identical to the fireflies but unblinking. And there it seemed to wait for me to notice it. Once my eyes had landed on its subtle brilliance, it moved up and down, reminding me of a finger beckoning me.

And then I saw it, something carved onto the tree. The natural path seemed to lead me directly there, making way for each of my steps.

I pressed my finger into the roughhewn letters and thought of the door to this building and the ones at home in Heprin. There was a dragon carved above. Or something dragon-like. It had clearly been carved by someone who was not a master at his craft, so the image was hard to make out.

And below the long talons stretched out in jagged lines were three sets of initials: TF + RP + GA.

The unnatural light moved down, bringing my gaze to a new set of carved words. These were done with a steadier, more skilled hand. "The old way is the true way."

I bent down to study the difference. I didn't know how I knew, maybe by the color of the bark or some buried instinct I didn't know I possessed, but I knew the initials were much older than the words.

The initials were cruder, awkward. Maybe carved by a child. Or children? And the words were . . . elegant. Meant to inscribe purpose and put meaning to the initials. If that was what they were. Maybe they meant something altogether different.

"What have you found?" Taelon asked over my shoulder. But then he read it out loud anyway: "TF plus RP plus GA. The old way is the true way."

"We are not the first to find your garden getaway," Caspian mused, sounding smug. "I don't think we want to ask questions about the three sets of initials."

"It is nothing untoward," Katrinka scolded, sounding sure of yourself. "Two of the sets are clearly our uncle, Tyrn Finnick. And our mother, Gwynlynn Allisand."

"And the third?" Taelon asked. "RP?"

I had been stumped by all of them, so I had no guess. Neither did Katrinka. But I had questions. "It is not very well done," I explained, although why I felt so desperate to remove my mother's name from the list, I had no idea. "I would have guessed a child carved the initials and the dragon. Our mother did not live at the castle when she was a child; if she had, her initials would have been GF, not GA."

And she had not harbored much love for Tyrn when she had been alive. Although I knew they had been close as children. But she had been disappointed and sometimes embarrassed by him as an adult. I remembered that clearly.

"Besides," I added. "If our mother had come all this way to carve initials into the tree, wouldn't she have done our father's? Why would she carve her brother's alongside her married initials?"

Caspian crowded near in order to inspect the carvings himself. "That is not a dragon," he said decisively. "I believe it's a bird. A crow perhaps."

Dread spiraled through me, and suddenly, I could not think of the initials on the tree without thinking of the assassins Katrinka had mentioned earlier.

Oliver spun around from where he'd been inspecting the stained glass along the wall. "I would wager it's a raven."

Not picking up the macabre meaning, Caspian leaned closer to the tree, his chest brushing my shoulder. "It's possible. Although I cannot tell the difference between real-life ravens and crows. So it's anyone's best guess which it might be here."

My balance shifted, and I swayed a little. Caspian reached forward, his body now fully wrapping around mine, and rubbed at the bark where the strange light had stalled. It disappeared beneath his fingertip, and he glanced skyward in search of a ray of sun.

He would not find one, and I knew that. But did he know what he'd just frightened away?

Did I even know?

The old way is the true way.

The old way of what? Could the initials really belong to my uncle and mother? If so, who was the third person? Not Fredricks Allisand, my father. So who?

Taelon reached for my hand, maneuvering it away from Caspian and into the protection of his grasp. "We should return to the luncheon," he suggested, allowing me to keep hold of his hand while I fought to regain my balance. "This has been an exciting adventure, but your uncle will be anxious about your absence."

"Yes, of course, you're right." I tipped my head back so I could focus on his handsome face. He smiled down at me, and it was tender and soft. I leaned against him for more support. I didn't know why this chapel had shaken me up so completely, but I felt upended by some fear I could not name.

Caspian's gaze had shifted to us and altered his temperament. There was something darker in his already dark looks, his bright, gray eyes almost glowing in the dim light. "Yes, it's a good idea. Also, I believe we managed to leave Tessana's guards somewhere behind us. And if we don't want them to ring the alarms and send an entire army to find us, I suggest we put them out of their misery soon."

We'd managed to lose my guards? But how had we done that? I

had totally forgotten about them on the walk here, but they were supposed to stay out of sight when I was in the company of others.

Katrinka moved toward the exit in a flurry of gray skirts and panic. "Hello!" she called to the outside. "We're over here."

Caspian gave Taelon and me one more long look, then followed Katrinka outside. I allowed Taelon to lead me back toward the door but remembered Oliver near the windows.

"Go ahead," I told him. "I'll follow right behind."

He leaned down and pressed a sweet kiss to my temple. "We will find time to catch up soon," he promised in a whisper. "Your uncle cannot get in our way forever."

I smiled at his back as he squeezed through the small opening. I hadn't liked the way Caspian looked at us. Like he knew something about us that he shouldn't.

Taelon and I hadn't hidden our affection for each other intentionally. We simply knew it could not lead anywhere. He had a kingdom to run. And I a realm. But that did not mean we could stop ourselves from moving toward each other from across the room. Or that I could stop my eyes from seeking his whenever he was near. It did not mean I could help feeling safest around him. Or that I could stop the frantic thumping of my heart when he pressed kisses to my temples, or hands, or lips.

But still, best not to let the realm think they could ship me off to Soravale and be done with me so easily.

"Oliver," I called, pulling him from intently staring at his hands. No, not his hands. A piece of stained glass he must have picked up from the ground. "It's time to return to the castle."

He looked up, shaking his head as if waking from a dream. He moved toward the exit, and I met him at the doors. When he approached me, I saw that he was still holding the glass.

"What is it?" I asked, nerves jangling in my belly like the alarm bell I feared would sound if we tarried any longer.

He tilted the glass so I could see it as it was meant to hang in the window. There was an image cut into it with different shades of color. But I could see the image clearly because it was a larger piece that had not shattered.

A raven.

Nearly matching the crude reproduction scratched into the tree. The colored glass was all triangles, so it was more rudimentary than classical, but the shape was clear. Wings spread wide. Talons long and sharp. In its clutches was a burst of light, like a star or sunburst.

I looked around at the other windows, now frantically searching for similarities, and found them everywhere. Cut into each window. At the front of the chapel. On the way out.

Oliver set the glass down as he very well could not carry it back to the castle, but my heart pounded frantically within the frail shell of my body.

TF + RP + GA

The old way is the true way.

But now, those haunting words felt familiar. I had seen them somewhere. Read them somewhere. Was it at the Temple? Or here?

We rushed back through the wheat-like grass to the stone path, where we nearly collided with our guards. They looked white as ghosts, pale with panic.

"Where have you been?" The question came from one of Katrinka's, who was clearly not as adept at hunting for her as mine were for me.

"We were just there," she said, pointing behind us. Her guard looked stunned into a stupor, clearly not understanding where she meant. "There is an old Temple," she added. "We were not far. We thought you were right behind us, Griffin. I didn't mean to startle you."

He was visibly sweating. And panting. But to my sister, he said, "It's nothing you did, Your Highness. It is my fault. I . . . I got mixed up. Thanks be to the Light you are unharmed."

She smiled reassuringly, and we all marched on. I looked back at the field of wheat grass once we'd made it up the hill a ways, but all I could see were more winding garden paths and rows of hedges. A chill slithered up my spine.

"Do you see that?" I whispered to Oliver, discreetly nodding behind us.

He nodded. "I noticed as soon as we were beyond the barrier."

"The barrier?"

"It reminded me of the Blood Woods," he whispered. "When we followed Arrick into the fog, his camp was waiting just on the other side. Do you remember?"

My heart kicked in concern. "Pagan magic, then?"

"The ravens, Tess. They must be . . . a calling card or symbol or something. Don't you think?"

The old way is the true way. "Yes, they must be. A symbol for pagans. But white magic or black?"

He was silent for a moment before he said, "Maybe both."

Then we both fell quiet. And stayed that way through the remnants of lunch, a scolding from my uncle afterward, and then I claimed a headache to avoid a late supper. I sent word to Oliver so he could skip if he'd like. I knew I had blown my chance of spending more time with Taelon that evening, but I needed to investigate something before I could recover my senses and engage with people again.

Once Clesta had forgiven me for leaving her to my uncle's wrath and helped take my hair out, I shooed her from the room and locked the door behind her. Digging out the grimoire I'd locked away, I flipped open the front cover. Incriminating initials were scribed in the upper right-hand corner. GA. Gwynlynn Allisand.

I flipped to the center of the book and found the same raven in flight that had been on the tree today. And in the stained glass.

It was identical to the book Father Garius had shown me at the Temple of Eternal Light. But more than this spell book had started to resemble my time at the Temple.

Then I flipped the pages back to where I'd left off the night I'd found it. There had been something that stood out just before I dozed off. A phrase in my own language. My mother's neat scrawl in the margin.

It took me a couple of minutes, but I found it. Next to pagan text and pictures of herbs and bones was the flourished lettering I knew belonged to my mother. "The old way is the true way."

She'd written it onto the page herself.

I sat in the middle of my bedroom floor, half undressed from the day's gown, with my hair a wild mane around my shoulders, and had to face the fact that my mother might have been more pagan than I had ever wanted to believe.

Not only that, but she could very well have been a part of the three initials carved on a tree in the middle of what appeared to be an abandoned witch's sanctum—an ancient chapel used by the pagans for spells, magic, and healing.

I only knew about them because my mother had told us stories of their power.

But had her words been more than just stories? Meant for more than to simply entertain us?

I had more questions. Why did our Temples of Light look so very similar? Had the Brotherhood of the Light simply copied an already established religion? Dumbed it down and made it more palatable for the masses? Created something they themselves did not believe in but would make a believable alternative for the people of the realm?

And beyond that, what did my mother have to do with any of it?

What did her death, and the death of my brothers and father, really mean?

The old way is the true way.

Was it her message?

Her faith?

Or was it her abandonment of them both so she could marry my father? If her initials were of her married name, did that mean she'd continued her pagan beliefs afterward regardless? I couldn't help but recall my parents' discussion again.

"Diamond for power. Ruby for love. Emerald for magic . . .

But in the old days, emerald was the power stone. The ignitor of all things magical.

I doubt the old ways have anything to do with these new days."

I hugged the grimoire against my chest and wished I could ask her these questions and more. Was this a mystery worth solving? Or should I let the dead remain dead?

One thing was for certain, I needed someone who could read pagan.

CHAPTER SEVEN

"Have they decided the date of your coronation yet?" the prince of Aramore asked as he twirled me around the dance floor. His name was Landrick Garstone, and he was the second son of King Henrik and Queen Lillibeth.

If I didn't know better, I would have thought he was waiting for me to arrive at the final ball of Tyrn's weeklong celebration. He seemed to appear out of nowhere as soon as the herald announced my arrival. And before I could even look around the room for Taelon, he'd taken my hand and asked for a dance.

Tyrn had answered for me, waving me away with an expression that reminded me not to mess this up.

"They have not," I replied with a bland smile. "We have been quite busy actually, acclimating to this new . . . arrangement. My sister had only just arrived. And I am not yet eighteen." Although I would be very soon. "My uncle is a pragmatic man. When I'm ready, he will decide the date."

"But even then, you will not be queen?" Landrick asked, his brow furrowing as if all these minute details were difficult for him to keep track of.

I tried my best to disguise my heavy sigh. "No, not even then. The coronation is more like a promise of future queendom. Or perhaps a seal of future power is more accurate. I will continue my education until my twenty-first birthday. At that time, I will step into power. Onto the throne, etcetera."

"Etcetera," he murmured, pleased with my answer. "Unless something happens to your uncle."

His words were ice in my veins. I did not especially enjoy Tyrn or his handling of . . . well, any of this. But he was my uncle. And he had held the Seat of Power for me, however unconsciously, all this time. Besides, even I could admit I was not ready to be queen. I liked that I had succeeded in securing my future. And I was proud that the Crown of Nine would remain in the Allisand bloodline. But I was not a fool. I had no royal or courtly training. I did not know how to command Shiksa successfully, let alone an entire army.

There was much to learn. And experience. But my time would come. Eventually. I just hoped it would be before the Ring of Shadows burned everything beyond the Marble Wall to ash. Or one of my many assassins made it beyond the castle drawbridge.

Landrick's confident smile wobbled for only a second before he asked, "And it is true that the council would like you married before you take the throne?"

It took all my self-control not to rip my hand out of his and run out of the ballroom screaming in horror. But Father Garius's fear control training served me well in almost every circumstance I had encountered so far.

Fear is not the enemy. The ancient Heprin Scrolls promised. *Your reaction to fear is your adversary. Face it or run from it. Conquer it or allow it to conquer you.*

"That is their wish," I told him, ducking my head and feigning a demure smile while bile rose in the back of my throat. It was not that I hated the idea of marriage. More like, I had seen through this smarmy second prince the moment he touched my hand and would never chain myself to someone so utterly full of himself.

The throne was a prize to him. A mountain to climb. A stag to hunt. I was the trophy he would mount on his wall and brag about to his friends.

He pulled me closer against his body, but because of the fullness of my gown, only our torsos touched. The cold, harsh buttons and meaningless military medals dug into the exposed skin of my shoulders and chest.

"And what do you want, Your Highness?" he asked in a voice I was sure he meant to be seductive.

Another glass of wine. But I couldn't say that and avoid a lecture from my uncle. So instead, I smiled brightly and said, "Whatever is best for the realm."

It wasn't a lie. But it also was most certainly not this spoiled royal. I glanced across the dance floor and briefly caught Taelon's eyes. He was dancing with a Kashan princess who was too beautiful for her own good. The dragon I liked to pretend lived inside me lashed out its long, spikey tail with a whip of jealous fury.

But then I had to smile. I remembered a conversation from long ago about Kasha princesses. And Taelon's sweet reply. Did he still think I was prettier than any foreign princess? Did it even matter?

My smile turned into another sigh, and I ducked my head to keep this Aramore prince from believing I was mad.

The orchestra finished their waltz in a crescendo of beautiful strings and timpani. I was finally given social permission to step out of Landrick's arms.

"Thank you for the dance," I said with all the poise and grace I could muster.

"You'll save another one for me?" he asked before I could sprint away. "Dancing with you has been my greatest honor. I am so looking forward to doing it again."

"I—"

"If there's time," Taelon answered for me. He stepped to my side and smiled down at me. "She's already promised me quite a few." He turned back to Landrick and said, "You know how dancing is the princess's favorite activity. It has made her very selective of her partners."

Landrick's brow furrowed with confusion again. He probably remembered all the times I stepped on his toes and tried to turn in the wrong direction. "Well, I'll find you la—"

The rest of his sentence was drowned out in the din of the crowd as Taelon turned me around and guided me to the balcony.

"This isn't the way to the dance floor," I noted.

His hand splayed across my spine. "I think what you meant to say was, 'Thank you, kind sir.'"

I bit my bottom lip to keep from smiling too wide. "Thank you, Rebel King."

His low chuckle vibrated through me. I had been waiting for this moment since he arrived in Sarasonet. Finally, we could have a few minutes to talk.

The ballroom was stifling with so many royals crammed into one space. And my massive ivory gown did nothing to regulate my body temperature. The dressmaker had outdone herself this evening. Folds of cream silk stitched with sparkling gold and silver thread. My arms were bare save for a thin, draped sleeve over my bicep that hardly covered anything. The tight bodice was meant to accentuate my curves and bust. It dipped down in the back, exposing almost everything, and pushed my bust up in the front so that, honestly, it gave a completely false impression of what I had to offer. But I supposed that was her plan.

I was, after all, on display this evening. Like a winter goose trussed up in the shop window for the Longest Night Festival.

Taelon and I lifted our faces to the cool night air once we stepped onto the castle balcony. We could turn around and watch the dancers in their finery through the floor-to-ceiling paned glass. But our eyes were fixed on the dark sky ahead with a thousand twinkling stars and the milkiest, fullest moon I had ever seen. Guards were positioned along the ledge, but they did not bother us as we moved to a clear space where we could look out at the blooming flower gardens below and the peaks of the Diamond Mountains along the horizon.

"You are truly a stunning sight tonight, Stranger," he breathed in a low whisper. "I have been desperate all night to speak with you but afraid words would fail me." He tucked a strand of styled hair behind my ear, his thumb moving in a slow caress along my cheekbone. "Sometimes I can hardly reconcile the woman I met on the road in Tenovia with the future queen you've become. If I had known what I know now, I think courage would have failed me, and I would not have chased you or captured you or . . . argued with you. I simply would have knelt at your feet and promised fealty right then and there."

"Are you saying I was ugly? On the road?" His compliment was lovely, but did he honestly think I would miss what lay beneath?

He laughed at my question. "No, of course not." Still, with more laughter, he added, "Travel weary perhaps." His thumb brushed over my bottom lip. "And a little dirty."

I folded my arms across my chest and feigned a pout. "You do not know what it was like. We walked across the length of Heprin. And then you chased us through the Blood Woods. In the dark! Find me a girl who could do all that and come out pristine." He opened his mouth, but I finished my point with a dramatic, "We outran a wildebeest that night, Taelon. Oliver and I had to scramble up into a tree to avoid having our brains smashed in. Excuse me if I was a little worse for wear."

His fingers pressed against my lips, silencing me gently. The look in his eyes was all adoration. "You were beautiful. Twigs in your hair and dirt on your cheeks. And I still thought you were the most beautiful creature I had ever laid eyes on. My point is that you have only grown more beautiful. The more I see of you, know of you, your beauty does not fade. You shine brighter than any star, bloom lovelier than any blossom, steal my breath better than any blow."

But it was me who was fighting to breathe. Because how could I after a compliment such as that one? "Oh."

His smile gentled, but the look in his deep-blue eyes darkened. "It seems your uncle has been intent on keeping us apart. My schedule has been filled with game hunting, card games, and diplomatic meetings."

"Meetings? I thought diplomacy was put aside for these ridiculous celebrations."

He lost the dreamy look on his face and frowned. "Your uncle is quite concerned with the Cavolia. And the Rebel Army. He wanted to talk . . . strategy."

Fear clawed at my heart. "Strategy?"

"He would like my help dismantling what he sees as our greatest threats."

"Taelon, you can't—"

He glanced around. "I realize."

"What about . . . ?" I raised a single eyebrow.

"He does not suspect," Taelon murmured in the lowest possible tone.

eret Grimsayer, Taelon's second-in-command of the Rebel Army, had been arrested during my Conandra trial for treason. But shortly after his imprisonment, eret had mysteriously disappeared. One evening, he'd been present to accept his supper of stale bread and gruel. The following morning, his cell had been empty.

It remained an unsolved case to this day.

Truly. Not even I knew how the Rebel Army had managed to make a full-grown man disappear from his cell without being seen and without damaging the cell in any way. But they had.

My shoulders relaxed some. I liked eret. But more than my good feelings toward him, I knew Taelon trusted him implicitly. And while Taelon had to be called away from their cause quite often thanks to his royal duties, the army needed eret to lead them.

"What will you do?" I asked Taelon, fear reappearing in the corners of my heart.

"Rely on diplomacy to drag out this process for as long as possible," he said with a gruff snarl. "And hope that my truest ally ascends the throne sooner rather than later."

I frowned. "Not until I'm twenty-one."

"Yes, but surely your uncle will include you more in court proceedings after your coronation."

"You would think. Two months from now, we will find out."

Taelon turned so he could lean his back against the balcony ledge. "At least celebrations have returned to the realm. You have already sparked change."

I turned to look at the packed ballroom and the realm's elite dressed in their finest. "Yes, look at my progress. I'm downright revolutionary."

He snickered at my sarcasm. "Well, you have to start somewhere."

"I would prefer to start with the starving and oppressed. Not extravagant parties and weeks of bum-kissing."

"That reminds me, Gunter has been pulled away for a while. There has been . . . some unrest in the north. The Cavolia have gone to see what's amiss."

"The north? Tenovia?"

He shook his head. "Heprin."

The wind whooshed out of me, and I fell back against the balcony too. "What sort of unrest?"

Taelon's expression flattened, but he offered only a small shrug. "I'm not certain. We have no contacts that far north and have never had the need to plant spies. The Ring of Shadows has thus far avoided the farthest kingdoms. But . . . Gunter has a woman. A pagan. She's . . . She's been having dreams."

My mind flashed with gruesome images of my own dreams. "A witch?"

Taelon didn't acknowledge my question. To do so would invite all manner of trouble. "Does she read pagan? This woman?"

He lifted one shoulder. "I don't know. Why do you ask?"

I thought of telling him about the spell book, the words I could not read. *The old way is the true way.* But I knew he would want to see it. And that would require me handing it over so he could look through it in private.

"The chapel," I explained instead. "From our excursion the other day. We had all assumed it was a Temple to the Light. But just before we left, Oliver found signs that it might have been a pagan chapel. There were images not connected to the religion of the Light. I thought she might be able to say for sure. And then we might better know whom the initials belonged to."

Taelon's blue eyes darkened with interest. "Do you think that's important information?"

His question was sincere. He was not dismissing me but genuinely asking if that was a mystery we needed to solve. My spirit swelled near to bursting. I had not felt validated in such a way since before I came to Elysia. Taelon's small show of confidence meant more to me than I knew how to convey. And while I regularly fought to give my love to him entirely, when he said things like that and showed how much he trusted and cared for me, it was impossible to withhold any of my heart.

"I can't explain why," I told him honestly, saving my useless declarations of love for another time. "But . . . I have this feeling I'm missing something. A key to unlocking a door. And it's found in those initials." I smiled sheepishly, a burn heating my cheeks. It sounded so silly now that I had said it out loud. "There are, of course, bigger matters at hand. I just thought if she accompanied Gunter when he returned, maybe she could show us something we're missing."

"Like why the palace grounds would have use for a pagan chapel?"

I nodded. "Yes, exactly."

His pinky finger reached out and caressed the line of my own. His expression changed from businesslike and stern to soft and sorrowful in the span of that one discreet touch. "Tessa, I have missed you more than words can say. It has been too long since we've spoken so freely."

I mimicked his pose against the balcony so we stood side by side, our arms less than an inch from touching. "Can I invite you to stay? To be my special guest? Once the rest of the monarchs leave, my life here will screech to a halt. No meetings, no luncheons, no balls."

He stared at the ground. "I received a missive from Gunter late last night. He's asked me to meet him in Heprin. I've delayed my leave so I could be here tonight."

"You should not have done that."

His touch moved to the center of my palm. The feeling of his fingers there, his light caress, made butterflies soar through my chest and belly. How long would it be till we could be alone again? How long would it be till I could be myself around him again?

Dragon's blood, I had missed this man. And now he was leaving again. After we'd just been reunited.

"How could I have done anything else?" he asked in a low murmur. Leaning closer, he whispered, "I will write to you from now on. I have placed a guard in your personal service. He's loyal to Arrick. His name is Finch. If you have anything you'd like to say to me, see that he receives the letter. No one but me will read it."

My spirit soared with his promise. I lifted my head, and our gazes clashed. So many unsaid feelings, so many choking fears. But now I could share them with him. I could hear his thoughts and get his opinions and read words he'd written with his own hand.

"Taelon," I whispered, my voice thick with joy.

He reached forward and brushed his thumb over my cheek. "I have missed you, Stranger."

"And I you, Rebel King."

Our bodies inclined toward each other as if we could not resist this intimate moment. Too many people were around, and we had too much at stake to be careless, but how could I care about any of that with Taelon so near?

Near enough to touch. Near enough to kiss.

"When I am not with you, it is as though a piece of my soul is missing," he murmured, his breath tickling my cheek, my ear. "I find it unbearable."

"Then stay here," I tempted him. "Let Gunter deal with Heprin and all of the realm if that is what it takes. Stay with me."

Instead of pulling away, he moved closer. His temple touched mine, the rough scrape of his jaw against the smooth line of mine. I wanted to turn and press my lips to his cheeks. To his lips. The realm and my future be damned. My self-control was held by the thinnest thread.

"You don't mean that," he murmured.

I bit out a frustrated growl. "No, I don't." I closed my hand around his wrist, the muscles and heat flexing against my palm. "I have this dreadful feeling that Heprin needs the Cavolia. Needs . . . you, Arrick Westnovian." I leaned closer, inhaling deeply as if I could always keep the feel of him and the scent of him with me. "But I find this unbearable."

"I will come straight back," he swore, his voice thick with promise. "I will leave tonight. And return as soon as I can. And then we will . . ." He hesitated, and I could feel the tension coiled tightly inside him. Because what could ever happen between us? He could no more promise me a place by his side than I could him a place by mine.

I pulled back, tears stinging the corners of my eyes. "No, you were right the first time. It is better if you—" This time, the sob that cut my words off was audible. I gritted my teeth, swallowing down the flood of emotion that threatened to spill over. "Better if you go. We both know this."

He straightened as well, but his hand reached down to take mine, hiding our entwined fingers behind the folds of my skirt. "I might know it, but I hate it as well." He dropped his head, his gaze finding his polished boots. "Would that I could take us back to the easy days of our youth. Would that I could make it possible for you to be mine again."

I squeezed his hand and drank in his lovely but impossible promises. "I will write to you regardless," I told him.

He turned his head to face me again, and I knew this was goodbye for a long time. "And I to you. I will let you know of Heprin as soon as I can."

My lips lifted in a wobbly smile. "Be safe, Rebel King. The realm needs you more than ever."

His mouth mimicked mine—a smile full of sadness and despair. "The same is true of you, Tessa. And if you need anything, ask Finch. He is loyal to me and will protect you at any cost."

"Let us hope it does not come to that."

His gaze narrowed. "Let us hope I will have someone in place to replace him when it does come to that."

"Taelon—"

He stood abruptly and lifted my hand to his lips. "We will meet again as soon as I am able, Princess. I give you my word."

Then he was gone in a flash of Soravalian colors, his brilliant blue-and-silver suit slicing through the crowd. I watched him until I could no longer see him. Until I could no longer feel him nearby. And with each step in the opposite direction, I felt my heart crack and split, whole pieces breaking off.

I cared for Taelon more than I should. Even if it was possible for us to explore a courtship, my feelings for him were too strong, too big. I must keep the realm in mind, the dangers that threatened it, and the future I wanted to make possible. The realm, my throne, the crown . . . were the only things that should demand so much of my attention and thought.

Not princes.

Not courtships.

And certainly not kisses.

I moved toward the ballroom again, knowing my uncle would be looking for me by now. My guards clicked into attention all around the terrace, but I hardly noticed them from the storm of my thoughts.

A figure stepped from the shadows as I neared the glass doors. I was startled from my misery and opened my mouth to scold a guard when a sliver of moonlight alighted Caspian's face.

CHAPTER EIGHT

My mouth snapped shut as I took him in. Unlike the other princes and delegates here tonight, he wasn't dressed in his kingdom's colors. Instead, he wore a dress tunic in all black, styled longer than the traditional styles I was used to. His pants were looser too than the majority of male leggings. And his feet were adorned in black silk slippers with delicate gold swirls embroidered on them.

His black hair was styled back, away from his face. And his pale gray eyes nearly glowed in the dim light.

He was a fearsome and beautiful sight to behold.

"Dragon's blood, Caspian, must you always sneak up on me?"

His lips twitched in a way I thought might have meant he was amused. "I stepped outside to ask her highness for a dance."

My already grim mood darkened. "You must forgive me. I'm not in the dancing mood."

"The talking mood, then? Or walking. I'm happy to escort the future queen through the gardens."

A stroll through the gardens would be better than suffocating in the full ballroom. But it felt like a betrayal somehow. An insult to the sweet and sorrowful moment Taelon and I had just shared.

"No, thank you. I think I will—"

He held his hand out in invitation. "Come now, Princess. I'm the only eligible bachelor who has not enjoyed your company this evening. Spare me a lecture from my brother on missed opportunities. Please."

I could not remember a time when I had ever heard Caspian use the word please. Both this week and when we were children. It was enough to pause my self-pity and give him my full attention. "As if your brother cares."

His smile turned self-deprecating. "If you do not think my newly kinged brother wants me as far from his kingdom as possible, you do not know Carrigan at all." I opened my mouth to argue, but he added, "And having an ally in the Seat of Power is also enticing."

My smile was somehow genuine. "But would you be an ally? To Vorestra, I mean. If your brother still occupies the throne?"

He lifted an arrogant shoulder and looked away. "As long as there is a possibility of being the queen's consort, my life is not at risk."

"That doesn't answer my question," I told him, ignoring the words queen and consort in the same sentence.

He met my gaze again, his all pale starlight in the dark night. "I suppose time will tell. First, I must woo the future queen, make her fall in love with me, and marry her. I say we tackle dancing tonight and worry about the rest in the morning."

I was taken aback by his charm. Had he been this enchanting since the beginning, I wondered if we could have started a friendship over the past two weeks. Instead, I was more skeptical of him than ever.

"Well, now that we know your true intentions, I believe I will stick with my previous answer. No, thank you."

Caspian nodded and stepped back, his face falling into the shadows again. But just as I was about to walk by him, he said, "He's betrothed, you know. Or very soon to be."

Dread pooled in my belly. But still, I managed to keep my voice steady. "Who?"

He leaned back against the castle wall and folded his arms over his chest. "Your Soravalian Prince Charming. There were rumors of a contract being drawn up between Soravale and Tenovia just before you reappeared."

My head spun with the possibilities. Taelon had never said anything about a marriage contract. Or about any other woman. And neither had Hugo.

Was this common knowledge? Did everyone know but me?

To Caspian, I said, "Taelon and I are friends. We've been friends our whole lives. What you saw—" I cleared my throat. "What you *think* you saw were two friends catching up after two long weeks of busyness. That is all."

"So you knew already, then. Surely, good friends—*lifelong* friends —would share things such as courtship and future nuptials?"

There were two ways to play this. I could pretend I already knew and potentially be caught in Caspian's outright lie. Or I could be honest and risk humiliation by omission. The hard truth was I already knew which way I would choose.

The humiliation had already occurred.

"He has not mentioned an engagement," I said in a small voice. "But I'm sure the subject is awkward for him because of our previous arrangement." I thought back to Hugo's promise of renewing the contract when I first arrived in Soravale. Had he been willing to embarrass Tenovia over my return? How would Tenovia have reacted?

Or had it been an empty promise from the start?

"Yes, you're right. Better to spare the princess shame than risk reminding her who she can never be with."

His cold words were like daggers in my side. "You've read this wrong, desert prince. We are friends. Nothing more." The words physically hurt to say. I had turned the dagger on myself. It was no longer in Caspian's hand but my own. My tone matched his cruelty when I added, "Your brother is wise in that this is the time to make allies. Soravale has succeeded where Vorestra has failed."

Even in the dark, I saw the line of his jaw flex with irritation. "Unlike Soravale, Your Highness, Vorestra values respect over pandering to spoiled princesses. And maybe I should remind you, you need our support as much as we need someone who is not even queen yet."

Fury burned through me.

I took a step toward him and pulled back my arm. My brain hadn't yet agreed to the punch my body had most definitely planned. There was a whispered swoosh from behind me that perked my ears. And then Caspian tackled me to the ground.

My back hit the balcony floor before I could land my hit. The breath was forced from my lungs, and my head bounced off the stone.

I gasped a foul curse, but Caspian's growl of, "Stay down," overpowered my will.

Something was wrong.

Caspian's whole body covered mine as he pinned me to the ground. I had pegged him for a lazy scoundrel who did nothing more than seduce innocent women and plot against his brother. But stretched out on top of me, all I felt was taut muscle and dominant strength.

A body fell to the ground next to us. I glanced over, ready to plead for help, but the person beside me could not answer. Glassy, lifeless eyes of one of my guards stared back at me, a dark arrow protruding from the side of his neck where blood seeped out and trickled down his throat.

The swooshing noise fired in the distance. *Swoop. Swoop. Swoop.* I was only mildly adept with a bow, but I recognized the release of an arrow. But never had I heard so many at one time.

"You're under attack," Caspian snarled at my ear.

I lifted my head and looked at the chaos bursting into action around us. Guards scrambled to dive out of the way of incoming arrows. But too many were slicing through the air and coming too fast. Wave after wave of ill-fated projectiles. I watched a young man who had only just been promoted from page to my protective service get hit in the chest and fall over the balcony's edge, his scream of pain and panic renting the air as he plunged to his death.

I clung to Caspian's tunic, terrified and shocked. Another body fell behind me. I did not have to look to know it would be another of my guards.

"Where are they coming from?" I gasped as an arrow crashed and toppled just feet from where we lay. We were high above the castle grounds, and no buildings or other structures were anywhere near this side of the castle. It was all gardens and rolling hills. And miles away, the sheer façade of the Diamond Mountains.

"The turrets." He ducked his face into my neck as another arrow whizzed by. It was the most intimate I had ever been with a man. Even Taelon had never pressed his face against my bare skin like this.

Obviously, now was not the time to be thinking of such things. Both of us could die in the next instant. Probably should be more focused on surviving than the way Caspian's rough jaw scraped against my throat or the way his chin dipped and brushed my bosom.

But then he inhaled deeply. I felt the breath move through him, down the length of his taut body.

He lifted his head again and smirked. "You smell of oranges and honey."

There was such an intimate knowledge of me in his voice that I nearly forgot about the arrows completely. Caspian wasn't like Taelon at all. That had been true since the first moment he spoke to me. But in this way especially. Taelon was nothing but a gentleman, proper, sweet, respectable. Yes, he was roguish and playful too. Clever. Calculating. Wise. But with me, there was always an invisible boundary of regard. Caspian was the opposite. His eyes glinted with carnal things, his hands flexing on my body where he held me—one hand on my outstretched wrist, the other at my hip. His voice was smoke and sandpaper. His skin hot against mine. And still, the arrows zipped by, miraculously missing us. But barely.

"We need to get inside," I reminded him.

He refocused and looked to the right and then to the left. The ballroom and its balcony were set into the castle, nestled between two gradually extending walls that ended in towering turrets. The design gave the ballroom privacy, tucking it away with only a view of the gardens. While I could see nothing but Caspian's profile and long neck, the bowmen must be set up in the guest rooms and using the windows to get a line of sight on their targets.

Swoop. Then a sick crunching sound made my stomach beat against my spine.

Caspian growled in pain, his body contracting from the impact.

"Caspian!" I shrieked as he became limp over me, crushing me beneath his surprisingly substantial weight. He did not answer. "Caspian, please!" He still did not answer. "Dragon's blood, Caspian, do not die on top of me!" Still, he did not answer.

I clutched his shoulders, my fingers brushing the hilt of an arrow on his right side. I breathed a small sigh of relief that it didn't seem to have gone through his heart. I stilled long enough to feel a shallow breath move his chest up and down. Shaking him gently, I tried to rouse him while the party inside finally realized what was going on.

Women screamed, glasses shattered, and guards began moving outside. But as soon as someone stepped onto the patio, they were felled by a barrage of arrows.

I heard someone shouting about the princess and wondered if they could even see me beneath Caspian's unconscious body.

"Caspian, please," I begged, shaking him again. "I promise, I will give you a fair shot at being my consort if you will just wake up!"

I knew he hadn't heard me, not really. But he did suck in a deep breath and make a pained growl against the pain.

His head jerked upward, and his gaze found mine almost instantly. "I've been shot."

It was inappropriate to laugh at a time like this. But was he serious? "I realize."

With strength I knew cost him much, he placed both hands on

the stone floor to either side of me and pushed his body weight off me. His right arm trembled from pain and effort.

"When I say run, I want you to get up as quickly as you can and move to where you found me. There is a hidden door to the ballroom, but you will be at an awkward enough angle where an arrow cannot hit you."

I glanced at where he meant and then noticed a door blended into the stone wall of the castle. It made me wonder how long he'd been watching Taelon and me. We didn't notice him because he hadn't come through the glass panes lit up by light from the party.

"What about you?" I asked, my voice tight with concern.

"I'll be right behind you." He winced. "Hurry, princess, or they'll get us both."

I nodded and reached for my gown. I pulled it up, past my knees as best as I could. But there was so much fabric. Whispering a quick prayer to the Light, I let him launch his body upward, his steps wobbling once he landed on them.

I rolled to the side and scrambled to my feet. Arrows started flying at double the speed they had been. I heard them everywhere. My feet tangled in my gown, but I lurched for the hidden door.

Caspian let out another grunt of pain. And then another. I turned to see that he had stepped in front of me, blocking my body with his own. There was a bloody line across his neck as if it had just narrowly missed catching him in the throat. Another arrow stuck out from his side.

He staggered on his feet, only barely keeping himself from falling to his knees.

I knew my life was more important than his as the future leader of the realm. He was a second son from Vorestra. But I could not leave him to die for me. Not after he'd only just saved me.

Running back to him, I grabbed his good arm and yanked him after me. He was too weak to fight me. Arrows continued to attack while guards continued to fall in their attempt to join the balcony battle.

But they had only swords. Which were not useful at this distance.

An arrow finally found me, lodging itself into my skirt. Thankfully the thick, layered material slowed its momentum, and I didn't even feel a scratch on my skin.

Maybe ball gowns were the way to go. *Well, in a bow and arrow fight at a distance, anyway.* Hand-to-hand combat, not so much given I could barely stay upright in the damnable thing.

A sharp pain on the back of my arm, where another one grazed my bare skin. And then another one just to the right of my head, barely nicking the tip of my ear as I yanked Caspian inside the hidden door.

We landed in some dark passageway. A small space between the ballroom proper and the balcony. I hadn't been gentle with him as I pulled him inside, and I knew I'd jostled his wounds against the doorframe in my attempts to save him.

He immediately collapsed on the cold floor, falling to his uninjured side. His arm curled awkwardly beneath him, but I could see he was in too much pain to adjust himself.

I knelt at his side, unable to stop the tears that had started to fall. "Don't you dare die, Caspian. I will not allow it. Do you hear me? Do not die!"

His eyes were closed, but a smile twisted his lips. "I would not think of it," he rasped, his voice as rough as gravel. "Not after the future queen promised to let me be her consort."

His teasing surprised me more than I wanted to admit, and I sat back on my heels. "I never said you could be my consort."

He rattled a sigh, his smile ticking wider. "But you said I could try."

Was it possible to be infuriated with a man on the brink of death? Yes, yes, it was. The passageway door was yanked open behind me, and a string of shouts and announcements were made as guards proclaimed I was alive. Someone put strong hands on my shoulder and started to pull me away from Caspian.

I fought them just long enough to lean down and whisper, "If I find that this has been orchestrated to win my favor, second son of Vorestra, I will finish this job myself."

His expression turned serene as he lay there, bleeding. "I knew courting you would be interesting. And to think I was worried you would be as boring as I remembered."

Losing the ability to think rationally, I kicked out at him, intending to embed the arrow in his side as deeply as it could go. But lucky for him, the guards pulled me back at just the right time, and my foot found only air.

When I was in the ballroom proper and fully surrounded by guards and generals and my uncle, I found enough composure to say, "I'm fine. Just a few grazes. But Caspian is bleeding out, and he happened to save my life. So if you could return the favor, I would be grateful."

My uncle's brow furrowed as he took me in. "You seem rather unfazed. You were nearly killed."

I let out a long-suffering sigh. "It is not the first time. Nor will it be the last. But I believe the assassins have infiltrated the castle and are using the guest bedrooms to attack the balcony."

My uncle nodded. "Yes, they will be captured forthwith. We've managed to secure this section of the castle. But we will wait here until a thorough search of the rest of the grounds can be accomplished."

"And Caspian?" I glanced nervously at the secret door that was now swung wide for everyone to see. As infuriating as he could be, I really did not want him to die. Especially after he risked his life so recklessly for mine.

"We will see he has the best medical care, Tessana. We will not let those bastards get the better of him."

It was the kindest my uncle had ever been. I closed my eyes as gratitude and relief washed over me. The night was far from being over, and I did not relish spending it here in this gown. I would much rather be recovering in the hottest bath I could tolerate. But I was not ready to be alone either.

Not after that.

I wished for Taelon, but when I looked around, I found only Hugo and Anatal. Hugo offered a short shake of his head. Taelon must have left immediately after speaking with me. At least he had not been injured. I may not wish death on Caspian, but had Taelon been the one riddled with arrows, I could not have borne it. Thank the Light, he'd escaped unharmed. Even if all I wanted was for him to be back with me now with his strong arms around me, giving comfort that would be void until his return, settling the violent nerves now trembling through me. It was better that he had left. That he was gone.

But Gunter was gone too. Caspian's presence had been a fluke. A providential coincidence.

My life was in danger, and I was the only one left to protect it.

CHAPTER NINE

The night rolled on with all the haste of a green-webbed tree slug. My peers were used to pampering and plush accommodation. Maids who would undress them. Servants to draw baths for them. Someone to turn down the covers. And bring them warm glasses of milk should they require a sleep aid.

Trapped in the ballroom while the royal guard searched the palace for the perpetrators, the party quickly dissolved from something beautiful and elegant to the inner realm of Denamon.

And it grew hot. We'd been moved to the room's inner wall, away from the glass windows and secret entrances. The guards had pushed us into a sweaty cluster and surrounded us with weapons and might.

I had spent the remainder of the night on the floor, my back pressed against the cool stone while an elderly statesman crushed my shoulder and sweated all over my once breathtaking gown. Oliver was to my other side. He was much less sweaty and offered a comforting shoulder for my body to smother.

At first, I was too concerned with Caspian's state to care much about the claustrophobic nature of our rescue efforts. But when word came from the master surgeon that he would be fine, I was forced to focus solely on all the bodies pushed against mine and the sticky roll of sweat down my spine.

I wouldn't need just one bath after this night. I would need several.

When dawn broke through the glass-paned windows, we all rejoiced. Surely light would mean release.

My uncle had disappeared with his contingent of the guard. I wasn't sure if he was hunting intruders or using his influence as King Regent to sleep in his own bed. But when he finally walked back into the ballroom, he looked refreshed and bathed.

How dare he.

He whispered something to the guards protecting us, and they began to help women and elderly men off the floor. It was apparently safe for us to return to our rooms.

"Thank you for being so patient with my guards," Tyrn said, addressing the large crowd. "We prepared for something like this to happen, but clearly, our enemies have more wiles than we gave them credit for."

"You mean, *her* enemies," the king of Aramore growled.

I felt the room of people collectively turn their glares on me. I was still on the floor, so the effect of Nine Kingdoms worth of royals, dignitaries, and states people looking down on me was poignant.

"An attack on her is an attack on all of us," Tyrn reminded the room. "Tessana represents the future of the realm. They are not simply attacking a girl. They are attacking our peace, our future, our power."

Well, that was a surprise. Tyrn usually acted with only cold disdain where I was concerned. To hear him speak about me and what I represented made me feel . . . surprisingly warm toward him.

The crowd did not exactly rally around his words, but they did disperse with quieter grumbles. For now, that could be considered a victory.

Oliver held out his hand to me so I could find my footing in the silky folds of my gown and helped me stand. My uncle moved toward me once the white-haired sweaty gentleman with many medals walked away. I was positive I smelled like a horse trough now. And I blamed him.

"Tessana," Tyrn greeted.

I staggered into a stiff curtsy. "Uncle. Were the men caught?"

He rubbed a hand over his jaw at my question, looking fifteen years older than he ought. "Yes, er, some of them. It seems they . . . were instructed to end their own lives before capture. We weren't able to restrain as many as we would have liked."

"How many?" The question felt important to me. There were a hundred other things to ask, but I needed to know this answer. When he didn't immediately reply, I clutched his forearm with both of my hands and pleaded. "How many, Uncle? How many were you able to capture?"

He held my wide-eyed stare. His pale-blue eyes drooped in the corners. "One."

"One? Out of—"

He held up a hand. "A battalion."

"How is this possible?"

"You are not safe here," Tyrn went on, ignoring my panic. "We still have not figured out how they got into Elysia, much less the castle. I have questioned guards at the wall, Sarasonet, here at the castle. I've sent riders to investigate the Marble Wall. There is more to inspect, but these . . . assassins seem to move entirely in secret. We had stopped plenty before last night. Yet the worst has happened."

"But Caspian will be all right?" I asked, even though I'd already been told he would be.

"Yes, he's recovering. But alive." His expression evolved from tired to grave. "But that is what we need to talk about."

Suspicion bled into my own exhaustion. "Caspian?"

"The attack meant for you, Tessana."

Well, that seemed obvious. But I still didn't understand. "I'm fine, Uncle," I reassured him, hoping this was his way of inquiring about my well-being. "I have been in battle before. I am not too delicate for a few misplaced arrows."

His frown deepened. "Your coronation is still months away. And even then, I am not sure I can keep you safe."

"But you have," I rushed to assure him. "You have kept me safe—"

He held up a hand, silencing me. "It's already been arranged. You and your sister will travel with Queen Ravanna to Blackthorne until your coronation. She will return you in plenty of time to prepare."

"Queen Ravanna?" I gasped, pulling plenty of attention our way. "You cannot be serious."

"Of course, I'm serious," he snapped. "Ravanna was meant to further your education as queen, and thus far, she has not been able to tutor you. This will give you the opportunity to take your duties as future queen seriously, reacquaint yourself with your sister, and see the kingdom. On the journey there, you will visit Barstus. And on the way back, Ravanna will take you through Kasha."

Now I was conflicted. I wanted to visit the realm and learn of the places I would soon govern with firsthand knowledge. But how could he send me with Ravanna Presydia of all people?

And then it hit me. Ravanna Presydia: RP.

The old way is the true way.

But how could it be?

I knew my uncle and her to be special friends. Had she not been needed back in Blackthorne almost immediately following Conandra, she would have stayed at Extensia and been his special guest. Whilst tutoring me.

Could it be possible that my mother was also her friend?

A strange feeling snaked through me, and it took several moments before I could identify what it was.

Loss.

Fresh grief.

The idea of my mother being friends with Ravanna Presydia

made me feel as though I did not know her. Maybe had never known her.

I thought about the spell book hidden away in my bed chambers and knew I was both right and wrong. I knew her as a mother, as a kind and compassionate woman who laughed easily and smiled even quicker. She loved my siblings and me. Would have done anything for us.

But she died when I was only a child. And the adult knowledge of her, who she was, who she knew, what her hopes and dreams were... were not for me to know then.

Would I ever discover them now?

My uncle grunted at my long silence, frustrated with me. "It has already been decided, Tessana. The maids are packing your trunks now. There will be time to bathe and change, but you will leave this morning."

"And Oliver?" I asked before I could think of a better way to phrase my desperate need to keep my best friend with me.

My uncle's annoyed glare flicked briefly to Oliver, who stood behind me. "Are you really asking Queen Ravanna to include your monk in her invitation?"

"Oh no, I just thought... I—"

"I must speak with your sister," Tyrn said, giving his answer to my question about Oliver without needing to say it. "And her father. Do not keep Ravanna waiting, Tessana."

"Okay."

"I will see you at your coronation."

He stalked off through the dispersing crowd to where the Barstus contingent still waited in a corner. When all Denamon had broken loose last night, and the party had been thrown into chaos, Katrinka had chosen to huddle up with her adopted parents. King Maksim and Queen Oleska had embraced her, albeit coolly, and allowed her to sit with them.

I turned to Oliver and threw my arms around his neck. "I'm so sorry."

"We knew this day would come," he soothed, his embrace as tight as mine. "We knew that if I wanted to be anything but a servant, you would have duties I could not be a part of."

I pulled back. "When I am queen, that will of course be different."

"But first, you must survive at least your coronation."

He was right. "Did you figure out the third set of initials yet?" I asked.

"I wondered if you'd realized the same thing," he murmured, pulling me away from the other lingering people so we could speak privately. "RP."

"Ravanna Presydia," I agreed.

"We could be totally wrong."

"I will find a way to ask her," I promised him. "While we're traveling together."

"That is a good idea. Ask about the ravens while you're at it. She seems to be especially fond of their feathers."

"Does that mean she loves them or hates them?"

Oliver stared at her from across the ballroom, where she stood in the place of a wife for Tyrn, instructing maids and footmen while they cleaned up the carnage from broken glass, blood, and bodies. "I don't know."

I nodded anyway. What choice did I have? "What will you do while I'm gone?"

He turned back to meet my gaze. "Don't be too terribly upset."

"What do you mean?"

"Well, I might ride to meet up with Prince Taelon. I'd like to check on Heprin as well. On the Temple. Make sure everything is all right. I've had a sick feeling in my belly since you shared with me last night. If Father Garius and the others are in danger, I need to warn them."

"Dragon's blood, I wish I could go with you." Never had I felt more frustrated or impotent. Just when I should have enough power and influence to help, I was locked away in a gilded cage and could do nothing to aid the people I cared about.

"No, your place is here. You investigate this mystery about the initials while I take care of the other." He put a hand on my shoulder and squeezed. "Be safe, Tessana." His gaze flicked toward Ravanna. "Watch your back."

"You as well, my friend," I told him. "Taelon told me of a way I can get secret letters through to him. I will send them to you in the same way. As long as you stay with Taelon, I can reach you."

He nodded. "I will do my best."

"And you'll be all right? He has a whole night's ride on you."

Oliver smiled, and it was all confidence and surety—a look I had not seen from him in quite a long time. "At least it is not two night's rides."

I let out a low growl. "Be serious, Oliver the Silent. You're a long way from Heprin. You traveled through the Blood Woods once, and it did not end up being quite as serene and placid as you expected."

He gave a careless shrug. "I shall take one of your horses. I hope you don't mind."

"Of course not."

"And I am a man of the world now. Not some sheltered monk who had never been beyond the market at Lishare."

"Mmm, a man of the world indeed."

"You be careful too," he admonished gruffly. "There are still assassins in Barstus and Blackthorne. You must be on your guard at all times."

"If you think there is a way to be off my guard when I'm in close quarters with RP, you are sorely mistaken."

He drew me in for another tight hug. "We shall meet again shortly. I will be back for your coronation."

"Come with Taelon. I'm afraid they will not let you through the Marble Wall if you try on your own."

He nodded against my shoulder. "Send word if you find out anything."

"You too. Finch is the guard's name. He will give me word if you try to reach me."

"Tessana," my uncle barked from across the ballroom. "Enough of that."

"I will miss you," I told him boldly before pulling away.

"And I you."

We stepped back, and my guards closed in as I marched toward my bedroom. How could I leave my dearest friend? How could we head to opposite sides of the realm? This seemed impossible.

More impossible than being stuck with Ravanna Presydia for the following months so she could teach me all there was to know about being queen. More impossible than getting to know the sister who so very clearly did not want to get to know me.

But I did need to hurry. There was one thing I needed to do before I could leave the kingdom. And it was not to take a bath.

I did stop in my rooms to peel out of my dress and rinse off as quickly as humanly possible. Clesta was there, managing the chaos of a room full of maids, trunks, and clothes. Shiksa sat on the edge of the bed, monitoring all the activity with a watchful eye.

I paused to nuzzle her nose with mine. "We're going on a trip, my love."

"You will be taking her, then?" Clesta asked, doing her best to hide the disappointment in her tone.

I smiled at her. "Yes, but I promise to bring her back. We will return shortly before the coronation."

"Aye, I've been told," she said dutifully. "Everything will be packed shortly."

I raised an eyebrow at her. "You'll be joining me of course?"

Her cheeks blushed crimson, and she began fidgeting in a way that conveyed both fear and disbelief. "O-oh, I wasn't sure if you—"

"Clesta, if I am to travel across kingdoms while preparing for my coronation, I will need you by my side." Her shoulders relaxed but just barely. "I trust no one else to do my hair quite so well as you."

Her tight mouth ticked into a small smile at my mild jest. "Of course, Lady. Of course."

"I have one thing yet to do before I leave, so I will let you finish packing for your favorite future queen." Her brow squinched in confusion, but I nodded to Shiksa, and she smiled.

"What do you have to do?"

I licked dry lips and asked a favor instead. "Would you mind distracting my guards? Just for a moment? I promise to be on my best behavior for the rest of my life. I just need ten, er, twenty minutes to... say goodbye to someone."

Her eyebrows now shot to her hairline. "Princess, I cannot—"

"I will be safe," I lied. "Completely safe." When she still did not look convinced, I added, "And I will buy you one of your own." I pointed at my white fox sitting like true royalty on a pile of silk pillows. "Any color you'd like."

Her expression immediately softened. "You can find one?"

"I'm going to be queen one day, Clesta. I could fill a stable full of kits for you to choose from." Total lies. All lies. I had no idea where to go about finding a fox kitling for her, but I would keep my promise no matter what it took if she would help me.

"You promise you'll be safe? That nothing will happen to you?" I nodded vigorously. "What do you need me to do?" she asked slowly.

"Draw them into the bathroom," I told her in a whisper. "I'll slip out the door." While she weighed the consequences of such deceit, I grabbed my purse from the closet. It was the same one Father Garius gave me almost a year ago, the one with the false bottom. "If they catch me, I will not blame you, Clesta. I shall take full responsibility for my actions. And omit you from any guilt."

She turned her back on me, walking over to Shiksa and putting out her hand. Quick as a cat, I opened my drawer and grabbed the spell book. A warm thrill of something slithered up my arm, but I quickly shoved the book into the secret compartment. It did not fit as easily as the Crown of Nine had, but I could hide it within the purse before Clesta turned around again.

"I cannot promise how long I can keep them here."

I retracted my hand from the purse and offered a pleasant smile. "No need. I simply want to say goodbye to an old friend."

"Prince Taelon," she assumed with a knowing look in her eye.

"Er, no, he's already left. But yes, one of our, um, mutual friends."

She moved toward the bedroom doors and shooed me behind them. Composing herself and breathing deeply, she suddenly lunged for the doors and flung them open. "Help!" she cried. "It's the princess!"

The guards burst into the room, flattening me against the wall with the door. They answered Clesta's plea for help as aggressively and hastily as I hoped they would.

"In here!" she ordered, running toward the bathroom. As soon as I heard their pounding footsteps, I slipped into the hallway.

I had more guards posted on me than just the two or three who always stood at my door. But if I was able to get past the guards who kept the closest watch, I could usually sneak by the others. Especially if they did not yet know to look for me.

So that was exactly what I did. Clinging to corners and dark shadows, I methodically yet quickly worked my way toward the dungeons. It was easier than it should have been. But I knew many guards to be following my uncle's orders around the kingdom and even the castle.

I had not known where the castle dungeons were for a long time. It wasn't something my uncle or anyone else at Castle Extensia made public knowledge. They were especially keen to keep the information from me.

There were certain prison cells I had been allowed to visit. While eret Grimsayer had been in residence, for instance, Tyrn had allowed me to visit him. But he had been kept in a civil court section usually reserved for local criminals in Sarasonet. The occasional rowdy town drunk. A cattle thief. A traveling con man.

It was the reason the Rebel Army was able to rescue him so easily. He had been arrested because my uncle had wanted to make an example of him, not because Tyrn thought he was truly treasonous.

But there were criminals within this castle's walls that my uncle did especially hate. And it was those prison cells I was looking for now.

Over the last several months, and with Oliver's help, we carefully narrowed our list of possibilities. And kept watch of the royal guard's movements and functions. As well as the kitchens.

Everyone needed to eat. Even the worst of the worst prisoners.

Even if it was only stale bread.

That was where we'd caught our break, actually. What exactly did a royal kitchen do with leftovers? Some were meant for feeding the stables. And some were meant for the poorest of the poor thanks to the local Temple's involvement in the process. And some, the worst of the leftovers, fed to prisoners.

And the worst of those leftovers fed the worst prisoners.

I moved as quickly and quietly as possible to a far recess of the castle. It was nearest to the river that ran around the front of the Keep. With the mountains in the back, Extensia only used a drawbridge in the front.

There, I found a door that opened to a stairwell that only moved downward. Sparse torches were lit and flickered in the dark but far enough apart that I could still blend into the shadows.

Surprisingly, no guards were positioned on the stairs as I moved down and down and down. My travel slippers echoed off the walls no matter how quietly I stepped. But I was in too big of a hurry to really take my time.

Instead, I hoped the time of morning and recent events last night would clear the way for me.

At the bottom of the winding staircase was an antechamber. I guessed there would be plenty of guards on the other side of the passageway, and I wasn't sure what to do. I needed to get by them without causing a scene or alerting my personal guard, who would be combing the castle for me right now.

"What should I do?" I whispered to no one. I already missed Oliver. He would have come up with a plan by now. Or sacrificed himself in order to distract the guards.

A play of light flickered out of the corner of my eye, pulling my attention. Just like all the times before, I turned, expecting to find natural light. Or a torch. But there was neither.

It was like the flame of a candle without the candle. It danced in the dark shadows on the wall. This time, I stretched out my hand to touch it. A ghost? Maybe it would feel ice cold. Or perhaps otherworldly. But alas, my fingers went right through it. I sensed nothing other than the cool, hard stone of the stairwell.

The light did move, however. Bouncing around the passageway until it alighted on the corner. It seemed to beckon me.

I gave it a look. Honestly, did it expect me to simply waltz right past the guards? It couldn't even tell me how many there were.

Gesturing to the other room with a wild hand, I made a face and prayed to the Light that no one was watching me. The little flame danced more frantically. I took a step toward it, and it settled some.

Okay, so it wanted me to follow. But why? Was it trying to help me? Or trap me.

CHAPTER
TEN

I pressed my back to the stone and slithered as close to the guard post as possible. A quick look around the corner showed five burlier and less civilized guards than usual. Their pale skin and yellowed teeth promised a hard life of hard work. They clustered around a wobbly table, cards being thrown between them and then swiftly picked up again while coins jangled and fists pounded.

Gambling by the looks of it.

Torches circled the room, offering more light than the stairwell. But to their left was a dark hallway that stank of bile and waste. I had found the darkest dungeons of Extensia, and they were a foul pit of despair. No light, no clean air, no hope.

The little light bounced around over their heads without them noticing. Their glassy eyes were fixed on the game. I watched from the shadows as it disappeared into one of the bright flames of one of the lit torches.

I wouldn't have believed what happened if I hadn't seen it with my own eyes. Suddenly and so quickly, I still wasn't sure what I was watching, the torch fell off the wall. In a stone structure as cold and damp as this one, it shouldn't have caused too much damage. Maybe one of the guards would have leaped to his feet and stomped it out. Or maybe, against that wall, where the press of the river seeped in through the cracks in the stone, it would have flickered out on its own.

But one of the guards had removed his cloak in the heat of the game and draped it over a chair that had been pushed away from the table. And that chair and cloak sat next to a small food supply in linen sacks piled on top of each other.

The torch fell directly onto the cloak, which seemed to explode with fire. Then quickly spread to the food. The five men shouted in surprise, jumped back from the climbing flames, and then burst into action all at once. A fire below the castle would be dangerous enough. But one that would set dangerous criminals free—or burn them to ash where they were trapped in their cells—was an entirely different emergency.

While the guards put the fire out, I slipped down the corridor toward the prison cells. Their shouts and orders echoed off the rounded ceiling, covering my noisy progress. Soon enough, I was hidden in the darkness of the passageway. As my eyes slowly adjusted, I became aware of how slick and sludge-like the floor had become.

Now I faced a new difficulty. The light had disappeared into the fire, and I had no idea where I was going.

Sensing a new presence, the prisoners began to stir. I jumped when one of them used a stick or pole to slide it along his cell bars. "Who's come to play?" he asked in a sickly sing-song voice. "Here, kitty kitty."

"Who's there?" demanded another gravelly voice. "You smell so very . . . sweet."

"And young," another voice taunted. "Come here and let me look at you, you sweet, young kitten."

I knew they were locked away. I knew that. But their voices were so close. And I couldn't see anything. A hand reached out and brushed my frock. I bit back a scream and tried to still my violent shivers.

"A kitten has come to play?" laughed another voice. "A kitten has come to play!" he shouted, then dissolved into maniacal laughter.

"Brahm?" I demanded in a harsh whisper, praying for a second miracle. "Brahm Havish?"

"Oooh, the kitten is here for the traitor," the first voice declared loud enough for the guards to hear. "Maybe the kitten is a traitor too?"

"Brahm?" I asked in a louder voice while the madmen began to cackle and taunt more regularly. "Brahm Havish, I need to speak to you. Please."

I could not stand much more of this. The voices began to echo and bounce off the ceiling, sounding as feral as a wild pack of jackals. It had become harder to walk too, my boots sinking deeper into the sludge that coated the floor. And the stench. Dragon's blood, the *stench*. How could anyone survive this for longer than a few minutes?

More than the awful smell, I knew the dark would make them mad. So dark you could not see a hand in front of your face. So dark that you could not tell what you were eating or drinking. So dark the days would blend into endless nights when there was no reprieve and no rest. The bugs and the rats and the creepy-crawly things that lived down here would become your only friends. And slowly, slowly, you would descend into an endless abyss of confusion and hallucination.

As was exhibited all around me.

Suddenly a meaty hand lashed out through prison bars and grabbed my hand. I could not help it when I cried out. But my plea for help only incited the surrounding prisoners to riot with crazed laughter. They beat on their cell bars and whooped and hollered mindlessly.

The hand held tightly to mine, though, unafraid of the crazed men around us or the ghosts I'd begun to imagine in every black corner. I found myself more afraid than I had ever been. More terrified than when I'd outrun a wildebeest. More shaken than when I'd fought Crenshaw. More unnerved than when a hundred arrows had flown for my head. At least then, I'd been able to see my enemy. I knew what I was battling. This bodiless hand could belong to a demon straight from the pit of Denamon, and I would still never see its face.

I began to tremble. My body could not hold the terror pulsing through me. A scream built in the base of my lungs, ready to unleash an ungodly shriek that was sure to get the guards' attention. Until a voice spoke in the darkness. It was a low, gruff rumble, but the face it belonged to was close enough to the cell bars I could make out his words despite the madness all around me.

"Who is here for Brahm Havish?"

I closed my eyes and hoped that this was he. That the miracle I'd prayed for had somehow found me in this cruel place. Dropping my voice and leaning in, I confessed, "Tessana Allisand. Daughter of King Fredricks. I've come to speak to him."

His punishing grip on my hand relaxed a little. "The Lost Princess? Why would you come to this place, child? It's not safe for you."

"I must speak with Brahm the Mighty," I told him urgently. "Please tell me you are him."

"Aye. Not so much the Mighty behind these bloody bars. But I once was. Is that enough for you?"

More than enough. He had no idea. He released my hand, but I still stepped closer to his cell, afraid the surrounding prisoners would keep me from hearing everything he had to say. "You knew my parents." It wasn't a question. "And you were there the day they died."

"Aye."

"Who ordered you to take my sister to Barstus?"

"No one," he answered easily. "It is why your uncle detests me. Or one of the reasons. I knew she wasn't safe. I knew if she stayed, they would find her too. I . . . Maksim Zolotov owed me a favor, and I cashed in. He raised the girl in secret. And she stayed alive. If I had known you were alive too, I would have—"

"No, please, do not feel badly. I was safe. More than safe, I was happy. You have no need to worry over what happened to me." I sucked in a deep breath and pressed on, "Were you afraid of my uncle? Who would have hurt Katrinka?"

"The same who killed your parents, my girl. There is a great desperation to end the Allisand bloodline."

"But why? The Allisands have ruled for thousands of years. Why go to war against us now?"

He was silent for a long time, so long I thought he would refuse to answer me. But finally, voice dropping even lower, so I had to strain to hear, he said, "The magic was moved. Before you were born. Someone moved the magic elsewhere. And there are people out there who believe the magic must rule."

"The magic?" I gasped. "What do you mean?"

"The Crown of Nine was bonded to a bloodline, not witchcraft. But there are . . . people out there who believe the Seat of Power must hold power too. Must hold the magic."

"When? When did this happen?"

"A century ago," he said, his words coming quickly. "There will not be official records. At least not detailing all of what happened. The Allisands sought to keep the magic to themselves, so the pagans intervened. There was war. Bloodshed. The rebellion was eventually squashed, but not before the damage was done. It was then that they banned magic throughout the realm. If the Allisands couldn't have it, no one else could either."

That was a history lesson I had never heard before. My mind reeled with possibilities, with different narratives than I had been taught.

"Was it pagans who killed my parents? My brothers?" I felt sick, and my head had started to spin. My mother had taught us to respect pagans. Or if not to respect them, to be empathetic toward them. My mother was different than my father in that. Where he had dutifully disregarded them, my mother had loved their ways. She had a soft spot for them and believed in their teachings, their healing, and their history. She'd wanted us to learn it, to be familiar with their ways. But she'd died before she could fully teach Katrinka and me what it meant to be pagan.

We'd been raised in the way of the Light. Separately, but similarly. And while I still held grace for pagans, I did not understand the importance of why.

"I do not know," Brahm said plainly. "There was magic involved. I could smell it in the air when we found them. The air was thick with incense and sulfur. But we never found a trace of intruders. No one we interviewed had seen strangers in the village or even in the kingdom. It was as though they appeared out of thin air."

His explanation made me think of the men last night. The arrows. The mystery behind their arrival. Had it been orchestrated by the same people?

Was it pagans after the throne?

Or someone worse?

A guard shouted down the dark corridor. Apparently, they'd contained the fire and wanted to know what had worked the prisoners up into such a frenzy. It was time to leave. By now, my guards would have alerted the army. And I needed to change shoes before I could get into a carriage with Ravanna. Lest I make everyone suffer all the way to Barstus.

I hoped my clothes didn't reek of this dungeon once I was out of it.

"One more question," I begged, leaning even closer to the cell. The stench was foul, and I caught glimpses of the shell of the man Brahm the Mighty had succumbed to. Even just months ago at the trial, he had been a robust, intimidating man, despite his age. Now he was nothing but skin and bones, his once manicured facial hair a scraggly, knotted mess.

"Quickly, girl," he ordered.

"Was my mother friends with Queen Ravanna of Blackthorne?"

He had not been expecting that question. How could he have been? Even I felt foolish for asking. What did it matter anyway? Maybe Ravanna was a different person back then. Maybe my mother brought out the best in her.

Maybe my mother was just like her.

The thought made my body jerk with a ferocious shiver.

"Why would you think I know the answer to that? I worked for your father. I hardly knew anything of your mother's personal friendships."

Now I gripped the bars and pressed my face against them, meeting his eyes in the darkness. "Please, you must have seen something. Seen them interact? Noticed something about the way they talked to each other? Did they seem like particularly close friends?" Close enough to carve their initials side by side.

He puffed out a harsh breath. Finally, he said, "In court, they hardly acknowledge each other. Your mother was notorious for calling her the 'Cold Queen.' It made people assume she hated Ravanna. And I would have agreed with them. Except early on in her marriage to your father, your mother and Tyrn, her brother, were especially close. They were often seen leaving the castle late at night, headed for the gardens without their guards nearby." He paused, trying to make sense of his own memories. "I know this because your father was aware of their activity and asked that I station men around the perimeter. He didn't want them to know, but he wanted them to be safe."

"There is a chapel in the gardens," I said, talking to myself more than Brahm. "I think it's pagan."

"Aye," Brahm agreed. "Ancient that one. There has never been a king willing to uproot it or tear it down. Superstitious about it, the lot of them." He sighed, and I felt it all the way to my bones. "But your mother . . . well, she still honored many of the pagan traditions. I think your father was charmed by the old ways. She never went out there often. Maybe for a few of the pagan holidays, or maybe if there was a reason to pray for something especially daunting. Except when . . . well, except when Ravanna was in residence at the castle. Then she would go out nearly every night. And more than once, I caught glimpses of Ravanna heading that way as well. Ravanna, your mother, and Tyrn."

The initials did belong to them. My head spun with possibilities. With questions. With confusion. Why would my mother speak about Ravanna in public one way and then sneak out of the castle to meet her? Carve her name beside hers?

The old way is the true way.

But what did any of it mean?

The guards' voices grew louder while the prisoners shouted about sweet kittens. My time was up.

"I'm leaving the castle," I told Brahm, unsure of the reason. "But when I come back, I will come see you again. What do you need? Let me bring it to you."

I could not see his face well enough to tell if he was smiling, but I heard his spirits lift in his voice. "Your presence is light enough to get me through for a while, darling girl. Don't worry about old Brahm. I'll manage."

I chewed my bottom lip, tasting the filth of this place. I would bring him a fresh blanket. And food. And clothes. And maybe a bar of soap. And a candle. I would take care of him even if my uncle would not allow it.

"Be safe, Brahm the Mighty. I will find a way to free you."

His hands slipped over mine where they held his cell bars. "They would be so proud of you, you know? Your parents. They would be so proud of the woman, the queen, you've turned out to be."

His warm sentiment made my eyes sting with tears. "Thank you," I whispered to him, not certain he could even hear me. "Thank you for your kind words and your help."

"What's going on down there?" a guard boomed. He had a stick or a baton, maybe a sword, but he hit it hard against the wall, and it was strong enough to echo all the way to my bones.

"Go," Brahm ordered. "But come again when you can."

I released the bar and found the center of the hallway again, where other prisoners could not reach out and touch me. Most of them had scurried back to their dark corners, afraid of the guards and their punishments.

But I wasn't sure quite why they were so afraid of the guards. Their captors seemed more spooked than anyone when I burst into the light again. They all shouted and jumped back. I sprinted for the stairwell while they shrieked in true terror and asked each other where I'd come from.

I heard them stand from the table and start to follow me when another torch fell off the wall and landed in the embers they had only just doused.

"Not again!" one of them hollered while I sprinted up the stairs.

"Leave her!" someone else yelled. "This one is worse than the other. We'll all burn to death if we don't get it put out."

I left them to their fires and cursing. At the top of the stairs, I slipped off my muddy shoes and left them in a corner for a maid to find later. Hurrying back to my bedroom, I was suddenly surrounded by my guards.

"Where have you been?" Curtis demanded.

"I, uh, I—" I looked down and said, "I can't find my shoes."

More guards clattered into the hallway, swords drawn. They all took a step back and let out a sigh of relief when they saw me.

"Your shoes?" Curtis nearly screeched. His face had turned a mottled shade of purple, and I had a terrible vision of being the reason he suddenly dropped dead.

I reached out and put my hand on his shoulder. "Were you worried about me?"

His eyes bulged. "Princess, I—"

"I know they're waiting on me," I said placidly. "If you'll escort me back to my rooms, I'll just put a pair of shoes on, and then I will be ready."

A new guard stood nearby. He looked as aggravated as everyone else and as winded. But he was younger than Curtis and leaner.

Finch, I knew immediately. This was the man who would get my messages to Taelon. I did not trust him as Taelon did, but I hoped he would prove himself.

Curtis did not continue to argue. Instead, he pressed his lips together and nodded toward the direction of my room.

Once there, I retrieved Shiksa from a harried-looking Clesta, a new pair of shoes, and some traveling gloves. After quickly saying goodbye to Clesta since she would ride in a separate coach, I allowed Curtis and the others to escort me to the waiting carriage.

Ravanna and Katrinka were already inside, and both let out annoyed sighs when I finally climbed onto my seat. Curtis reluctantly relinquished his oversight of me so he could take his place on the back of the impressive transport that managed to be both luxurious and formidable.

"So nice of you to finally join us," Ravanna sneered. "We thought you had run away to avoid us."

"Oh, no," I rushed to tell her. "I just had . . . one last goodbye to make."

"This is so exciting!" Katrinka gushed suddenly in a burst of optimism I had not yet seen from her. "I cannot wait to show you both my home."

The door to the carriage closed, and Ravanna reached over and locked it. Katrinka opened the shades to her window while she tried not to bounce up and down in her seat.

"This is your home," I told her as the carriage lurched into motion.

She blinked at me, trying to process my words. "Well, yes. But, you know what I mean. Barstus has been my home for so long that . . . well, I am looking forward to showing it to you, is all."

I regretted stealing the optimism from her voice. Of course, she was excited to return to the place so familiar to her. I would have felt the same if we were headed toward Heprin.

Attempting a smile, I said, "I'm also looking forward to it." I turned to Ravanna. "And to seeing Blackthorne of course."

Her icy gaze swept over me, and she said, "You have black smudges all over your face."

My hand flew to my face as I realized the prison bars had left marks. I rubbed blindly and tried to picture my mother enjoying this woman's company.

Brahm Havish's words haunted me. *". . . when Ravanna was in residence at the castle. Then she would go out nearly every night. And more than once, I caught glimpses of Ravanna heading that way as well. Ravanna, your mother, and Tyrn."*

It did not make sense. Why would the three of them spend time together in the pagan temple? And why would my mother lie about their friendship to everyone else? Or lack thereof?

And if they were so close, why do my uncle and Ravanna despise me now?

I was missing too many pieces for even part of this mystery to make sense. I had hoped Brahm would give me answers. But I only had more questions. And now, I had been left to Ravanna's care until my coronation.

Whatever relationship she'd had with my mother, it was clear she did not want to continue it with me. Even now, as she settled across the carriage, her lip curled with barely restrained disgust, and her gaze bounced around the small space looking everywhere but at me. The next couple of months would be as trying for her as they were for me. She had no interest in tutoring me. Or training me. Or even spending time with me.

The Cold Queen indeed.

CHAPTER ELEVEN

We approached Gray Cape, the capital of Barstus, in the dead of night. We'd been traveling for days, only stopping when it was necessary. I'd spent much of the journey napping, still trying to recover from two weeks of festivities and a night spent on the ballroom floor.

The border crossing between Elysia and Barstus had been smoother than when Taelon had tried to get through the Marble Wall on the Soravalian side. But the Wall was as dilapidated and gray as it had been there too. My heart sank to see the dirty sight of it, so much worse for wear than when I was a child.

I thought of what Brahm had told me about the pagans removing the magic from the Allisand bloodline. Was that why the wall seemed to be aging so quickly now?

We were not planning to stay long in Barstus, but I wondered what Bale's library would be like and if it might contain information about the pagan rebellion. My hand rested on my satchel, where the spell book remained hidden away. Would it have anything to say about the pagan's opinion on the Allisand bloodline and the Seat of Power?

How did one get to know a pagan? How could one even find a pagan?

I missed my mother. For more reasons than just the answer to this question, but not knowing who or how to ask someone for this information made my grief for her a sharp pang slicing through my chest.

Glancing at Ravanna across the carriage, the question bubbled up in my throat. It would take almost nothing to break the tense silence and ask her a simple enough question. *Did you know my mother?* The answer was even obvious. Of course she did. They had ruled kingdoms at the same time. They would have crossed paths willingly and unwillingly. That was the nature of their power and influence.

But I couldn't manage to get the words beyond my lips. It was more than just approaching Ravanna's ice-cold demeanor, though. It was that I wasn't sure I wanted to know the answer. I partly suspected Ravanna of trying to have me killed six months ago. I partly suspected she still wished for my death. To know my mother was her particular friend threatened my very memory of her. All that I knew to be true of her. And I was not ready for that.

It was late, and the road was exceptionally bumpy. We'd left the Diamond Mountains three days ago, but earlier this evening, we'd reached the foothills of the Ice Mountains. A steady rain fell outside, and a chill had crept into the carriage, despite the fur blanket I'd laid over my lap and Shiksa curled up beneath my chin.

Katrinka had warned of this bone-deep chill, even if she had not known I would soon be introduced to it.

Because of the constant rain, the main roads had been packed with gravel in order to keep them from washing away. The carriage wheels were able to find purchase, even while going up a steep incline, but it made for rough travel.

Still, Katrinka slept soundly to my right. She'd sprawled across the bench in her seat, so I sat huddled against the window. If we were more familiar as sisters, I would have laid her feet across my lap and moved toward the center of the bench so I could escape the damp seeping in through the carriage window and door. But we did not have that sort of relationship yet, so I tried to avoid touching her when I could.

I wasn't sure if it was the chill outside of the carriage or within, but it made me angry. I had lost my parents and brothers nine years ago, but as Brahm reminded me, my sister had also been taken from me. Physically. Emotionally. *Would we ever recover from the separation that neither of us chose? Would she ever cease to hate me for the trauma we'd both faced?*

"This is one of my least favorite kingdoms," Ravanna Presydia declared from across the cabin.

I had not known she was awake, so her stark declaration startled me. "Barstus?" I managed to squeak.

"I have never known constant rain like this damned country. All day and all night, it is nothing but rain and chill. We'll be lucky to leave without fevers and chest rattles."

Her complaint surprised me. I knew nothing about her, but she seemed like the kind of person to enjoy gloom and gray. "I have never been."

Her head dropped back on the black velvet seat, and she closed her eyes but not out of exhaustion. There was an irritation to her that seemed to smother all the air in the carriage. "You will not be sorry you waited so long."

I licked suddenly dry lips and asked a bold, albeit childish, question. "What is your favorite kingdom in the realm?"

Her eyes snapped open, and she leveled me with a harsh glare. "My own."

"I've never been to Blackthorne either," I told her, sounding more foolish than ever.

She closed her eyes again and settled heavily against the seat. "Yes, you have. You might not remember, but your family visited mine more than once when you were a child before . . . well, before."

My heart jumped in my chest. This was the opportunity I had

been looking for. "Did you know my parents then? When they were alive?"

"You cannot rule a kingdom in this realm and not know the king of it," was her terse reply.

"Oh, yes, of course. I just meant..."

"You meant to ask if I was friends with your parents. If I knew them intimately." She had not moved from her relaxed position, not one muscle. But despite her easy façade, she did not sound calm. Instinct told me she was coiled like a striking viper. When I remained quiet, unable to respond properly, she let out a short sigh and said, "Not friends. With either your mother or your father. Your father was not the type to keep female friends. He hardly tolerated me from a distance, so no, when we found ourselves in close quarters, we were not friendly. Although there were a few times I considered us civil."

Well, not a glowing recommendation for their relationship. But it was more than nothing. Still, I had to ask, "And my mother? I know you said you weren't friends, but did you know her?"

Her eyes opened again. Slowly, as if fluttering awake or slipping into a dream. Only she did not look at me, she gazed out the darkened carriage window at the rivers of raindrops and blurring scenery. "Sometimes, I think she was the only person I have ever really known. The only person who's ever known me." Her voice was quiet, reverent. I wondered if she even remembered that I was still here, still listening. "We weren't friends. What a foolish word for what we shared."

My frantic heart stuttered. I knew what that was . . . to be more than friends, to share something that transcended a colloquial definition. I had it with Oliver. And this distance between us, distance we had not suffered since the day we met, had been punishing and cruel. And it had been less than a week.

But my mother's voice echoed in my head. "The Cold Queen." I had never heard her speak of Ravanna with anything but disdain and irritation.

Ravanna seemed to read my thoughts. "At least when we were

children. After she became queen, we were . . . less so. I suppose she had your father then and didn't need me. But I never forgot the girl she used to be. The power she used to wield."

My eyebrows furrowed together as I played that over in my mind. "The power she used to wield." As queen? When she married my father? Or before?

I knew she had been a foreigner to Elysia. That had never been kept a secret from us children. But now, I couldn't seem to remember where she was from. I was only half Elysian. There was something else in my blood, some other kingdom. But where?

I wanted to ask Ravanna and press her with questions until she ordered me to stop. But the carriage came to an abrupt halt, and voices started shouting back and forth across a distance.

We'd reached Castle Bale's outer ramparts. Soon enough, the loud whining of wheels and clicking of spindles drowned out whatever conversation we could have had as the drawbridge was let down for us to pass into the renowned seat of Barstus.

I had never been, not even as a child, I knew that. My mother had been reluctant to bring us to the dreary kingdom, but I could not remember why. My governess had once told me it was because of the gargoyles. And now, as we moved slowly toward the castle proper and lightning flashed in the sky, I could see why she thought that. Statues of the gruesome goblins sat on nearly every structure. Hanging from the drawbridge portcullis to the pillars that lined the drive toward the castle.

They were nestled in hedges and lined along the outer-edged battlements. Guarding the steep, pointed roofs of the towers. And all around the borders of the bailey once we were inside. Some were short and fat. Others were as large as a grown man. They sat in the windows of the parapet. And I had no doubt they would even live in the castle's Temple.

Although they were made from stone, so I'm not sure what my mother's prejudice would be against them. An eyesore for sure, but hardly dangerous.

Katrinka stirred next to me, finally waking once we'd come to another stop. She stretched in a delicate yawn. "Oh, we're home."

We were not home. That was certain. But instead of arguing, I asked, "Did you really live among the hobgoblins, sister? They are quite fearsome."

She laughed easily. "Oh, yes. But they are hardly frightening when there is no lightning streaking the sky. We're old friends. I'll introduce you in the morning."

Ravanna frowned and sighed again. "The Zolotovs are a superstitious lot. The gargoyles are meant to scare away evil."

Katrinka frowned, not liking Ravanna's harsh tone, I guessed. "It is also quite common for the lords and ladies of the land to gift them to the king on the winter solstice. It has become somewhat of a competition between them to see who can commission the ugliest, most terrifying."

I smiled. That was a contest I would like to see. "So they are a joke?"

Ravanna snorted a laugh as Katrinka frowned again. "Well, no, not a joke. They're not meant to be funny. Just . . . a sport of sorts."

I wanted to ask what they won, but I was afraid I would offend her again.

Finally, under the portico, footmen appeared to let down the stairs and help us onto the carpet. My legs felt wobbly beneath me as I struggled more than I would have liked to walk normally. But the long several days in the carriage had made me stiff and sore.

Katrinka bounced forward, clearly energized to be back at the home she had only just left. I scowled, worrying that this adjustment back to Elysia had been harder on her than I gave her credit for.

I had also hated leaving Heprin and the home I'd known for eight years. But I had a purpose in front of me, a reason to adapt to castle life. Katrinka was not given that same purpose, except for distantly. She did not feel the same call to power I could not deny. Nor the same sense of responsibility.

She had been happy here, anonymous.

I let out a weary sigh, not knowing what to do with that.

Inside the doors, the royal family waited to greet us in luxurious furs meant for this cold weather. King Maksim stood next to his wife, Oleska. And next to her were their children. Six princes lined up by height and battle medals.

Katrinka had shared their names shortly after we left Sarasonet, but I could not remember them now. I was surprised that some were my age and older yet had not joined Katrinka and the king and queen for the last couple of weeks of celebration.

"Welcome," Maksim greeted us formally. "We are happy to offer you accommodations."

They must have flown to get here before we did. Or they had only just arrived themselves. Maksim and Oleska looked utterly exhausted.

"Thank you, Your Highness," Ravanna purred, sounding more pleasant than I had ever heard her. "We're grateful for your hospitality." She moved to the queen, taking her hands in her own and bowing her forehead to them. "You have a lovely home, from what we've seen."

The queen looked shocked at her compliment, forgetting to hide her wide-eyed look of astonishment. And then her furtive glance around the foyer at all the shadowed gargoyles watching us. "Thank you, Your Majesty," she managed to murmur. "May I introduce you to our sons. The Crown Prince Alexi and his brothers, Prince Andretzo, Prince Anton, Prince Akim, Prince Aleksander, and Prince Ashka."

"Does our sister need to be introduced to us?" Prince Anton asked. He seemed to be about Katrinka's age, maybe a year or two younger than I was, with wiry curly black hair that stuck out everywhere. He wore wire-rim spectacles almost identical to Katrinka's and a teasing smirk that endeared him to me immediately. "Has she already forgotten her family?"

"She is not our family," his older brother, Andretzo, scolded. "She is certainly not our sister."

"Andre," his mother admonished, but then Katrinka was laughing, and the declaration felt less of an insult and more of something else.

"Andre has never claimed me as his sister," Katrinka explained to Ravanna and me. "He is afraid I will taint the Zolotov line."

Andre met my eyes and offered a shy smile. "It is because she is too beautiful to be a Zolotov. No one would believe us."

Katrinka's pale cheeks heated with a pretty blush. And she turned away to push her glasses up her nose.

"No," Alexi, the Crown Prince, agreed. "Clearly, she is an Allisand." He took my hand in an elegant way and pressed his lips to the back of it. "Their beauty is famed for good reason."

Shiksa, cradled sleepily in my free arm, watched his gesture with her insightful gaze, and moved up my arm, toward my shoulder, farther away from the prince and his kisses.

Alexi's compliment was kind, but I knew myself to be ragged from travel and gaunt with sleep deprivation. I pulled my hand away. "Thank you, Prince Alexi. I am not sure about our beauty, but when I look at my sister, it is my mother whose face I see most clearly." Katrinka's cheeks burned a brighter shade of red as if she did not quite know what to do with my compliment either. I stepped back from the Crown Prince and addressed his family, "But I must thank you all for taking such good care of my Katrinka. I can see she was in good hands while she was here."

"It was our pleasure," Maksim said. "She has been sunshine in our dreary kingdom since the day she arrived."

Katrinka fidgeted next to me, and I got the distinct impression she was doing all she could not to flee this embarrassing account of her praises.

Ravanna yawned beside me. "This is all wonderful, but I wonder if we can be shown to our rooms now? Before I pass out from exhaustion and must be carried there."

Oleska clapped her hands, and her boys stood straighter and jumped into action. "My sons will show you your rooms tonight. I know Katrinka could do it easily enough, but this feels more formal." She smiled adoringly at my sister, who beamed back.

Katrinka seemed to have really been loved here. Their affection for her eased some of my regret and worry.

The youngest son, Ashka, stepped forward to take her hand. And Alexi and Andretzo stepped out of line and waved toward the corridor we were meant to take. They led the way while the other three middle boys followed, Anton jumping right to Katrinka's side. They began to speak in hushed whispers while Andretzo shot furtive looks at them over his shoulder.

So many siblings reminded me of my own family, my own brothers. I remembered them being thick as thieves, always getting into some kind of mischief. And usually blaming it on me. Not that my mother ever believed them.

Ravanna's knowledge of my mother had made me doubt what I knew of her, made me doubt that I knew her at all. But my memories were not false. I had enjoyed a very happy childhood and a very loving family.

That was why the pain of their absence stung so sharply now. If I had loved them any less, the grief I felt even to this day would be less too. It was because I loved them so dearly that I could not stand to be parted from them. Even nine years later.

Heprin and my time at the temple had taught me to be grateful for grief and the weight it left me carrying. The priests taught only great love could bring great pain. And that the depth of our grief was a measure of our affection for those lost. A life with little grief was not a life well lived.

It was the sad soul, the longing soul, the heavy soul who had so many opportunities to love and be loved that their life had become a lament.

The lives most celebrated in Heprin were the lives marked by tragedy and loss. It was those sorrowful souls who were thought to have experienced and celebrated the best this world could offer.

I thought about Oliver and the absolute suffering I would face if I lost him. Or Taelon. I knew what it was to love deeply. So I would always know what it was to suffer deeply. I would write a letter tonight for Finch. I had no idea how he would get it to either of them, but I trusted Taelon. So I would trust Finch too.

"Your rooms," Alexi announced with a flourish of his hands. Andretzo was showing Ravanna her room. And Anton and Katrinka had their heads bowed together while exchanging furtive whispers at her door.

I paused at the threshold to watch them for a minute. Alexi glanced over at them and sighed. But even in my tired state, I could tell he was annoyed at their closeness.

"They have always been trouble together," he murmured so they could not hear. "Always sneaking off to where they should not go. Anton is... not the obedient son he would have our parents believe. I thought Katrinka's departure would make him more compliable. But with my mother and father's recent absence, he has become wilder than ever. If you care for your sister, you will keep her close to your side while she is here."

Andretzo left Ravanna's room to stand by Anton. His eyes followed Katrinka's movements, her face, her laughter like he was a dying man in need of a life-saving drink of water. He smiled when she smiled. Laughed when she laughed. And I wasn't even entirely sure he knew what she was laughing at.

"It pleases me to see how friendly your brothers have been to her," I told Alexi, ignoring all the other things he'd try to accuse her of. "She is very dear to me."

He moved closer to me, our shoulders brushing as we watched them from across the dark hallway lined with gargoyles and candelabra. His head dipped even closer to mine until we were uncomfortably intimate. "As she is to us. It seems now that your bloodline has been restored, our families are inextricably linked."

He reached out to pet the top of Shiksa's head, but she recoiled, scrambling higher up my body. I laughed to cover my worry as I pulled out her tiny claws from the fabric of my traveling dress. "Elysia is fortunate to have an ally in Barstus. I can see that."

I remembered Conandra. Maksim to my uncle's left. Blackthorne to his right. Had they not already been close friends?

Alexi stepped fully in front of me so I was forced to look into his eyes. "I hope we can be more than allies, Your Highness." My mouth dried out at his unspoken implication and the way his brown eyes seemed to heat with something I didn't want to face. But he finished mildly with, "Friends. I would love for us to be friends."

I offered him a tight smile and then abandoned my sister by ducking into my bedroom. The fire had been lit, but only recently, for it had not chased the chill from the room yet. Or maybe the cold, sickly feeling washing over me had more to do with the Crown Prince than the temperature.

Katrinka seemed so at home here, but after being introduced to this kingdom, I found myself agreeing with Ravanna. I would be much happier when we were on our way again.

CHAPTER TWELVE

Clesta was there to wake me in the morning, for which I was grateful. She was still mad at me for the scene I'd convinced her into causing the day before. But this was not the first time she'd refused to talk to me.

Nor would it be the last.

But still, she did her duty and shook me awake. The sky was still too dark for me to have noticed sunlight, and I woke on my own. In fact, the constant rainfall disoriented my sense of time. I had no idea what hour it was. If I had slept until supper. Or if it was first thing in the morning.

I had not even been in Barstus a full day yet, and already I was tired of the rain, the bone-deep chill, and the gargoyles.

More looked at me from around the room. Carved into the marble fireplace, hanging off the four posters of the large bed, snarling from the bath foot claws, or embroidered into my pillows.

Everywhere I turned, a ferocious beast was staring back at me, maw yawning wide to reveal its razor-sharp teeth.

Sitting in bed now, I wondered how Katrinka could have survived this place. Last night, seeing her with the Zolotov sons, I felt warmth for her and her sanctuary. But in the gray light of day, I worried about what it would be like to live here all the time.

"They will be waiting for you to start breakfast if you do not hurry, Lady." Clesta's reserved admonition held her ire and her duty all at once.

I sighed, knowing she was right. "When I am queen, I will make a royal edict to move breakfast one hour later. Then I will never be late."

She snorted quietly. "When you are queen, that will be your prerogative. Although I'd like to see you get the farmers to agree. They have to be up with the sun. I don't suppose they'd like waiting till nearly supper time to break their fast."

It was my turn to snort. And to hide my smile. She was not very good at holding a grudge against me for long. I suppose that was the best I could ask for in a maid.

I certainly wouldn't stop asking her to distract guards for my benefit. Or lying for me.

"Will you make sure the bath is extra hot this morning, Clesta? Please? I cannot seem to get warm." I was still under many fur blankets and had gone to sleep with an extra shawl wrapped around my shoulders.

"I'll have to ask a footman for more heated water. It does not run directly to the rooms here. They must bring it up from the kitchens."

Her complaint could not move me. I wanted pink skin and banished chill bumps before I dressed for the day. "I'm sorry to inconvenience you," I told her sincerely.

She gave me an assessing look before saying, "The Barstus maids believe that's a sign of black magic."

Her words were so out of place that I could not make sense of them. "What do you mean?"

"The chill. They call it the goblin wind. It's supposed to be brought on by the keepers of the castle." Her head tilted toward a particularly gruesome-looking hobgoblin statue near the threshold to the bath. "It's supposed to ward away those that wish evil on the house of Zolotov."

My body jerked with a shiver, and I picked up Shiksa from where she slept next to me so I could hold her against my chest. "How do you know that?"

"The maids' quarters are bunk rooms," she said, sounding righteously annoyed. "They believe your sister is possessed by magic. She has borne the chill the whole time she lived with them."

"What of the married families?" I asked, ignoring what she'd said about Katrinka for the moment.

"They are not allowed to get married," she said plainly. "Servants in Castle Bale remain celibate as long as they're in service."

I struggled to process both revelations. The first, that Barstus would force its servants to live together on top of each other and not give them their own separate quarters. Or let them get married. It seemed a cruel standard for someone who lived their life washing bedpans and dressing spoiled royals.

The second, that the servants here thought my sister was possessed by black magic.

"Never mind about the hot water," I told Clesta, quickly jumping from the bed and facing the not-nearly-warm-enough bath anyway. Ravanna also hated being here, hated the chill. Did I believe in being possessed by black magic or haunted by stone statues of demons?

No. Not particularly.

The old way is the true way.

But I did find it fascinating how many superstitions these royal houses clung to. Magic had been banished a hundred years ago, so shouldn't these castles have moved into a more modern ideology?

I bathed and dressed as quickly as possible. Thankfully Clesta had thought to pack my wool stockings and fur-lined cloak. By the time I was ready for breakfast, I was dressed as though it were the dead of winter. Only none the warmer for it.

The Zolotov sons were sent again to escort us to breakfast. This morning though, it was Anton outside my door. Alexi waited for

Ravanna and Andretzo for Katrinka. I was the first one in the hallway, so I had the pleasure of watching Andretzo fidget nervously while my sister dallied.

"I must insist on knowing how Katrinka is being treated in Elysia," Anton murmured in a harsh tone, pulling my focus from across the hall to the middle Zolotov. He was taller than I was but still scrawny from youth. I was positive I could take him in a fight.

Sparing him only a glance, I said, "She's treated like a princess. How else would you expect us to behave toward her? She is one of two remaining Allisands. She has anything she desires."

"She does not desire much," Anton said defensively. "And she will not ask if she needs something, so you must pay attention to her."

"Of course, I will pay attention to her." I tried to keep my tone more even than he had, but I was struggling. Anton Zolotov was not her family, no matter how many years she'd spent in his castle. She was *my* sister. I would go to the ends of the realm to protect her. Fight dragons for her. Ascend to the Seat of Power to ensure that her bloodline was secure—and, therefore her own dynasty.

Anton was not convinced. "One spring, she broke her glasses, accidentally stepped on them. Instead of asking Father for a new pair, she pretended she had outgrown the need for them. She had us all convinced until she added salt to her tea instead of sugar. It had been months that she'd been blindly feeling her way around, too upset over the idea of asking for help than simply replacing her glasses."

My mouth opened and closed as I decided whether to stay annoyed with this boy who clearly cared for my sister or make him an ally. Finally giving him my full focus, I met his gaze and asked, "Truly?"

His lips twitched with an affectionate smile. "Truly."

"And she does need her glasses?"

"Oh, most certainly. She's as blind as a two-headed river rat without them."

I did not know what a two-headed river rat was, but I believed him. She finally emerged from her room and immediately turned the color of a ripe strawberry when she found Andretzo waiting for her.

"Oh, and she's in love with Andre."

His comment was so careless that I almost didn't believe him. Except I could see my flustered sister just across the corridor. She nervously pushed her glasses up her nose and tried to meet Andre's eyes by staring at her feet.

A small laugh escaped me. "You don't say?"

"My brother is in love with her too," he continued in a confident whisper. "But for as long as she's stayed with us, she was promised to Alexi."

"Promised to Alexi?" His expression told me to keep my voice down, but he was a wealth of information I did not know to expect.

"It's why my father agreed to take her in. I think he thought he could make a play for the Seat of Power if she married his eldest son. But then you showed up, and my father realized you're the better choice." He cleared his throat. "As far as power goes."

"Was it made official?"

He shook his head. "More like expected. My father is nothing if not opportunistic."

"And Alexi?"

"Just like him."

"What about Andre?"

His narrow mouth split into a grin. "He takes after my mother."

Across the hallway, Andre tugged at his collar while we waited for Ravanna to appear. "Why are you telling me all this? Surely your father would be unhappy if he knew what an... open book you are."

He smiled wider, and I felt a pang of endearment. "Katrinka was the best thing that has ever happened to my family. My father is a very serious king. And this kingdom is no less severe. With her love of books and muddy walks along the moors, Katrinka disrupted the natural order of things."

"You love her." I could not believe this. "Truly."

"No," he argued, throwing his hands in the air and pulling furtive glances from his brothers.

It was my turn to smile. "Not like," I dropped my voice, "Andre. But you do. As a sister. A friend perhaps? But yes, this is clearly love."

He rolled his eyes and tugged at the hem of his tunic, straightening something that did not need straightening. "Love is not a concept we promote in Barstus. In case you haven't figured that out by our decorative demons. Fear, yes. Loathing, of course. But we do not love."

Except hadn't he just told me Andre was in love with my sister? "Of course. Obviously."

He hummed a disgruntled noise.

"Speaking of your, er, decorative demons. Are they truly cursed?"

"Cursed?" He huffed a laugh. "Cursed to be ugly perhaps."

"I didn't mean cursed. I meant . . . spelled. Or enchanted?"

"Oh, you mean the goblin wind. It's a myth. Nothing more."

"Your maids seem to think it's real."

"Yes, the maids. But aren't all maids superstitious? Anything to perpetuate gossip."

I had found that to be true. But still, I had felt a chill the moment we crossed the border into Barstus. Even now, I wished for my warmest cloak and hot stones for my feet. "So you don't believe Katrinka is full of black magic?"

He laughed outright again. It was an easy, lighthearted sound for someone brought up without love. "Katrinka? You're serious? She once fell down a set of stairs by simply trying to walk down them." I must have made a horrified face because he quickly added, "It was a small set of stairs. And she only suffered a twisted ankle. Nothing more serious."

Nothing more serious. Was he serious? "So you don't believe in the goblins?"

His smile turned into a weary sigh. "I believe my father uses them to play power games with the nobles. And I believe Katrinka is too sweet and good-hearted to be twisted with black magic. And I think you are too smart a princess to believe gossip by maids."

He was right about that.

But...

Finally, Ravanna's door opened, and she stepped into the hall truly wrapped in a black fur cloak that looked almost as heavy as she was. At the looks of surprise from around the corridor, she tilted her chin higher and tugged her cloak around her shoulders more tightly. "I will never survive this damp land," she told us by way of explanation. "There is not a fire hot enough in this entire kingdom to chase away this chill."

I looked back at Anton and watched his eyes go wide. It might not be believable for Katrinka to be filled with black magic. But it was much easier to believe someone as dark and cold as Ravanna Presydia could be.

A shiver rocked through me at the thought, and I wished I was as brave as Ravanna to wear my cloak to breakfast.

So what did that say about me?

Was I too full of black magic? Had the goblin wind sunk under my skin and twined through my bones?

The old way is the true way.

The words came unbidden into my thoughts. What was the old way exactly? Black magic? Or something more? Something that was not quite so damnable?

Anton leaned forward and whispered, "My father will never let Andre marry her. Not without a suggestion from someone powerful."

He meant me.

We began walking toward the way we'd come last night, but he and I lingered behind so we could continue our secret sharing in private.

"Why did you not come to Elysia? If your father wants Alexi to try for consort?"

Anton snorted. "My father is a greedy man, but he's also proud. He thinks parading his sons around in front of you is beneath him."

"Ah. So he brought us here instead to parade me around in front of them."

He grinned again. "I did not think you'd make a good queen at first. But maybe I'm starting to change my mind."

I had not expected to like anyone in Barstus. I was glad Anton had changed *my* mind. I was also beginning to understand why Katrinka hadn't wanted to leave this place for the unknown in Elysia. In the wake of our tragedy, she'd been surrounded by protective brothers with whom she shared genuine affection.

She also might have been afflicted with a goblin's curse for the last nine years, but it was a small nuisance compared to the happiness she'd been given.

My time in Heprin had been equally filled with affection. But maybe not as much happiness.

I thought back to the long hours in the library and the punishing lessons Father Garius put me through. He had not thought to marry me off to a rich noble. He had always known I was destined for the throne, and he'd done his best to prepare me.

Now, able to look back, I was incredibly grateful for the time and effort he'd poured into my training. But my first impression of Heprin had been bleak. Used to rowdy brothers and constant companions, the silence of the Temple had been a stark contrast to my life with my family.

It wasn't just that I'd lost those most cherished and was suddenly alone. It was that I'd left a life brimming over with love and loud affection and been thrust into an unknown and silent new world.

The monks were always kind, but they were not doting until much later in my life. And while I never went without at the Temple, I was also not spoiled, pampered, or coddled. I learned to do whatever I needed done on my own. And more than that, I learned to carry the communal share of burdens.

I did not leave one family for another. My family, and my happiness, were stolen from me. And I'd had to claw and fight my way back to any kind of meaningful relationship with other people. By the time I left the Temple, I knew those that lived there to be beloved. But it was a long, arduous journey from loneliness to friendship. From mere nuisance to precious sister.

But that journey had also given me Oliver.

And he was worth so much more than a whole kingdom of affectionate but fake brothers.

In the breakfast room, Maksim and Oleska were already sitting at the heads of a long table crafted from iron and laden with a breakfast spread. Gargoyles decorated this room as well, from the legs of the table to the backs of the iron chairs, to the knobs on the curtain rods where draperies had been pulled back to reveal a dark morning of steady rainfall and crackling thunder.

A herald announced us as we largely ignored him and found seats around the table. The food smelled fishy. And looked as gray as the landscape through the wet windowpane.

We'd mixed up again. Alexi sat to my right. The youngest of the brothers, Ashka, sat to my left. His head barely reached over the lip of the table, and he had to continually push his wild Zolotov hair out of his face while he waited to be served with a fork in one hand and a sharp-looking knife in the other.

Examining Maksim at the other end of the table, I had to believe the unruly locks came from their mother. She had her long blond hair wrapped in braids this morning, but there were signs that her mane would be as untamable as her sons. A loose curl here. A halo of frizz. She was a striking woman, but Queen of Barstus ensured she remained composed and mostly silent.

Even though Katrinka's hair was more chestnut than onyx, it was easy to see how she'd been mistaken all these years for Maksim and Oleska's daughter. With the matching glasses, Anton gave a false impression of similar facial features. And her springier curls seemed to match those of her adopted brothers and mother. Had Brahm chosen Barstus for her with this in mind? Or were the similarities a gift of the Light?

"What is it you are focusing on so intently?" Alexi asked in a subdued tone.

I turned to look at him, searching for signs of what kind of man he was. I had not enjoyed speaking to him last night, but I had been in a foul mood and utterly exhausted. Maybe I had been ungracious.

"Your mother," I admitted. "She is beautiful."

He smiled at my compliment, looking more like her than he had previously. His own hair was cut shorter than his brothers, his curly blond locks tamed somewhat at this stubby length. He wore a scaled bronze band for a crown that resembled a snake, the head positioned in the center of his forehead with an amethyst for its eye. Gray and purple were Barstus's colors, and they considered themselves defenders of the Serpent's Sea. Maksim wore a similar crown. And Queen Oleska wore a daintier bronze diadem with a larger amethyst in the center. It did not appear to be a snake.

"Thank you, Princess Tessana," Alexi answered. "You compliment my father as well, as he chose her for her beauty." He gestured around the table. "And her breeding."

At just that moment, servants stepped forward to lift the covers of the breakfast dishes, revealing boiled sea snakes and stuffed octopi. I had to press fingers to my closed lips to keep from gagging. But I wasn't sure if it was from the seafood or Alexi's assessment of his parents' marriage.

"So not a love match then?" I managed to ask while a servant cut the thick head of a sea snake off so he could offer me part of the body.

"You're lucky," Alexi told me while I watched in horror as the slice of flesh was deposited on my plate, spreading black ink across the width of it. "The neck is the best part." I nodded and attempted to smile. "To your question, no, not a love match. I don't suppose many of the royal houses are love matches." He laughed at the absurdity. "They're ruling kingdoms, after all, not frolicking through fields as love-sick youth."

He was right. I knew he was right. But still, his utter disbelief in the possibility of love made me feel toward him what I felt toward the still bleeding sea snake turning everything else on my plate a chalky gray.

"My parents were in love," I insisted. When it was clear he didn't know how to respond because they were dead, I added. "Hugo and Anatal are in love. Very much so."

He deftly sliced through an octopus tentacle, filleting it open as if he'd done it a hundred times before. I consoled myself and the poor octopus that at least if I ended up marrying this man, we would live in Elysia, where the food did not resemble the sea monsters of the deep.

Talking around a giant bite of tentacle, he said, "Maybe they have affection for each other now. But not when they first wed. How many royals do you know who have spoken to their bride or groom more than a handful of times before their wedding day? Not many."

He had a point. Even still, I had known Taelon well before . . . well, when we were betrothed. My father had gone out of his way to include the Treskinats as often as possible because of our future nuptials and our countries' relationship.

Back when I wasn't heir to a throne or future queen of the realm. Back when I was just a daughter to a king looking for solid allies. Back when Taelon had needed a smart match to help him rule his own kingdom. Back when it was expected to leave Elysia. Not sneak back in and demand to rule it.

Still, I had known even then that I'd been lucky with Taelon. I thought about Caspian as a child, throwing that shield at his older brother, hoping to kill him. My match could have been so much worse.

If my father had loved me any less, my whole life could have been void of emotion.

Alexi went on. "My point is when you are a king"—he inclined his head to me—"or even a powerful queen in your case, love is more of a curse than a blessing. The kingdom and the realm must come before everything else."

He made a good point, but my heart still squeezed in my chest. I had not truly thought about love or loving someone else too often. There had been other things. But I did know what it was like to have a strong affection for someone else, the seedlings of love. And those feelings were important to me. But they did not overshadow the realm I wanted to rule.

He continued, nodding toward where Ravanna sat next to Maksim. "Take the Blackthorne queen, she chose her kingdom over her husband, and it has served her well. Blackthorne had never seen the power they wield today until she took the throne."

I picked at a bite of sauteed mushaboom that had somehow managed to escape the salty ink of the sea snake. "Ravanna had a husband?" I gasped, keeping my voice low.

Alexi shot me an odd look. "How do you think she became queen? Until her, no kingdom had allowed a queen on the throne." His voice dropped to a snide murmur. "Although now it appears it is common practice."

I ignored his highhanded dig. Was this honestly how he sought to win my hand? I resisted an eye roll and said, "I do not know."

"Blackthorne had been ruled by the Presydias since the Marble Wall was erected. It is said they've sat in power as long as the Allisands. So Ravanna marries, er, what's his name. King, uh—"

"Mynot," Ashka put in. I was surprised to find him listening at all.

"Yes, that's right. Mynot. She's from some powerful family from Blackthorne. Not nobles, but wealthy merchants or something. He's seduced by her beauty and wealth. She wants power. So they marry. She's determined to expand Blackthorne's power and make them formidable in the realm. Mynot is content to be left alone and mostly ignored by the other kingdoms. She started to go to council meetings for him, throwing her weight and money around, using connections to move Blackthorne up the ranks. You know what I mean." I did not, but he wasn't exactly waiting for me to confirm or deny. "Well, Mynot finds out what she's been doing and tries to regain his power.

Tells her, she has to stay home while he deals with the council and whatever else." He pauses to tear an impressive bite of tentacle off his fork with sharp teeth stained black from sea snake ink. "Then he dies."

Next to me, Ashka makes a sound in the back of his throat while dragging his thumb across his neck. I flinch at the brutality of this child whose feet hardly dangle off the ledge of the chair he's sitting in.

Alexi leans even closer. "Well, we can't prove that she killed him of course. But that's what everyone believes."

"Everyone as in..."

"The rest of the council. Honestly, try to keep up. This is all common knowledge."

Common knowledge, maybe, but was any of it true?

I looked across the table where Ravanna sat deep in conversation with Maksim. Her face was tilted proudly upward, her meal sat nearly untouched in front of her, and she'd pulled her black feathered cloak off her shoulders to reveal a pale slash of skin.

Could I believe she was capable of killing her king husband to gain his throne? Absolutely. But did I believe she did it?

It was hard to say.

"How did she manage the throne?" I asked, remembering my own lengths to secure mine. "Surely it would pass to the heir?"

"Ah, you're smarter than I gave you credit for." I ignored his rude comment and waited patiently for him to divulge more information. "She had no son. Or child for that matter."

"She can't have children," Ashka intoned dryly. "Witches can't have children."

"That's not true," I told him. Although I wasn't sure if I was arguing that witches can have children or that Ravanna was not a witch. He didn't seem to care what I had to say either way.

"And there is no council of nobles or army in Blackthorne to vote or stop her. Ravanna simply took over. No one could tell her not to. Well, I suppose your father would have had to step in. But I have never heard of him even trying to intervene." He sat back, slouching in an arrogant kind of way. "Lucky witch. Imagine what you could do with unlimited power as queen of the realm? If no one tried to stop you?" He became aware of what he was saying and added, "Imagine the progress you could make without needing a council's approval."

Well, if I had not been convinced he was not a consort I could tolerate before now, the greedy look in his eyes as he talked about unlimited power would have been enough. "The council is important for accountability. Unlimited power becomes a curse when not kept in check."

He laughed, low and condescending. "I'll be sure to ask your opinion again once you've truly had to deal with them. They're all old, out of touch, and too happy to sit back and get fat than make real progress for the realm. They can't even stop the Ring of Shadows. What if Kasha's civil war spreads? Or the famine in Vorestra? What if Aramore ever comes clean about their gold running out? Do not underestimate the lengths these council members will go to ensure their comfort is not interrupted."

"And what would you do? Unlimited power and the famine are spreading throughout the realm. What is your solution?"

"Easy," he sneered. "The crown takes food stores in every kingdom and distributes it based on worth. If you have something to offer, your family can be fed. Should you be a worthless lout, then you'll learn to work very quickly. Fair distribution based on merit will build a realm of hard workers and motivated neighbors."

Maybe. If corruption were not as human a trait as breathing. "And what of children? Your brother, for instance?" I gestured toward Ashka. "What can he offer the crown so that he can eat? The disabled? The elderly? How will they work for food if they cannot get out of bed?"

My questions didn't seem to bother him. "The children will be cared for, of course. They will one day be the workers so they will need their strength. As for the others, what do we need of the disabled and elderly if they cannot work? What value are they if they do nothing?"

His words sent a sharp shiver sliding down my spine. This wasn't mere speculation. Alexi had thought about this. And because I wasn't willing to take him as my consort, he would one day sit on the council with me. The small amount of breakfast I'd eaten rotted in my belly. I felt sick.

Somehow I managed to keep my composure. "Well, you certainly have many thoughts on the realm."

He smiled at me. I could see that there was a handsome man somewhere in there. But it was blotted out by his pride and twisted ideals of life, of living. "You certainly don't have enough. But worry not. It will be my pleasure to guide you."

I looked away from Alexi so he could not see my expression of horror, and my gaze clashed with Ravanna, who looked on the verge of laughter. It was such an odd expression for her usually serene face that I lost all control of my facial muscles. I could not have said what I looked like, but I seemed to amuse her even more.

With a subtle incline of her head, she glanced at Alexi and then rolled her eyes. Had she heard him offer to guide me? Had it annoyed her as much as it had annoyed me?

I closed my eyes and made a show of sighing. She dipped her head to hide her smile, then turned to Maksim when he demanded her attention once more, totally composed.

Had I just shared a moment of brevity with the Cold Queen? I could hardly believe it. But if anyone understood the needlessness of a man's advice to come to my own opinion, it would surely be a witch who murdered her husband so she could ascend his throne and take over his kingdom.

Breakfast ended shortly after, saving me from more strained conversation with the Crown Prince of Barstus. And shortly after that, Katrinka said goodbye to the family she loved so dearly, and we left the kingdom altogether.

There was a moment, as I climbed into the carriage and caught her clinging to Anton's neck, when I regretted her company. Maybe it would have been better for her to stay with the family she cared about so deeply. And who clearly cared for her just as strongly.

But being alone in the carriage for just a minute with Ravanna made me thankful for her company. And not just because I was reluctant to be alone with RP. I wanted what Katrinka had with her brothers. I wanted that closeness. That affection. I wanted a sister who acted like my sister. Who loved me like a sister.

I had lost my family many years ago, and now I had the chance to have at least part of it back. And I refused to pass up that chance for an easy solution.

Just as I'd battled my way into a comfortable existence with the Temple monks, I would fight tooth and nail to have a solid relationship with Katrinka again too. It might take years, it might even take a lot of years, but one day we would be thankful for each other. And I couldn't wait for it.

I was quiet, lost in my many thoughts, as our caravan of royal Blackthorne carriages traveled over the vibrant green moors of Gray Cape that rose up all along the southern border of the kingdom. Before we reached the border, we stayed two more nights at Barstus Inns and eventually caught a glimpse of the Serpent's Sea. The highway winded right next to beaches that were as wet and muddy as the constant rainfall would suggest they would always be like.

When we finally crossed the border into Blackthorne after days of shivering misery, the sun shone through the clouds and finally chased the chill away.

And I was left to wonder if it was the change of landscape or the goblin's curse.

CHAPTER THIRTEEN

Blackthorne was as diverse as all the other kingdoms I'd been to. But where most of the other kingdoms gradually changed over distance, Ravanna's kingdom was an abrupt departure from the gloom and greenery of Barstus.

Immediately, the scenery changed from drizzling and dreary to sunny and clear blue. And so did the landscape. From green and vibrant to stark and desolate.

The highway was rough and cobbled together with broken stones. And for miles in either direction were the remains of what used to be fields and forests.

Charred earth and broken trees. Gray and black and colorless.

Blackthorne was famous for its White Oaks. As famous as Tenovia for its Black Cedars. But the White Oaks were especially breathtaking to look at. Pure white bark with pale pink flesh. And clear leaves that glistened in the sunlight. I had seen them in the gardens at Elysia and been awed by their otherworldliness.

But here ... they were the opposite of beautiful. This was death and destruction on display. Had something happened while Ravanna was away? Was this why she hadn't been able to tutor me before? Because her kingdom had been under attack?

Katrinka was the first to find a way to voice her concern. "What happened?" she gasped, pressing her forehead against the coach window.

Ravanna glanced out the window. "This is an old scar. Older than you two. Older than even me."

"War? From before the wall?" Katrinka guessed.

"War, yes. But much after the Marble Wall. This was thanks to the Century War, a couple hundred years ago."

"When the magic was taken from the crown," Katrinka said, clearly calling on her better education.

Either Father Garius had purposely omitted the Century War or we had not worked up to it yet. Either was possible.

I felt Ravanna's cold glare on me. "I'm not so sure the magic was stolen after all. Hidden, perhaps. But how else is Tessana here and still alive, after everything?"

"You think the Crown of Nine has something to do with my Conandra?"

She laughed, but it did not hold any humor. "Sure, the trial. Your escape all those years ago to a little forgotten kingdom where nobody would think to look for you. Your travel back to the Seat of Power. Surviving several attempts on your life. Even now, the land sings of your arrival, Tessana Allisand. The Crown has protected you all this time." Her gaze flicked to the fox curled up in my lap. "Even your pet purrs with some greater connection."

I recalled the goblin curse but thought better than to bring it up now. "I'm not trying to do any of this."

"But that's the point, isn't it? Despite your fumbling and flailing and utter ineptitude, you remain unharmed. That's magic, my dear, if I've ever seen any."

Fumbling? Flailing? Utter ineptitude? Tell me how you really feel, Cold Queen. Was that the purpose of the Crown of Nine? To protect the royal family? My family? "But what of my father? If the crown still held the original magic, wouldn't it have saved him all those years ago?"

She turned away again, releasing me from the unrestrained intensity in her gaze. "That's what I can't figure out. Either the crown noted that you would be a better ruler than your father and acted in a way that would protect its longevity or your father had betrayed it somehow that released it from his service."

"And then it skipped all of my brothers?" My voice was a harsh whisper, trembling and weak. How could she even suggest that I had been spared because of a mystical power in the crown?

What nonsense.

Ravanna frowned deeply and then sighed. Turning toward the window once more, she changed topics. "The land was cursed. The pagans who manipulated the crown, in whatever way, cursed the land so the rest of the realm would not follow them into Blackthorne. It was their last line of defense against the approaching armies."

"This land is cursed?" Katrinka gasped. "How?"

"Death, my child. The only curse that matters."

"I'm sorry, I have more questions. Why would the pagans hide the magic? Why not remove it?"

"Maybe they couldn't," she suggested. "Magical objects are tricky things. More so, cursed objects. Or even blessed ones." Her gaze never strayed from the window. "Take these lands, for instance. Blackthorne has worked tirelessly since the fall of the pagans for the land to be restored. We've gone so far as to hire new pagans to extract the curse and breathe life back into the land. But no one has been successful. No animal can skitter across it. No seed can be planted in it. No man can walk it. Everything withers and dies." She breathed deeply and continued, "But consider this highway. No carriage will break down upon it. Nor man or beast grow too tired to travel it. No creature that alights on it will meet its end. And no bad weather will ever prevent anyone or anything from using the road. It has been blessed, and blessed it shall stay."

"Your failsafe from the surrounding cursed lands," Katrnika guessed.

"We could not leave our land for a very long time. The witches cursed the ground in such a way that kept everyone else out. But also kept the people of Blackthorne inside. We call that time The Darkness, for the people of Blackthorne barely survived it. In a time when freedom and travel were myths of the past, people began to group together in small units, some forsaking society altogether. So you will not find towns like you are imagining in the other kingdoms. Or even a thriving society. But you will find resilient people who will do anything to protect their homes and their lifelines no matter the cost."

Yet this was Ravanna's favorite realm. So strange. The more I learned about her, the more I wondered how she and my mother were once friends.

The carriage fell silent while Katrinka and I absorbed the full weight of what happened. News may have never reached Heprin of this war between pagan witches and the Crown of Nine. I wished I could ask my father about it. Wished I could read his face and see if he was as heartbroken over the loss of lives and the loss of relationships as I felt now.

I thought about how much the people of Blackthorne must have suffered as prisoners in their own country. And how many lives were lost not just during the battle but in the time since then? How many families died off over that time, ending their lineage?

Outside of Heprin, magic was becoming a very real thing. Even in the safety of the Castle Extensia, I had grown up knowing magic was banned. But not why. Nor at what cost.

"You feel the pain of this land," Ravanna noticed as green grass began to appear and pale barked trees could be seen in the distance. "It is not just speculation for you. You feel it here." Her hand pressed against her heart, pale, porcelain skin against the black of her feathered corset. And her black eyes were on me.

"How could I not? There was not a victor in such a war as this."

Whether the witches removed the magic or simply hid it, too many lives were lost for the pursuit of greed."

"You think the Seat of Power should have given up the Crown of Nine?" Her tone sounded genuinely interested in my opinion for the first time since I'd known her.

So I chose my words carefully. "I think there is never a reason to justify so much bloodshed. And I think unlimited power is only useful when it is useful for all people. I don't know all the facts, but I do know that my ancestors turned their power on people they were meant to protect and lead. Whatever the reason the pagan witches had for moving the magic must have been significant enough to go to war."

"You side with the witches?" Ravanna sounded as if she could not believe me.

"I side with those I feel have been wronged." I gestured out the window. "Your kingdom has been wronged. No one should have to live like this. No one should have to fear the land they come from."

Ravanna turned to Katrinka. "And what do you think?"

Katrinka nibbled on her bottom lip and pushed her glasses up the bridge of her nose as she thought over her answer. With a nervous glance at me, she said, "My sister is right. We are missing facts. But the Crown was forged for a reason. Many, many people already died to build the Seat of Power. The witches seem to have sought to undo all the good that had been done. I cannot say for sure, but surely, they brought some of this on themselves. The innocent lives lost both then and since then are on the pagans' hands. Not the Allisands."

Ravanna's lips twisted into a sneer. "You're right, Katrinka. The witches did bring the war here. And they are the ones who cursed their own land." Her focus fell to me and stayed there. "But you are right as well, Tessana. The Seat of Power had grown ill with greed. And it remains that way to this day. Unlimited power can only corrupt. And this is your first lesson of being queen. You must face the corruption and decide to work with it or succumb to it. Your days of good deeds and kind thoughts are coming to an end. There are many problems in the realm such as this one, and not one has a clear, happy solution. To rule over many is to know that you must sacrifice some. So ask yourself now, Tessana Allisand, future queen of the realm, how many pagans are you willing to martyr for the greater good? How many kingdoms are you willing to let curse themselves as they try to protect themselves from you? When will you decide enough is enough? When the world has been crushed beneath your boot? Or when someone asks you nicely to hand the power over to them? There is hardly any middle ground between the two. As you well know."

I tore my gaze from hers and looked out the window, watching the scenery change and evolve into something ethereal and wild.

The rest of the drive to Ravanna's home, Fenwick Keep, Katrinka asked Ravanna questions about the Blackthorne people, but I could not look away from the splendor of the land. The Blessed Road, which Ravanna told Katrinka was the official name for the highway, did not pass any towns or cities like she'd said. Instead, the land rolled with untouched forests of White Oaks and glistening lakes. Flowers as purple and pink as the most vibrant fabrics crawled over the ground instead of grasses or crops, making a contrasting blanket of beauty against the stark whiteness of the short, twisty bleached trees.

The road remained rough and bumpy, but I stopped paying attention to the way my body bounced around the carriage as I desperately tried to drink in as much of Blackthorne as possible.

Ravanna explained that the people here lived together in territories instead of villages. It was still a struggle for her as queen to get them to communicate. Skirmishes often arose between the territories, and she was called in to mediate.

That was what called her away those months before. The faction from inland had started using land near the Serpent's Sea to harvest an algae known for its healing powers. But the territory that controlled the beach wanted to trade for it instead of letting the inland territory simply take it. Neither side had been willing to compromise and had gotten to the verge of war. Ravanna had stepped in and helped the inland territory see reason. Now they traded algae for a rare flower that does not grow near the icy sea with its tempestuous weather.

As we neared Fenwick Keep, the landscape changed again. From clear lakes and white-capped rushing rivers to marshes and swamp land. The crawling flowers from nearer the Barstus border faded away, and pale-pink vines covered the landscape instead. I found it fascinating to be in a place where humans truly had not touched it. The wild was everywhere. Even here on the road, now that it was no longer cursed land. The uneven, poorly made Blessed Road became almost intolerable as the vines stretched over the highway itself. More than once, we had to slow to a stop, and the guards would get out to lift the carriages over particularly thick obstructions.

And then there was the Keep, rising from the flattened landscape. It was shocking obsidian in a world of white and pale pink.

The outer walls and battlements were as smooth and glossy as the Marble Wall had once been. A burbling moat of mossy swamp water left a wide berth between the castle and the rest of the land. And as we drove over the drawbridge once it had been let down for us, I noticed the stillness of Ravanna's home.

There was no hustle and bustle of servants as we arrived. No royal guards or military to salute us as we pulled up in front of the massive castle proper with its pointed center and imposing outer towers. It reminded me of a crown, a perfect circle with evenly spaced points.

Yet there were no people anywhere to be seen.

Now that I thought about it, I realized that Ravanna had no people with her. No maids or courtiers. Not even footmen to help her down from the carriage.

We'd traveled in her carriage, but it had been Elysian guards that had escorted us and driven the caravan. The only maids belonged to Katrinka and me.

The door to the carriage opened, and the footmen released the stairs. I waited for a servant or an advisor to greet us, to show us inside, but Ravanna led the way. And as we marched away from the carriage, up an endless set of obsidian stairs so steep and smooth I worried I would slip on them and fall to my death, our own servants and guards disappeared into their duties so that Katrinka and I remained with Ravanna alone.

A whisper of fear curled through my belly. My head was still sore from where Caspian had tackled me to the ground to save my life. Had his bravery been for nothing?

What was more was that there was no furniture either. No sideboard tables holding lit candelabra. No overstuffed chairs or elegant rugs. No paintings of old, dead people decorating the walls. Or tapestries hanging from the ceilings. The inside of Fenwick Keep was as stark and black as the outside. The only light filtering in through the long narrow windows spaced evenly apart.

Ravanna did not explain. She simply moved forward at a quick pace, leaving Katrinka and me to hurry after her. I started to worry we'd have to sleep on the floor and make our own supper when Ravanna pushed through giant black doors four times the size of any entrance at Extensia and led us into the throne room.

I was relieved to find a throne in the room. Although it sat alone, in the center of the hexagon-shaped space. There was a rug beneath it, feathered like everything else Ravanna wore. And overhead, a wide chandelier in the same shape as the room held half-burned candles, their dried wax running down the iron sides of it.

Ravanna paused in the center of the room, remembering we were with her. Turning slowly, she glanced at the chandelier over our heads and said, "You may take the evening to refresh yourselves. Your maids should have your things in your rooms. I will summon you for supper but expect it to be after sundown. The days are longer in Blackthorne and the nights much shorter. It will take some adjusting, but I have no doubt you girls will manage."

Katrinka cleared her throat and said, "Excuse me, Queen Ravanna?"

"What is it?" the Cold Queen murmured, already annoyed with our presence.

"I haven't seen any servants. Or other people in the Keep." Katrinka tucked her hands behind her back and averted the queen's eyes.

"I don't hear a question," Ravanna snapped back.

"Are there servants? In the castle, I mean?"

If Ravanna wasn't annoyed before, she very much was now. "Of course there are servants. What kind of question is that? We simply prefer they stay out of sight in Blackthorne. I know in other kingdoms, the servants prance around as though they are one of you, but here, they know their place and stick to it. Which is why you don't see them now. They're being respectful of your rank."

I shared a wide-eyed look of terror with Katrinka before she said, "Of course. I just had not seen anyone yet and—"

"Here is Mrs. Blythe to take you to your rooms now." Her tone was so condescending and dismissive that I felt my face burn with shame.

Katrinka wouldn't look at anyone, not even me or Mrs. Blythe.

Mrs. Blythe was an older woman with a severe expression and snow-white hair pulled back into a tight bun at her nape. I was instantly terrified of her.

But Ravanna wasn't finished with us yet. "And Allisand sisters," she called. We turned to look at her in unison, and I had no doubt both of us were trembling in our traveling boots. "Just because Blackthorne is the poorest kingdom in the realm doesn't mean I can't afford to keep help. Even though we pay the highest taxes to the Seat of Power."

Katrinka practically sprinted to Mrs. Blythe's side. I followed quickly after. How had we managed to learn more about Ravanna than I knew possible and infuriate her in the span of one day?

Just before I left the throne room for the hall, I braved a glance back to find that the candles on the chandelier had all been lit. But when?

And by who?

I thought of the pagan witches. Magic in the Crown of Nine. A war over a magical object. And cursed lands and blessed roads.

Magic had always existed in my world as something from the past. An outdated construct that no longer held any authority. But here it was. Alive and breathing. Still a thing from the past, but a strong and powerful enough influence to still affect things today. And not just something used hundreds of years ago that still held power in modern things, but something actively used and manipulated now.

The Crown of Nine hiding away for so long, then falling into my hands.

The goblin's curse.

The Blessed Road.

The chandelier that had not been lit and then was after Ravanna Presydia had merely glanced at it.

Magic was not a myth. Magic was real. And the chill from Barstus meant something I could not yet face. Something that tied my mother and Ravanna together. Something that would change the world should I sit in the Seat of Power.

Was the old way the true way?

And if so, what did that mean for me?

CHAPTER
FOURTEEN

A knock on my door had me jumping from where I sat cross-legged on my bed with Shiksa curled up in my lap, the spell book laid out in front of me. Clesta had gone to find someone who could help her track down Finch. I had a letter to give him, but he hadn't been around since we'd arrived in Blackthorne.

I was worried about him but desperate not to draw too much attention to him. My other guards, Curtis and Dover, didn't seem concerned about him at all. But surely, if something had happened, they would notify me.

Besides, Clesta didn't knock.

Before I could hide the spell book or move off my bed to answer the door, Katrinka pushed inside. She looked agitated and pale with worry, so I immediately forgot about trying to decipher pagan and was concerned over her.

"What is it?" I asked, tensing for something horrible.

She glanced around my bedroom. Despite Fenwick Keep's rather stark décor around the rest of the castle, our rooms were outfitted nicely. They were still simple and practical per the rest of the castle's style but also tasteful.

I had made sure Katrinka wanted for nothing. And I had found my own stay last night to be lovely. I had slept harder here than I could ever remember sleeping in my life. No dreams about ravens following me around or killing my family. No icy chill to keep me tossing and turning to get warm. I was not on the road—either by foot or carriage—and I had not found my mind spinning with all the things to do and discover and uncover. I had simply relaxed into a deep, dreamless sleep that had left me well-rested and comfortable.

In fact, the only times I found myself uncomfortable in this castle were at the mealtimes Katrinka and I shared with Ravanna.

The queen was clearly not used to constant houseguests or other people sharing meals with her. She kept forgetting we were at the table, only to look up and startle every time her gaze alighted on us.

It probably didn't help that Katrinka and I were being as quiet as possible so as not to annoy her. Supper last night had been painful. And breakfast this morning was something more than excruciating. So much so that I had suggested to Mrs. Blythe that Katrinka and I could eat earlier or later than the queen so as not to disturb her. But Mrs. Blythe had only looked at me like I was a fool and continued walking.

"I am wondering . . ." my sister started with a trembling voice. "If you would go for a walk with me. I know you are fond of exploring the grounds. And I just . . . I just can't stay inside much longer, waiting for her to yell at us."

"Or talk to us like a decent person," I added, understanding her pallor now. Katrinka offered a meek smile. "I would love to go for a walk. There is nothing a little sunshine and fresh air cannot cure."

I slid the spell book under the covers and hopped off the bed. Shiksa sat up abruptly, shaking off her slumber. She had been restless since we arrived at the Keep last night, but she could at least stop her pacing when she was with me.

Apparently, when I left for a meal, she would pace the room and scratch at the door. Clesta was worried she'd gotten pregnant somehow. And I had to keep assuring her that would be impossible since we hadn't seen any male foxes since I found her as a baby.

Scooping up Shiksa, I decided to take her with me. She wouldn't wander far if I let her walk. And it would be good for her to stretch her legs after so much travel.

"Should we tell someone?" I asked as we navigated the winding hallways of Fenwick Keep toward the throne room. Neither of our guards was permitted on this side of the castle because Ravanna insisted that hers didn't need their help, so ours had been forced to guard the foyer. They were ill pleased with the setup, but I relished the freedom.

Or at least the façade of freedom.

Ravanna's whole employ had learned to stay so well out of sight. The only other people we had seen since Barstus was Mrs. Blythe and our maids.

We got lost somewhere on the way, though, and ended up in a different part of the castle. When we tried to turn around and go back the way we came, we found the ballroom. Katrinka stepped inside first, smiling at me.

"Ballrooms always lead to gardens," she whispered.

I knew her to be right, so I followed. Both of us gasped at the sight of the ballroom, even in the light of day. It looked like the night sky but as though we were aloft in it. The same black marble that made up seemingly the entire Keep was more speckled here. There were sprinkles of gold and silver and white saturating the glossy obsidian. Everything around us sparkled in the sunlight, a breath of whimsy in an otherwise dark existence.

And sure enough, along the back wall were glass panes that showed us the gardens.

We hurried for doors that had been left open to the afternoon breeze and slipped outside, breathing deeply. I had not realized how tight my chest had coiled until the sun was on my skin again. Even Shiksa stretched in my arms and tipped her face toward the sky.

Katrinka sighed happily beside me. "Thank you for joining me.

My head feels as though it's been spinning for months, and this . . . this place is too much for me to comprehend. I felt as though I was going mad in there."

I smiled to myself at her admission. It wasn't much, but this was a small step toward trust. Sure, her other options for companionship were Ravanna Pressydia or Mrs. Blythe—the ancient servant who refused to speak to us—but I would treasure this small victory. This tiny invitation to be more than acquaintances.

We walked down onyx cobblestones and stepped onto a garden path with trellises on either side, splendid with climbing flowers. Shiksa wiggled until I let her jump from my arms. She landed gracefully on the trail and began trotting happily in front of us, leading the way.

Katrinka and I were silent for a few minutes, but this question about magic was scratching the inside of my mind. I needed a second opinion. There was a letter for Taelon in the deep, inset pockets of my dress, but until I could find Finch, the topic seemed to swarm throughout my body like an angry hive of bees.

"What did Barstus teach you of magic?" Her head snapped quickly to the side so she could measure the severity of my question. "I'm quite serious, Katrinka."

"Well, like the monks in Heprin, I'm sure you learned the same thing. Magic was once vibrant in our realm, but after the war and the Marble Wall was built, the Seat of Power, etcetera, it was used less and less. And eventually banned." She plucked a flower from the hedge, rolling it carefully between her fingers. "I had heard of the Century War, but what I read was diluted compared to what Ravanna shared on the way here. And I had never heard of magic being attached directly to the Crown of Nine. Hundreds of years don't seem very long ago in the grand scheme of things."

"My thoughts exactly."

She hummed thoughtfully, then glanced over her shoulder. "Did it seem that Ravanna thought there might still be magic in the

Crown of Nine? She seemed . . . I don't know, confused or particularly thoughtful about the subject."

"Yes, you're right. I had not thought of that till now. I suppose, if you believed in magic, it would matter greatly if it had been removed from the Crown or merely hidden. The difference would be great."

"But why, Tessana? Why would it be great to someone who would never wear it?"

I remembered my trial and said, "She nearly did, though. Before I arrived in Elysia, the council was set to vote on a new Seat of Power. They were going to move it from the Allisand bloodline. I had thought it was meant for Uncle Tyrn. But do you think . . . ?"

She pressed her lips tightly together and considered. This was the most the two of us had spoken to each other without interruption, and my heart swelled at the possibility of a more familiar relationship. "Do you know, I blamed you for sending me away to Barstus? Well, not specifically you. But my family. I foolishly blamed them for getting murdered because it made my life so difficult. In the early years, when I was so cold and so alone, I would think things like, why didn't they love me enough to take me with them? Why would they abandon me in this wretched place? Why would they do this to me?" She laughed quietly and pushed her glasses up her nose. "Dreadfully selfish, I know, but I couldn't imagine life without the family I loved so much. I couldn't reconcile why they'd been taken away from me and why I'd been left to navigate this cruel, harsh world all alone. But then, well, then I got to know the Zolotovs. They were kind to me, accepted me as one of their own, and became the family I had lost. When Maksim offered to marry me into his family, I leaped at the chance. I . . . I didn't care about losing Elysia or the realm or the Seat of Power. All I cared about was staying at home." She cleared her throat and added, "Although I had truly never expected him to have Alexi in mind. I thought . . ."

"Andre," I filled in for her when she trailed off. "Anton told me."

She blushed the color of the rose in her hand. "He has such a big mouth."

Nudging her shoulder with mine, I couldn't help but laugh. "He cares for you. He wanted to see what I could do to make it happen."

"Of course he did."

"And I told him there was nothing I could do. At least not yet. But check back with me in a couple of months."

"Tessana, you did not!"

I grinned at her. "Why should I be the only one to marry a second son? They seem to be much nicer than their firstborn brothers. Andre might not be heir to the throne of Barstus, but he genuinely cares for you. And in my opinion, that is more important than the potential power he might wield one day."

"Isn't that the truth?" She spared a quick glance in my direction. "Is that what you're hoping for as well? A love match?"

I thought of Alexi's harsh beliefs that royals weren't allowed love matches. And then I thought of Taelon and all I would give up to be with him. And all that I would not give up—the Crown of Nine for instance.

"I don't think I'm allowed to hope for a love match. I don't even get to have a king. Consort. That's what they're calling him. The Queen's consort." I shuddered. "It sounds ridiculously torrid to me."

She snickered into her hand. "So not a love match, but a lover."

A surprised laugh burst out of me. "Dragon's blood, Katrinka! No!"

She giggled harder. "Queen of the Realm and her assigned lover."

I couldn't help but laugh. "You're going to make me sick. Now I'll be alone forever just to avoid anyone calling him that."

"You won't be alone forever," she said sweetly but sincerely. "And I don't think you'll have to worry about forsaking love to find someone worthy. Too many are already in love with you for that to be the case. The right man will make himself known to you, Tessana. Love and power. I believe you can have both."

Her words were surprisingly thoughtful. And I somehow felt more optimistic about my future. Even while I wondered if she meant Taelon. Or had she mistakenly assumed Oliver was a potential husband.

I quavered again. Arrows and assassins might not have been able to take me out yet. But much more talk of Oliver as my lover would surely be enough for me to drop dead on the spot.

We'd started to sort of follow Shiksa as she led the way through the winding maze of flowers and cobblestones. The sun was warm in the blue, blue sky. And it seemed a perfect day for a walk.

"You know our mother used to speak of magic. Often really."

"I remember," she said. "And I don't remember much, but that . . . that I can conjure as clearly as if she were still alive today. All of us sitting at her feet while she spun tales and told stories from that great big book."

It was on the tip of my tongue to tell her it was a spell book. And that I now possessed it. But something held me back. Fear that she would think I was as mad as Ravanna. Or insecurity that she would tell our uncle.

"I'm glad you're here, Katrinka. This isn't at all what I thought it would be. And I don't know how I could do it without you."

"I'm glad I'm here too. You're right to think that way. I don't know how you could do this without me either." Her smile was as wicked as I'd ever seen it, and it made me laugh. "She's terrifying. Isn't she? One second I feel as though I'm safe, cared for. The next, I feel the urge to hold my neck lest she chops it off because my breathing bothers her."

"You're not alone in that. I haven't heard Mrs. Blythe speak once. Probably for fear of having her tongue cut out."

We'd come to the end of the hedge maze. The black cobblestones ended, and a forest of White Oaks with fluttering clear leaves began. Where fallen leaves blanketed almost every forest, the translucent nature of these made it seem as though this forest floor was glistening in the sunlight. It was too enchanting to resist exploring.

I remembered the massive moat we'd crossed to get onto the

castle grounds, so I knew we were still well within the protection of the Keep.

"Should we explore the woods?" Shiksa had already started pawing at the ground, making sure it was safe. "We won't go too far."

My sister looked around uncertainly. "I remember our father taught us to love long walks."

I smiled and took a tentative step forward. The ground was not too spongy for our elegant slippers. "You're right. He would leave his duties whenever there was sunlight and gather us up from our lessons so we could explore a new part of the castle grounds."

Katrinka followed me off the path and onto the wild earth. "Mother was always so vexed with him." She laughed and then mimicked our mother's voice. "They will never learn to read, Fredrix, if you're always running off with them."

I joined her as we wandered aimlessly through the pretty forest. "I remember them arguing over it." I laughed with her because it wasn't a real fight. I couldn't remember them ever having a mean-spirited row. But this was a strong marker of my childhood.

Katrinka rubbed a hand over her heart. "By the Light, I'd forgotten how much I missed them. Just being with you has unlocked a door I did not know still lived within me."

I knew what she meant. "It's good to remember, Kat. Even if it's painful." I hadn't called her "Kat" yet, not since we'd been reunited. I waited for her to rebuke me or complain about the childish nickname, but she instead linked her arm through the crook of my elbow and laid her head on my shoulder.

"I don't like the pain," she admitted. "It hurts too much, cuts too deep. I would much rather be able to shut it all up again and not think of it anymore." I had just opened my mouth to argue when she added, "But I loved them more than I want to avoid the grief. We were so lucky back then. So loved. What I wouldn't give to feel that again. To be able to crawl onto Papa's lap. Or watch Mama get her hair braided again. To follow Papa into the woods while he shouted orders to look for fairies and dragons. Or listen to one of Mama's stories about the pagans while we stretched out in front of the fire. I learned to love my life in Barstus, but nothing can replace those happy days at home."

My eyes stung with tears, so instead of saying anything, I simply nodded. How I had often yearned over the years to simply hear my parents' voices again. To hear their laughter. To feel their touch on my cheeks in love. To get in trouble again because of my brothers' nefarious plans. To have them tease me once more. To have them near me. Several tears rolled off my cheeks, but my smile was relentless.

But even more than the gaping sense of grief and loss was this new, fragile connection with my sister. I talked about my family with others in the long span between losing them and being reunited with Katrinka. I had shared with Oliver, especially, told him stories, and remembered them. But he could only sympathize. With Katrinka, we shared this grief. This tragedy. When we spoke of our parents, our brothers, they were memories we both had and treasured. I had not known to miss this connection. And if I had, my mourning would have been exponentially worse. But now that I had it with Katrinka, I would forever and always be reluctant to let it go.

I needed Katrinka for the future, for all that lay ahead. But now I knew I needed her for the past too. For all that had already happened.

Glancing back over my shoulder, I noticed the Keep was no longer in sight. Nor were the gardens. We'd been wandering without much thought to where we were going. Shiksa was just ahead, carefully stepping over fallen branches and larger rocks. She had her nose to the ground as if she'd caught a scent that required all her attention. And we'd been thoughtlessly following her in her pursuit.

"Do you think we've gone far enough?" I asked when a trill of unease spiraled through me.

Katrinka lifted her head too. She'd been as intently focused on where she stepped as I had been. "I-I don't know."

The trees in this part of the forest had started to change. There were not fewer of them, but they were barer. Not as though their leaves had fallen off, but as if they had no leaves at all and hadn't for a long time.

The ground was less cluttered too. Without the sparkling leaves to act as a carpet, the ground was a mixture of dry and cracked earth with wet, soggy mud. We'd begun leaping from dry spot to dry spot, hurrying after Shiksa, who was picking up her pace.

"Does she often run off?" Katrinka asked, grabbing a low-hanging tree branch for balance when she'd leaped over a particularly wide puddle. The dead branch gave way beneath her weight, and she swayed wildly before practically hugging the tree trunk to counterbalance her momentum and avoid plopping right down in the gritty mud puddle.

When I was satisfied she wasn't going to face-plant in the mud, I said, "No, never. She always stays right by my side. Unless she's at Extensia. Then she prefers to hunt down her dinner. But she always comes back."

"Could that be what she's doing now? Hunting?"

I watched the fluffy white tail of my pet fox twitch with agitation as she leapt onto a fallen tree and tiptoed over moss and musha-booms to the other side.

"Shiksa!" I called. But she only briefly glanced back at me.

"Let's get her, then head back." Katrinka sounded as concerned as I was becoming.

"Good idea." We hurried after the fox, hoping she would eventually see reason.

But she didn't. The terrain grew more difficult and much less beautiful. The spring breeze picked up too, whipping through the bare trees and pulling chill bumps from my arms.

I called her name again and again as Katrinka and I held our skirts high and tried to avoid the mud by jumping and climbing our way over the now stark trees. It was growing futile, though. Both of us had stepped in so much mud that our slippers, stockings, and hems were now thick with blackish muck. I had no idea how we were going to explain this to Ravanna.

"They're dead," Katrinka finally exclaimed. "These trees are dead."

A sickly realization doused my good mood. I had been holding a tree branch and let it go as quickly as possible. Then I wondered if it wasn't the tree that was the problem but the ground. So I grabbed the branch again, with two hands this time, and tried to hold up my weight by leveraging my feet on the trunk.

The branch snapped instead, and I landed in a heap on the ground, in the grime and dirt. Now it wasn't just my dress and silk slippers that were filthy, but my hands and bum as well. Clesta was going to give me an earful as soon as we found our way back to the Keep.

If we found our way back to the Keep.

If we did not simply die from walking on the cursed ground. Because that was what this had to be—the cursed ground. Forests did not just die like this.

"How much time do you think we have?" Katrinka asked in a choked whisper. Her thoughts had been exactly where mine had been.

But still, I played dumb. "Time for what? Before Ravanna comes looking for us. Hopefully only minutes."

She looked as aggravated as I'd ever seen her. "No, not Ravanna. The cursed ground. Are we going to die, Tessa?"

I took a deep breath and searched my mind and body for signs of pain or disease. I felt as normal as I should. But then again, I wasn't entirely sure what dying from a curse entailed.

"This is not cursed ground," a bodiless voice said.

We looked around, searching for the person it belonged to. It wasn't a voice I recognized, so I didn't know if it was friend or foe. But it did sound . . . old. So I wasn't sure I needed to be so on guard.

"Who said that?" Katrinka demanded, sounding bolder than I

had ever heard her. But then she pushed her glasses up her nose and left a smudge of dirt along her cheekbone, ruining the effect.

There was a fluttering in branches overhead. It was abrupt and aggressive, so much so that the light flickered around us. We spun in circles, searching for signs of life, when suddenly an elderly woman appeared. She had arrived behind us, so when we turned around after sensing her, it was impossible to tell if she'd simply manifested out of thin air or walked around the corner.

"Who are you?" I demanded before she could answer Katrinka's question. She looked as old and creaking as her voice had sounded. She was wrinkled everywhere and dressed in thin black cloth that I could see straight through. Although she'd been wrapped in layers from head to toe, so she wasn't indecent. In fact, even her head was covered in black cloth.

Her skin was dark brown with white powder streaking over her cheeks and forehead. Her lips were painted a dark burgundy with a single line of white marking the center of both the top and the bottom. And she had small rings piercing the length of her ears and along her eyebrows. The little hair I could see had turned gray, frizzing where her head covering had pulled back over her forehead. Tightly coiled curls escaped around her temple. She was old, I could tell. But she held an heir of authority that put every royal I'd met thus far to shame.

"This is my land," the woman said with a bob of her chin. For as old as she was, she did not stoop or hunch but stood ramrod straight. "So I will ask you the same question. Who is it that trespasses in my bog?"

"Your bog?" I gulped down a big breath and looked around, seeing it again from a different perspective. This was not the full forest near the Keep with its petal-like leaves blanketing the ground. This was, in fact, a swampy, marshy bog. How had we wandered so far from the castle in such a short time? "This . . . er, bog is your territory?"

"I'm the Bog Witch, child. Of course this bog is my territory."

Katrinka and I shared another look. The Bog Witch? What did that mean?

"I will ask you one more time," she said coolly. "Who *are* you?"

This time, it was not me confessing my identity impetuously. But my sister.

Kat burst with, "We are princesses from Elysia. Guests of your queen."

If possible, the Bog Witch's nose lifted higher. "She is not my queen." Katrinka reached out and grabbed my hand. "As for the princess part . . . I have been under the assumption Elysia has no princesses. Not since they killed the king's family. So you're either lying to me or deluding yourself into thinking something entirely untrue."

CHAPTER
FIFTEEN

I realized all at once we were facing an enemy. And if not an enemy, then someone who could become one quickly. I wasn't sure what Katrinka's training had been like or if she'd ever been prepared for combat, but my entire body flexed and tensed in wait for what was ahead.

My sword was back in my room. Packed away thanks to Clesta, who always insisted that I did not need it. Well, Katrinka and I had found ourselves in the middle of a witch's territory without a weapon or guard. I wished Clesta was here to witness it just so I could prove my point.

"We are true princesses of Elysia," I told the Bog Witch with as confident of a voice as I could manage. "Our family was killed nearly nine years ago. But my sister and I were saved. We've grown up apart from the capital, but we have come home to claim our birthright." I cleared my throat and added, "We have no reason to lie to you. We're guests of Queen Ravanna. We had no intention to cross into your territory. We are here quite by mistake, I assure you."

Her intense gaze moved over us as if measuring our worth and weighing the truth in our words. Shiksa had disappeared. But movement behind the surrounding dead tree trunks had me on edge, waiting for the attack.

"Daughters of Elysia?" she asked, considering. Katrinka and I nodded. "Then you've come to claim your mother's birthright as well. I tell you, I will not give it up easily."

I shared a look with my sister, unease unfurling inside me with wings as mighty and powerful as any dragon. "Our mother's birthright? What do you mean?"

She began to walk, evenly spaced steps as she circled us, and it was like branches of a tree swaying in the wind. Her lithe body moved liquidly over the ground as if she was not even touching the soft earth. But the menacing smile in her voice made chills rise on the back of my neck.

"You're like newborn babes. The two of you. Thrown into the middle of your destiny by fate yet uneducated in the ways of your blood. How will you take either of your thrones if you are so naïve to what lies ahead?" She paused, thinking. "Or what came before?"

Either of our thrones? What could she mean? A throne for me? And a throne for Katrinka, assuming she married a king? But what had she meant by claiming our mother's birthright? More questions to add to the litany of others. And at the center, more mystery about our mother. What I wouldn't give to ask her all these myself. "What came before?" I asked.

At the same time, Katrinka said, "What lies ahead?"

This made the Bog Witch laugh. "If you are home again, in Elysia, do you possess the Crown of Nine?" Neither of us answered her. We'd positioned ourselves back-to-back while she continued to walk slow circles around us. "You do. Of course you do. No one would accept your legitimacy without it. But you are still missing a crown. It is the one your aunt seeks even now. The Crown of Nine is only half of the puzzle."

"Our aunt?" I blurted, hardly believing the words this strange woman was saying. "You can't mean?"

She paused, turning to meet my eyes and, once again, search for the truth. She must have seen honesty in my face because her ringed eyebrows dipped over her eyes. "She has not told you? Do you really not know?"

"Know what?" Katrinka gasped, unraveling under the pressure of this meeting.

"There are always two to a family. Witches, I mean. There is one to wield the light and one to balance the dark. This has been true even after the Century War when magic was banned. But the night your mother was born, there were two moons in the sky. Rather, a full moon, cut in two. One side was much greater than the other side. A bulging sphere to a sliver of insignificance. It was said about your mother that she would restore magic to the realm and balance the opposing forces. The light with the dark. The land with the kings. The past with the future. But we knew another would come after her. And when her sister was born, the moon was absent from the sky. And the stars hid behind storm clouds. She screamed her way through the veil and shook her fist at all that would oppose her. Still, your mother loved her. Cared for her. Cherished her. They were inseparable.

By the time your uncle came along, they had already decided how they would rule the world. But the little moon did not like being outshined by the larger moon. She did not like having little moon power or getting lost in the light of the big moon. And no matter how much magic the little moon gathered, the larger moon always had more. If they had loved each other less, they would have seen the danger ahead of them. But their love for each other blinded the need for balance. And so it was all for naught in the end. There is no balance. The magic has not yet been restored. And the crowns that could save their mission grow dimmer and dimmer."

She'd spoken in too many riddles. I could not comprehend what she meant. Or who was my aunt? I glanced over my shoulder, hoping to catch Katrinka's gaze and see if she understood any of this better than I did. She was already looking back at me, brow furrowed, mouth in a flat frown. The look on her face betrayed her confusion as well. How were we to understand any of this?

"It is here," she continued. "The crown your aunt seeks, the one she hopes will revive her kingdom. It lives among the dead."

It lives among the dead? "Please, speak plainly," I begged her. I knew what she was saying was important, but my mind struggled to understand it all. "Name our aunt. We do not know her."

She smiled, and the movement between the trees grew more frenzied. Bodies wrapped in similar thin cloth as this lady ran in circles, hiding behind the tree trunks and dead shrubbery. "You are her guest, child. I should hope you know her."

Ravanna Presydia. Our aunt? I would have rejected the entirety of such a preposterous idea, except for those initials. TF + RP + GA. Tyrn Finnick plus Ravanna Presydia plus Gwynlynn Allisand.

The old way is the true way.

"You're saying our mother was a witch?" Katrinka demanded. "And that she was from Blackthorne?"

"Not just a witch, darling child. A witch of the highest order. She was the Moon Priestess."

I had no idea what that meant or how to interpret this information. "But she married the king of Elysia. Our father enforced the ban on magic."

Her dark eyes glimmered with memories. "She was negotiating peace for her pagan people. And she was killed for it. There are those out there who cannot tolerate peace. Who will not abide by it, even now."

"You're saying someone killed my family because of my mother's desire to bring magic back to the realm?" The world dipped and faltered in front of my eyes. Had Ravanna known that? Had Tyrn? Had my father?

"Your mother died because she believed peace was possible. She believed in the magic she wielded. And your father believed in her. When they died . . . even the land gave up hope." She reached out to rest her fingers on the barren branches of a dead tree trunk. But as she held her hand there, a new leafling began to sprout and grow with fresh life. "But here you are. A larger moon and a smaller moon alive and more formidable than all who came before you."

A power thumped in my chest. It was my heart, I realized. But beating in a way I had never known it to before.

Shiksa finally reappeared. She pranced over the puddles, as white and pristine as she'd always been. The bog had not touched her. She climbed up a fallen log and then leaped into my arms. She was not a weapon, not sharp like my sword or quick like a dagger, but I felt better protected with her nearby.

"What is this?" the Bog Witch asked with renewed curiosity.

I held Shiksa closer to me. "My fox."

"Your fox?" she repeated, extending her elegant arm so Shiksa could sniff her. At this distance, I could smell her too—wet earth, smoky campfire, and dried leaves. She smelled as though autumn had sprouted legs and began to walk around. She smelled of incense too. Like the Cavolia, only fainter.

I held Shiksa closer to my chest. "I found her in the Blood Woods when she was a kitling." I didn't know what possessed me to keep speaking, but I felt the incessant need to explain why I'd taken something from the wild. "Her family had been killed by a wild animal. She had no one. She would have died without me."

"You found this pure beauty in woods of blood after her family had been killed in the same manner as your own." Her explanation sounded like a question, but it was not one. She wasn't asking. She was telling me something I had not understood before. "She is yours, future witch. Yours to command. And you are hers. Hers to protect. If you do not believe in magic, your path with hers will show it to you."

"I believe in magic." My voice was sharp, defensive. But I had been unable to deny it since I left Heprin. "I'm learning to, anyway."

Her smile was back, but it was condescending. "As you should, since it's as deep inside you as the blood in your veins and the marrow in your bones." She stepped back and looked between Katrinka and me. "You must finish what your mother started. It will not be easy, and you might die before you see it to completion, but it is your legacy to take hold of, your mantle to carry."

"We don't know what she set out to do, though," Katrinka argued. "And who is there to tell us? If Ravanna is our aunt, not even she has been willing to admit it. And Tyrn hardly acknowledges we're alive. There is no one left to interrogate."

I thought of Brahm Havish in the castle dungeons. He'd known Ravanna and my mother were close, but he had not known they were sisters. Had anyone? What about my grandparents? We had never met them before. Only my father's mother had been alive while I was also, but she'd died peacefully in her sleep when I was very little.

"There was a spell book. The Fenwick Grimoire. It should have more answers than I can give you."

"A spell book?" Katrinka gasped. "Where could we possibly find that?"

I did not say anything, so the witch turned to me. "Your sister knows."

"It's in a language I don't speak." I felt Katrinka's gaping stare on my face, but I held the witch's gaze. "It tells me nothing if I cannot make sense of it."

The Bog Witch looked down at Shiksa and spoke in words that sounded like trills and curls. She held out her hand, and my fox nudged it with her little pink nose, seeming to give her permission of sorts. Then the witch rested her hand over my forehead and continued speaking in that same foreign language, her voice growing stronger and more confident.

Shiksa stretched up to lay her head in the crook of my neck as if assuring me all was well. I closed my eyes as an unseen power seemed to wash over me. She was casting a spell on me.

"Wait," I gasped as it seemed to take hold. But it was too late. The witch's hand dropped over my eyes, and her words held more force, more... magic.

Then I heard her say, "Let their meaning be clear. Let the

language she does not know be the voice inside her head, inside her heart. Let the spell book bring her near. The old way is the true way."

The witch pulled her hand away, and I opened my eyes just in time to see her flinch in pain. A slicing pulse cut through me as well, stealing my breath in a single gasp. I stumbled back, and Shiksa pressed into me even more, seeming to somehow absorb part of the blow.

The Bog Witch doubled over, losing her poise for the first time since we'd run into her, and said, "Your power is . . . too much. You are not the moon, but the sun." Her ragged breaths scraped through her chest as she struggled to stand upright once more. She glanced fearfully between Katrinka and me, a new fear twisting her features. "Your mother and aunt were pale moons that destroyed what they touched instead of saving it. If you two, as bright as the sun is in the sky, fail at what you set out to do, you will not just destroy a family. You will destroy us all. The land will never recover from your scorching."

Fear, cold and raw, burst to life in my blood. I shared another look with Katrinka and wondered what she thought of all this. "What did you do?" I asked the witch.

"Gave you true sight. The grimoire is yours to use now." She stepped back, her eyes flickering to the sky in a nervous sort of way. "The magic called to them. They're on their way."

"Who?" Katrinka asked.

Shiksa had begun to look at the sky in the same way, afraid, cowering.

"The Raven Queen's army."

She meant Ravanna. I didn't know if it was true sight or the evidence I'd gathered on my own, but I knew the Raven Queen was my aunt.

"Go," the Bog Witch ordered. "Tell her of none of this. And do not share the grimoire with her. There must be two, but she would cut you both down and take it for herself."

"Take what for herself?"

"The Seat of Power. The Crown of Nine. The Crown of Sight. The realm. The sky. The sea. All of it. She will take it all and swallow it whole."

The steady beating in my chest became a wild roar. I clutched Katrinka's hand as the air seemed to come alive with movement. Wings flapping. Birds cawing. A swarm of ravens so thick and numbered, they seemed to blot out the sun in the distance.

"Go!" the Bog Witch shouted. "Go, before it's too late."

Movement on the ground too. The people of the bog who had been in poor hiding while she told us her tales began running away from this place. They fled all at once, surprising me with their number and ability to stay hidden in the feral land of the marsh.

"What about the Crown of Sight?" Katrinka demanded, her feet planted firmly where we stood. "How can we find the dead place where it lives?"

I had nearly forgotten about this second crown. And had yet to understand why it was even important. We had the Crown of Nine, which secured the realm. What other crown was out there? And why had no one else heard of it?

"It's closer than you think," she said, swirling her arms in a purposeful kind of way. "But I cannot help you find it. Send the fox. Or let it find you. Now go. I will hold them off for as long as I can."

Our feet seemed to release at the same time, whether held by fear or by magic we had only just noticed. Both Katrinka and I turned and fled back the way we came. Shiksa leaped from my arms and sprinted ahead, seemingly wanting us to follow.

Not knowing what else to do, we did. She found the driest paths and the surest footholds. She avoided low-hanging branches and other obstructions, quickly leading us back the way we'd come.

There was a great cacophony behind us. The sound of birds screeching and wind rushing. I dared not look back while we moved so quickly forward. Something unseen urged Katrinka and me on. An urgent need, a new purpose, an old magic we had only just met. Maybe all three. Maybe more than just those.

And then, out of a wall of fog, just like the Blood Woods and our own castle grounds, we stepped back into Fenwick Keep's gardens. Our feet touched smooth, black cobblestone again, and the trees beyond the fog seemed to set themselves right once more.

We did not speak as we caught our breath on the steady walk back to the castle. No one seemed to have been looking for us, nor had we set off any sort of panic. The gardens and castle were as empty and quiet as we'd left them hours before.

The only difference was the one singular raven that landed right in front of us once we were nearly inside the castle. Katrinka screamed in surprise, but it only cocked its head and danced around on its little bird feet before taking flight again.

We clutched each other once more and then hugged each other.

"What does any of that mean?" she rasped in my hair.

I trembled against her, my mind racing to understand all that had just happened. Meeting a Bog Witch on any day would have been enough to upend the natural order in which I understood the world.

But what she'd assumed about me. About Katrinka. What she'd . . . *revealed* about us both. How did she know us? How did she know so much about my mother and Ravanna?

Ravanna, who was my aunt.

Ravanna, who was the Raven Queen.

And what did it even mean to be the Raven Queen?

Was it a simple moniker that described her love of feathers? Or something infinitely more nefarious and wicked?

Instinct whispered the latter. But I still had more questions than I had answers. And if the title of Raven Queen did decry evil . . . in what way? And how did it affect us? How had it affected my mother?

My family?

My knees wobbled, and I nearly fell to the floor. Katrinka was there to catch me and hold me up. What would I have done without her here? If for no reason other than to assure me that all that had happened had been real.

"I had no idea." I gasped for breath. My vision swam. "I had no idea there was power within me. Or our mother was... was..."

"Me neither." Katrinka hiccupped. "There were times. Moments, I mean... Things have not always made sense. Both when she was alive and since then. But I never thought... I never believed it could be..."

"Magic," I whispered, finding the courage to spit the word out. "You never believed it could be magic." She shook her head frantically. "Me neither, sister."

"But what does any of it *mean*?" she begged. "The Crown of Light? Power as great as the sun? Ravanna being our aunt?"

I felt sick to my stomach. Nausea rolled through me, and dark spots danced in my eyes. She was right to ask that question. Now that we knew about magic. And that we had magic. What did it mean? What were we supposed to do with any of it?

And what, especially, did it mean that Ravanna was our aunt?

I had set out to discover if she had simply known my mother. But I had never thought to expect this. Her words in the carriage came back to me.

"Sometimes I think she was the only person I have ever really known. The only person who's ever known me... We weren't friends. What a foolish word for what we shared."

They hadn't been friends, of course. Because they had been sisters. And now, my own sister and I were to carry on what they had begun. But what exactly was that?

"We must find out," I told Katrinka, finding solid ground beneath my feet again. "We must get to the bottom of it somehow. Lest we... Lest we..."

"Scorch the whole earth," Katrinka finished dryly.

"Yes, that."

"The grimoire," she suggested. "The Bog Witch spoke of a grimoire. Maybe it will have a solution? A plan? A guide to... what is next? Do you truly have it?"

"I will show you." If it was the spell book that would give us answers, I could at least show her that. "Come with me."

But the door to the gardens burst open, and Ravanna pushed through, looking more harried than usual. "Your uncle has arrived," she panted. "Come along. He's not doing well."

CHAPTER
SIXTEEN

Ravanna didn't give us time to respond. She simply turned around and left us to follow. Shiksa slipped into the castle and disappeared down one of the dark hallways instead of investigating what was wrong with Uncle Tyrn.

I was too worried to call her back. I had not expected to see him for another month. What had made him come all the way here? Follow us so quickly?

And more than that, if he was truly ill, why had he risked travel at all?

He must not be so very sick. Otherwise, he wouldn't have survived the journey.

So even more pressing than my uncle was that Ravanna might be my aunt. And not just my aunt, but the other portion of my mother's power. Even if only a fragment.

My mother had been a pagan witch. How could I have not known? Had father? Had my brothers? Tyrn must have known then as well.

The old way is the true way.

Had Ravanna and my mother set out to rule the kingdom? One

queen on the Seat of Power, the other with the Crown of Light? What could they have been capable of then? What was Tyrn's role in all of this?

"Tessana, are you ill?" Ravanna demanded from down the hallway.

I hadn't realized I'd stopped walking, too wrapped up in my thoughts and all the possibilities. I looked up and found Katrinka's eyes on me, her face tight with worry.

"I'm so sorry," I blurted. "I . . . I . . . I was lost in thought. Is Uncle Tyrn okay?"

"No," she hissed. She spun around again and tromped down the hallway. The servants were nowhere to be seen. Not that I had yet to see them before now.

I hurried to catch up to Katrinka, but I was struggling to concentrate now that I was moving again. The black walls and doors I'd previously passed without thinking much about any of them had painted markings on them. The floor. The ceiling. The . . . chandeliers.

The markings were familiar. And while it took me a few minutes to place them, I soon realized they were the ones in my mother's spell book. Runes.

Why had Ravanna painted runes all over her castle? Was Tyrn maybe physically fine but in danger instead?

And then I realized they were meant to protect the castle and all living within. The entire Keep was painted in protection charms. I caught a glimpse of Mrs. Blythe near the door to the dining room, and even she had a rune painted on her forehead.

The Bog Witch had not just given me the ability to read the pagan language but she'd also given me the ability to see it where it had previously been hidden.

As we stepped into the dining room, I took a steadying breath and leaned against a sideboard. Tyrn sat at the head of the dining table with his head in his hands. There were no guards in sight. No food in sight either. Just my uncle pulling at his hair with two fists and making sounds that made it almost seem as though he were crying.

"What have we done?" I heard him hiccup on a sob. "The children. By Denamon, Ravanna, the children."

"There, there," she soothed, gesturing for us to come closer. "Here they are. The children are fine, Tyrn. They are right here. You're mistaken. They're right here."

He wailed a sound that sent chills skittering down my spine. But then he listened to his sister and looked up. His gaze found Katrinka and me, muddy slippers and all, standing in front of him. For just a second, his vision cleared, and he released a trembling smile.

"They're here," he said on a ragged breath of relief. "Oh, thank the Light, they're here."

Ravanna reached out and patted his cheek. "Right here, my love."

"It was just a nightmare," he continued, new tears for a new emotion. This one delighted relief. "I only dreamed they had been killed."

"Yes," Ravanna whispered soothingly. "A dream. Nothing more."

But then his expression twisted with rage, and he pounded the table with his fist, jostling the elaborate candelabra in the center. "They want to take my throne. They want to take it from me." Spittle flew from his lips, and his cheeks burned red. "They've come to take everything from me. They want to kill me, I think. They want to murder me!"

Instinct propelled me forward, and I knelt before him, laying my hand over his. "No, Uncle, we do not want that at all. The throne is still yours. *Will* be yours for years yet."

Katrinka joined me in front of him, humble and meek, exactly the way he needed to see us. "We love you, Uncle," she promised him. "We would never wish you harm."

His expression screwed up again, this time from fury to distress. "Do you see this, sister? Do you see what I must tolerate day and night? They are just like her! They taunt me with their goodness . . . with their power. How can anyone stand this? How can anyone survive this madness?" He dropped his face into his hands and let out another wail of agony.

His cries made my skin itch because they were so very tortured. He wasn't just upset about something. Uncle Tyrn was going quite mad.

Ravanna stepped away from the table, looking as distraught as I'd ever seen her. She whispered words and moved her hands over his head.

Tyrn somehow noticed what she was doing and kicked out at her. She dodged his attempted blow easily and shot him a disappointed look, but he was back to weeping again.

"Please, no more. I can't take anymore." He sucked in a rasping breath that made it seem like he was drowning. Even though there was no water in sight. "No more," he begged and begged, repeating it over and over.

Ravanna stepped back, tears clearly falling from her eyes, although she made no sound with them and her expression remained placid. She continued to whisper as she moved around the room. Tyrn's violent weeping turned to softer cries that shook his shoulders and made him whimper. It was less shocking but no easier to watch.

"He needs an elixir I make for him sometimes," she said absently, reaching for the handle of a far door. "Sometimes he gets lost between the past and the present, sometimes even the future and the present. And this . . . this helps him find his way again. I'll be right back. Please, make sure he doesn't leave."

Katrinka called for her to wait, but she'd already stepped into the hallway. Very suddenly, we were left alone with our uncle and a side of him we'd never seen before.

Tyrn hiccupped a series of sobs before coming around to his senses again. He plopped his chin in his hand and rested his elbow on the table, looking very much like my brother Benedict used to when he was pouting. The sight of him so upset, and so familiar, made my heart ache for his pain.

And even though he had treated me so poorly since my return to Elysia, I couldn't help but feel true sadness at his state. He was so different than the man who locked me away and treated me worse than a slave all those months ago. The man whose right-hand man had tried to assassinate me. *He seemed so . . . burdened.*

"It's too heavy," he murmured. "The weight of it is tearing me apart." His gaze focused on me in particular. "You'll see what I mean soon enough. The power is broken. We tried to fix it, but"—he started sobbing again—"but we broke it worse." Tears streamed down his gaunt face and pooled on his tunic. He was barely dressed in a simple white tunic and leggings. But all his clothes were dirty from what I assumed was his hasty travel, wrinkled and splattered with mud. "It's a broken crown. And the broken pieces of it, they dig, and they dig, and they *dig* into your mind until your head is as shattered as the gold." He made claws with his hands to illustrate and tore at the make-believe head in front of him. "It will break you too, niece. You are not the rightful heir. You are a girl who should be dead. And when they put it on you, it will smash you into pieces so small and useless, you'll never find yourself again."

Tyrn's prediction somehow put all the other revelations from this day to shame. How could I face my looming coronation with a prophecy such as this one? Oh, how I longed for Oliver to be near. By now, he would have said something funny and broken the tension with his witty sense of humor. Reminded me that it could not be as bad as Tyrn made it out to be. Or if it was, we would find a way to stop it. Together.

Instead, only Katrinka remained at my side, and she was as pale as a ghost and looked as though she was on the verge of losing her breakfast.

"I am not just a girl," I told Tyrn. "I'm an Allisand. I do belong on the throne."

His laughter was the thing of nightmares. His head tipped back, and he slapped the table as though I'd truly entertained him. "That's what my sister said. She thought marrying into the line of arrogant, power-hungry devils would solve her dilemma. But look how that ended. She got herself and her entire family killed." His eyes were wild with madness, unfocused and glossy. And somewhere else entirely. His expression turned pained again as he seemed to walk through the awful ordeal in his mind. "Besides, it's not the blood that makes you friends with the throne or crown. It's not you at all. The crown decides who's worthy. And I can tell you right now, it will not choose a girl from the same family it only just murdered."

Had he really meant to say that? Did he really believe the Crown of Nine was what murdered my family?

No. No, I didn't believe that. It couldn't both kill my family and lure me back to Elysia, surely. Or was he speaking in metaphors? Of power and greed and the natural end to so many unchecked rulers?

Of all the things I expected from this trip to Blackthorne, it was not more questions to my already impossible unanswered list. But that's all I seemed to unearth. One question led to a hundred more. One answer to a locked door and more confusion and too many mysteries that did not seem to have solutions.

Ravanna hurried back into the room, her voluminous black skirts swishing as she moved. For once, she was unadorned with feathers of any kind. And somehow, she seemed more approachable this way. Not kinder exactly, but . . . less severe.

Tyrn noticed her immediately and started crying again, more the style of his distraught weeping than the enraged sobbing. She wrapped her arms around him as soon as she was close to him. And it was the gentlest I had ever seen her.

"There, there, brother, there is no reason for all these tears. You are the king, remember? The most powerful of them all. You should not be crying. You should be ruling."

Katrinka grabbed my hand, and we took a step back together, both physically hit by the confirmation blow of Ravanna's words. *Brother.* Which meant the Bog Witch had been right. Ravanna Pressydia was our aunt.

I was breathless and dizzy all over again. Even though I had suspected this truth, I could not reconcile with it. My whole life felt like a lie. My mother felt like a liar. And all those between then and now are accomplices. How could we not have known?

Why had no one told us?

The questions running rampant through my mind now had teeth. Sharp, jagged ones. They were more than mysteries now. More than uncertainties. They were a path that led into the unknown. An undeniable fate where my destiny might not be as bright and happy as I had once hoped.

Tyrn was right, after all. The Crown of Nine would tear me apart. And it started before it was even mine.

"No one listens to me," he wailed. "No one ever listens to me! I told Gwynnie not to do it. I told her not to leave home. She didn't listen. And now look! Now, look what's happened."

Katrinka squeezed my hand tighter at the mention of our mother. Was anything he was saying true? Or was it all just ramblings of a madman?

"She was always headstrong, brother. You know that." Her gaze met mine, then Katrinka's, almost as though she was apologizing to us for all of this. Her expression seemed to say she had meant to tell us. And that she had never meant for us to find out this way. She looked as tortured as Tyrn. "She loved you, but she did not listen to you."

He cried harder. "And now you won't listen to me either. I need you, sister. Make the pain stop. Make it go away!"

She kissed the top of his head. "Of course, darling. Of course, I will." Who was this suddenly compassionate woman? She had dropped her cold, distant façade sometime during her concern for Tyrn. And behind that icy wall was an attentive, humble sister who seemed to genuinely love her brother. Pulling a vial from her pocket, she held it out to him. "This will make the pain stop. Drink it down, brother."

His eyes cleared again for just a moment. And he stared at the small glass bottle with something like resilience in his hard gaze.

Shaking his head, he turned away from her. "No, thank you." With great effort, he seemed to pull himself back together, sitting up straighter and adjusting his facial features into the semblance of someone I recognized. Still, his voice shook as he said, "I realize I've been foolish. The pressure of the crown sometimes, it . . . well, it sometimes gets to me."

Ravanna shushed him patiently, like a mother taking care of a sick child who didn't like the taste of the medicine that would make him well. "Now, now, brother, please do not be difficult. Let me help you."

Tyrn's gaze met mine once more, and I was surprised to find it still clear. "You have to help me—"

She touched the lip of the bottle to his lips and tipped it. He resisted for only a moment before accepting the sparkling contents of the flask. He calmed down almost immediately. His shoulders straightened out, and his head lifted again. But his eyes . . . his eyes were more lost than ever.

My heart squeezed in agony for him, but I couldn't say why. Mrs. Blythe appeared again, stepping to his side to help him to his feet.

"He'll be a little unsteady," Ravanna explained. "Katrinka dear, could you help Mrs. Bythe take your uncle to his room so he can lie down?"

"Oh, er, of course." Katrinka jumped to her feet so she could support the other side of him. But her expression revealed she was as perplexed about the term of endearment Ravanna had used for her as I was. Our gazes clashed, and I tried to silently convey the need to play along for now. I wasn't sure if it was an obvious solution to all that we had just witnessed or if she was able to read my thoughts the way we used to as children. But either way, she did as Ravanna asked.

Tyrn dutifully draped an arm around each woman and let them lead him from the room. He'd calmed down dramatically. His tears had stopped falling, and his face looked more composed. There was a stillness to him that did not at all seem natural. He had only just been on the brink of total hysteria. In some moments, he'd succumbed to it entirely. But now, he was as docile as a lamb.

I felt more anguished than ever for him. At least when he'd been railing, his behavior seemed to be his own.

It was a spell of some sort. A potion. I was sure of it.

Assessing the room, and more specifically Ravanna, I decided to compose myself as well. If I played this wrong, Ravanna's mask would slide back into place, and my thousands of questions would remain unanswered. I needed to stay calm and diplomatic. I was a future queen, wasn't I? There was no better time to practice my statesmanship than the present.

After they'd left the room, and I could no longer hear them in the corridor, I turned to Ravanna and asked, "What can I do to help?"

Her measuring glare was cold and unexpected. I was too late. She was back to being herself. Whatever remnants of nurturing had been there with my uncle had already faded.

"Take a walk with me," she said, "I'd like to show you something."

I had stopped being afraid that she would kill me today. I didn't know when exactly, but probably somewhere around when the Bog Witch confirmed she was my mother's sister, my aunt.

If I was honest with myself, I could admit that I had a suspicion there was something more there since we'd found the initials in the abandoned chapel. Even if I hadn't wanted to admit it, even to myself. Maybe I didn't put together that she and my mother were quite that close, but I knew there had to be an explanation for why my mother had been aligned with her.

But how did she fit into my mother's death? And the deaths of my father and brothers?

There was only one way to find out. And it would start with taking this walk with her.

I followed her out of the dining room through the door she'd used earlier. It led us into another part of the Keep I had yet to explore. Our heeled slippers clicked against the polished floor, and I said a silent prayer that I wasn't leaving a trail of mud and dirt in my wake.

At long last, she led me into a library. The doors, like the Temple in Heprin and the chapel at Elysia, had carvings. Dragons, mermaids, sea creatures, and even beasts that I could not name. And now, with this magical sight, I could see that each represented a different charm.

There were runes inlaid over the top of them. And all of it worked together to make the library a special, safe place. These runes were not as abrasive as the ones around the Keep. They did not force others out with power. They gently let all who seek inside.

Now I wondered what the doors in Elysia would say. Or in Heprin? Would they be as welcoming and kind as they were here?

Inside the library were stacks and stacks of books and scrolls. There was hardly any organization in the massive room. Just books everywhere. And places to sit on the floor near precariously towering piles.

Toward the back of the room were stone tables covered in glass bottles of differing sizes and shapes, all holding liquids. Potions, I realized, when I read some of the rune inscriptions. I did not have to ask to understand that she'd given Tyrn something from over there. Something she'd concocted for him.

His words haunted my thoughts. "You have to help me." Help him do what? With what? From the potion? Or the crown?

Ravanna moved gracefully around her stacks of books. I followed her—less gracefully—but managed to avoid toppling any piles. We headed for the balcony. It was a cozy thing through paned glass doors. And bare except for us. It looked out over a graveyard. Each grave was marked with a rounded white stone.

The sun was dipping below the horizon. I had not realized how late it had gotten. We must have been in the forest for hours today. And now my stomach was growling because we hadn't eaten anything since breakfast.

"This is the castle cemetery," she explained, although I'd already figured that out on my own.

"Oh." I wasn't sure what else to say.

She took a deep breath and pointed at a far corner. "Your grandparents are buried over there. If you'd like to read their headstones, I can show you tomorrow. They died before you were born."

"Oh," I repeated, but it was a stronger, more intent sound. My grandparents? Maybe she was about to—

"I wanted to bring your mother back here and bury her," she confessed with a hitch to her voice. "I begged the council to let me rest her here, where I could continue to watch over her. But Elysian custom is to burn the bodies. They would not let me have her." Her fist had balled up where it rested on the balcony ledge, and now her voice did not just have a hitch but it was also whet through and through with emotion.

"You really are my aunt, then?" I asked, afraid she would try to deny it.

Her dark eyes met mine in the twilight. "Yes, your aunt. I suppose I am. It just feels . . . strange to admit that. Gwynlynn and I spent so much of our adult lives denying our familial bonds so we could marry kings, I suppose." One side of her mouth lifted in a smile. "Not that marrying well was our only goal. Although nothing is wrong with enjoying royal life, mind you." The other side of her mouth joined the first, and I admired how beautiful she was when she actually smiled. "But we'd both wanted to help the realm, and we thought we could do that best as queens. Tyrn, well, Tyrn just didn't want to be left behind. Although I wished he would have married. He liked a girl once. She was sweet. Very shy. But so sweet. They could have built a home here. Enjoyed a quiet, happy life. He wouldn't have ever had to—" She cut herself off and looked back down at her hands.

I had many questions about Tyrn. But I was finally facing the answers to the things that burned hottest within me. There would be time for my uncle. Later. Right now, I must stay focused on the most pressing matters. "So my mother was from here?"

She smiled again, softer this time, and looked out at the graveyard. As the sun set, lights started to glow over each grave. No, not lights... flowers. I leaned forward to marvel at petals that seemed lit like candles. Only these flames burned an ethereal blue and purple.

"What is that?" I gasped.

"What I wanted to show you," she said. "The people in this area plant them after someone dies and is buried. The petals soak up the sunlight all day long, then slowly release it through the night. And while they do, we're treated to this breathtaking sight. It's amazing that something so full of life could exist in a place so full of death."

I thought of the Bog Witch's words. "It lives where everything dies." Could this be what she meant? Was it really so simple?

But to Ravanna, I said, "What was my mother like?"

"Headstrong, impetuous, stubborn." She laughed—actually laughed. "Sound like anyone else you know?" I blushed at her insinuation. She softened again and added, "But she was also gracious and kind. She mothered Tyrn and me incessantly, but we never complained. Our own mother died in childbirth, so she was all we ever knew. And she was always negotiating with anyone willing to match wits with her." She took a deep breath as if preparing for something hard. "And she was the most powerful witch I have ever known." When I didn't immediately respond, she added, "You come from a long line of pagan witches, Tessana. Magic is in our blood. We are meant for power. And you, my dear child, are no different."

At her term of endearment, I felt my face screw up. "If you're my aunt, why did you use Conandra to try to keep me from the Crown of Nine? Why have you been so distant? So... so..." *Cold*, I wanted to say. *Cruel*.

Her smile faded, and her expression became the hard mask I recognized. "I... I was afraid at first, I suppose. Afraid to get my hopes up. That it was truly you. That you were alive after all this time. And then afraid for your future, of what the Seat of Power would do to you. The Crown of Nine. I watched it kill my sister. And I've watched it turn my brother into a madman. And while I could not reveal myself to you, I sought to protect you in whatever way I could."

My heart stuttered in my chest, stumbling over whether to believe her or not. I wanted her explanation to be true. Oh, I desperately wanted for her words to ring genuine. But . . . "Why since then?"

Her eyes flashed with pain, deep sorrow. "Well, I suppose after it was proven you are who you say you are . . . I wanted to protect myself. I have lived a lonely life, Tessana. My parents, my sister, and even pieces of my brother have all died. Have all left me. It wasn't that I wanted to treat you poorly. I was afraid to open myself up again after finally learning to live on my own."

An instinct to hug her rose within me, to throw my arms around this poor, lonely woman. I knew what it was like to lose my parents and my siblings. I knew what it was like to be afraid to trust again, hope again. Hadn't I been battling the same internal beast with Katrinka—desperate to love her again and terrified of it at the same time?

But I held back. I still didn't understand the need for secrecy. For lying.

"Why did no one tell me? Or my sister? Why was your relation to us kept secret?" I could come to terms with this magic, this line of witches. But how was I to reconcile the silence?

"There is an unspoken rule in the royal families that two sisters shall not be queen at the same time. Kings, of course, are descended from the lands they rule. So with each royal family, they house one king at a time. But queens are often married from other lands. Elysia already has the Seat of Power. None of the Nine want to give that much power to any family. They would have gladly accepted my sister as Elysia's bride. But had our relation been known, I would have been destined for a second son at best. More likely a duke or distant noble. The other kingdoms can hardly stand being under the thumb of Elysia. The council would have never allowed the Finnick family to put royals on multiple thrones. It was too much of a threat. They would have seen it as a coup of sorts. Finnicks ruling Elysia and Blackthorne. We might as well have handed Aramore to Tyrn and burned the rest to the ground. The lot of them are so bitter about the power the Allisands wield that they will never allow another family to grow that powerful. Jealous pigs, the whole bloody council."

I thought back to my childhood, the way my father would take us around the realm in the hopes of finding good families. But I remembered tension too. And now I understood why my father had first intended me for Caspian, a second son. A spare heir. Being betrothed to Taelon all those years ago, the Crown Prince of Soravale, must have caused an uproar. It would have meant an Allisand king on the throne of Elysia. And an Allisand queen on the throne of Soravale. I couldn't remember who my brothers had been betrothed to. But I knew there was talk of Katrinka marrying a wealthy merchant's son from Sarasonet.

"But more than that," she went on, "there were the rumors about my family in particular. That we were pagans. That we were witches. Our name used to be Fenwick. Until the Century War. We ruled Blackthorne for millennia, all the way to before the Marble Wall. When the Crown won the pagan war, they blamed my ancestors for the witchcraft that had stolen the magic from the Crown of Nine. And for cursing the land here. Dragon's blood, they blamed my family for inciting the war, to begin with. And disrupting the peace of the land. Peace that was a farce from the start. The only people who know peace in this realm are the wealthy, the elite. You've seen what it's like in the villages, how the people suffer, how they starve. It was the same back then. If the Fenwicks were behind the war, it was because the war was necessary for change." She had grown passionate as she exclaimed the history of the war. Her porcelain cheeks had blushed crimson, and her eyes sparked with zeal. She gasped for breath and seemed to come back to herself. Her hands brushed down the front of her skirts, smoothing them, and she straightened her shoulders before she continued in a calmer tone. "As punishment for the war and the curse, the council took the throne from my ancestors and handed it over to the Presydias. A noble family with great wealth and promises of loyalty to the Seat of Power. My family was made pariahs, enemies to the people of this land. We had tried to make the world better and were hated for it instead. Meanwhile, the Crown grew more powerful even while the magic diminished throughout the realm. Even while my people, not just the Fenwicks, but pagan witches of all kinds, of all kingdoms, were hunted and killed. Or locked away. Stripped of their power. Of their dignity. Of their . . . will to live." Tears of empathy glittered in her black eyes. "The exiled king and queen changed our family name from Fenwick to Finnick to avoid further shame. Our lands were taken. Our wealth stolen. And we were blamed for the cursing. They were forced into hiding. They took to the marshes, to the secret places of the kingdom, places beyond the curse. And that is where they rebuilt, regathered their strength. And their power. When they rejoined the world, sometime before your mother was born, they were more powerful than ever before. They might not have had titles or coin, but they had magic. Magic in spades. By the time Gwyn was born, we were back to being a noble family but still not trusted. We had real power, and we had some social power. But the people of Blackthorne had bought the lie the Crown sold them. To this day, they still blame us for the cursing. For losing the magic. But then there was the prophecy."

"The prophecy?" The Bog Witch had spoken in many riddles, but she'd mentioned a prophesy too. I hoped Ravanna would speak plainly about it. But I'd also lost my fear of asking her anything. She had shared more with me than I'd ever dreamed she would. Or could. Now was my chance to get as many answers as possible.

"When a witch is born, a circle of witches gathers to oversee her birth. It is common practice and has always been this way. Even now, throughout Blackthorne, those who practice the pagan arts still practice this ritual as well. As they sit, they also cast, making sure the child and mother are healthy and safe, making sure all goes as planned, and sometimes a telling will cease them, and they will speak words over the birth. When Gwyn was born, there were two moons in the sky. An already interesting omen, but she was born casting."

"What do you mean?"

"Magic, Tessana. She was using magic, even as a baby. The circle of witches said they had never seen anything like it. The magic, as harmless and weak as it was coming from a baby, took hold of them all. And then the prophecies began. They said she would be beautiful beyond compare. And she was. They said she would have unmatched power. And she did. And they said she would restore the magic to the realm." She looked away, her eyes searching the graveyard with its lit flowers. "Which she could not. Because they killed her."

"Who? Who killed her?" My voice betrayed how desperate I was to know the answer. This one question had followed me to Heprin and back and spanned nearly a decade. Yet I still did not have an answer.

Her jaw tightened, a muscle ticking near her ear. "Would you like to learn to use it?"

I thought I could not be distracted from this one question, from this one mystery that had upended and directed my entire life. But I was too taken off guard to keep my tongue quiet. "Use what?"

She turned back to me, the tension fading into a radiant smile. "The magic, Tessana. Would you like to learn how to cast?"

The temptation of magic was so strong I felt swallowed whole by it. I had not known I wanted to use magic until now, but how could I say no to such a promise? My mother, the most powerful witch. It hardly seemed possible.

But still . . . "Do you know who killed my family, Ravanna? My mother? Please, tell me."

Her face flushed with unspoken emotion, and something harsh and furious flashed in her eyes. "I have told you much, child. I have spoken of things I buried long ago. My heart is tired. And my mind is too saturated with worry for your uncle to speak of such things. The short answer is that I would like to know as well. The long answer could be discussed and debated and speculated upon until we are both old and gray."

My face fell at her decided answer. My entire spirit crumbled.

She noticed and reached out to lay her chilled hand over mine. "We will speak of it, of course. I will answer as many of your questions as I'm able. And when Tyrn is feeling better, we will enlist him in our investigation as well. But for now, allow me to let my ghosts rest. Allow my heart to be warmed by your presence. And the truth that we can now know each other as family. I want to teach you our ways, Tessana. I want to show you the power you come from. The way of the women in your family. The way of your ancestors. Please allow me this one thing."

It was on the tip of my tongue to agree. Of course I wanted to learn all she had offered to teach me. But there was a hole in my chest where my family should be. And now that Ravanna was here, confessing all of this, I struggled to let my questions go. Even though there was a promise of more answers later.

At my hesitation, Ravanna said, "Your mother might not have been able to restore magic, but you are about to do a thing that no queen has ever done before. You will sit on the Seat of Power and wear the Crown of Nine, Tessana. Your mother's legacy lives through you. You are the only one who can bring magic back to the people. You alone can erase the bans and biases the men before you have built. You can make a new way for the people of this realm. For the kingdom of your mother's birth. You have the power inside you. I felt it the moment we first met. And it has only grown every day I have known you since. I will teach you to unleash it and then wield it to your advantage."

"What about Katrinka?" I asked, still struggling to agree even though I had never wanted anything more in my life.

"Of course, she can learn too. She might not be as powerful as you, but she was born to magic. She will get the hang of it eventually."

Her smile made me hold back. It did not seem genuine. Something to her promise didn't feel...

"The Crown of Nine calls to magic," she continued. "And since the pagan war, it has been in decline. It is why your uncle suffers so. He is not the rightful heir. If you are to wear it, Tessana, you must be strong enough to resist the darkness within. You must wield the power that is already rightfully yours. Wield it to your advantage. To the advantage of the realm and its people."

Now, I felt the opposite of before. These were true words, true statements. The Crown of Nine was not something I could just put on my head and hope that everyone kneeled to it. The Crown required power, a force I did not yet possess, magic to mirror whatever made it so special.

Tyrn's state, the awful way his mind seemed to fracture, did not bode well for my future. If magic could protect me from the same demise as my uncle, I would need as much of it as I could get.

"Yes, all right," I whispered, feeling something permanent press down on my shoulders and tighten around my chest, squeezing the breath from my lungs. "I would like to learn," I rasped anyway. "Please, show me."

CHAPTER
SEVENTEEN

For the next three days, Ravanna worked with Katrinka and me to bring out our magic. She was surprised when I told her I could read runes, but she did not ask how it was possible, nor did I tell her about the Bog Witch. But Katrinka could also read them, so I thought that might have been more mysterious than even my knowledge.

Later, when I asked her if she'd had done to her what the Bog Witch had done to me, she said she hadn't. That she had always just seen the runes and thought I could too.

Tyrn was said to be resting while we learned and practiced our new skills. I asked if he had ever used magic, but Ravanna explained that magic was for women. Men had other powers, such as greed and oppression. And each of us should stick to what we're good at.

I did not wholly agree with her. While I knew some kings to be cruel and power hungry, I also knew many who were not, who loved their lands and their people, and wanted the best for both.

Taelon. I knew Taelon. And I knew him to be fair and just, loyal and kind. He was not swayed by the promise of power or the intent to hurt others. He wanted what was good for the people of this realm.

Even now, he fought to rid the realm of the Ring of Shadows. Even now, he was in Heprin, answering Gunter's call.

I knew Hugo too. And my father. He had been a good king. A fair king. I did not remember all, but I knew he was not an evil or oppressive man.

I knew Katrinka also struggled with the Cold Queen's assessment, but we chose not to argue. Instead, we simply learned as much as we could from her.

Katrinka was much faster at learning her spells and casting her magic. By the end of the first hour of practice, she could light a candle from across the room with just a wave of her hand. It took me all day to light a candle right in front of me.

Ravanna assured me that it was normal for someone as old as me, who had never been exposed to magic before, to struggle. I struggled because Katrinka was only two years younger than I was.

"First, you have to make magic possible inside your own head," she'd explained. "And then it *will be* possible in the world."

But that was where I struggled. I hadn't only been in the dark about magic and casting and my mother's pagan line. I had grown up in a monastery for the Light. The Brotherhood shunned all magical things and would have handed any proclaimed pagan over to the royal guard.

Katrinka, who had been left to her own devices and libraries full of books that spurred on her imagination, did not make mental boundaries for what was possible and what was not. She simply believed anything could happen.

Also, I suspected her to have a natural talent for it. But Ravanna never allowed her to rest in the ease of inherent ability. She pushed both of us to our limits.

By the end of the third day, I could feel the power surge through me when I spoke charms or incantations. I could do little more than light a candle and then move it across a table. But it was more than I had ever believed was possible before.

We had just worked through a protection charm that was supposed to keep one from contracting sickness when exposed as Mrs. Blythe appeared at the library door. She didn't make a sound, but Ravanna looked up and moved toward her.

"I'll be right back, girls. Your uncle needs me."

She left abruptly, and Katrinka and I were suddenly alone in her private space, surrounded by her potions and elixirs. I felt the urge to rifle through everything but knew it would be a terrible idea. There was no other possible outcome than getting caught right in the middle of my snooping. I didn't need magic to know that.

Katrinka looked at me and smiled. "Did you ever imagine such a world existed? Real magic, Tessa. Real magic."

I grinned back. "Not a clue."

She sobered and looked seriously around the room. "I suppose we must be careful. This must be why Mama died. Why Papa and our brothers died too."

Opening my mouth, I intended to agree with her, but something held me back. The mystery of our family's deaths was not that simple. I knew that in the center of my being. This was part of the reason, but not the whole of it.

As if to confirm my suspicions, a beam of light caught my attention. During the day, this room was flooded with sunlight. Ravanna often kept the balcony doors open so more light would flood the space and we could catch the afternoon breeze. But now we were in twilight hours. It was growing late enough that I was anxious to look at the cemetery again.

Watching the bulbs of the flowers spark with light had become one of my favorite things about Fenwick Keep. And it never failed that they would start to glow at exactly the same time as the first stars made their appearance for the night.

Ravanna's home was cold in so many ways. But then there were bursts of warmth and allure, just like the queen herself.

The light that did not belong at this hour danced along the wall where books were piled high. Shelves could have organized them, but Ravanna had stacked them hastily on the floor instead, as though she'd been working through them book by book.

I walked over, intrigued by what I might find. Ravanna had always been with us in this room, so I had never taken the opportunity to see what she liked to read. But now I could see that almost all tomes were written in runes.

Spell books and texts on the theory of magic, histories of kingdoms, and especially Blackthorne and Elysia. Ancient books about the Marble Wall and the war that nearly destroyed our realm. Odd books from beyond the Crystal Sea. Several books about the Cavolia. And one particularly large book about the Crown of Nine and the magic used to fashion it.

But the book that caught my attention was an identical grimoire to the one I had in my own possession. In fact, it was so similar I worried for a moment that Ravanna had rifled through my things and found it hidden away in my satchel.

But now that I could read runes, I saw that it was her name scrawled across the front. Ravanna Celestly Finnick.

I wished I'd made time to look through my mother's. The last three days had been taxing, and by the time we'd finished supper late into the night, I'd been too mentally exhausted to do anything but go straight to bed.

"What are you doing?" Katrinka asked from behind me.

I picked it up and brought it to the table where we were working. "Ravanna's spell book," I explained. "Look, her name from before she was married."

Katrinka ran a finger along the binding. "The old way is the true way."

As my sister spoke the words aloud, they flickered and glowed along the cover. We took a step back, not expecting the book to come to life.

I opened it. Unlike my mother's book that I'd started from the beginning and was slowly paging through, Ravanna's opened in the middle directly on a spell.

Pictures of naked men were on one page, and I felt my cheeks grow hot at the sight. Katrinka gasped and reached out to turn the page. But the image directly across from it made me put a hand on hers, stalling her.

There, across from the naked men, was an entire page covered in ravens. Their diagrams were drawn out exactly as the men had been sketched. Anatomy and biology and notes scrawled in someone's, *Ravanna's*, own hand. And at the bottom of the page, the words, "How to raise an army."

I immediately thought of Crenshaw. Of when he'd thrown himself out my bedroom window after he'd tried to murder me. Of the scene I'd witnessed during Conandra when it appeared my uncle was talking directly to a bird.

Could it be possible?

"I don't understand," Katrinka said plainly. "This can't mean what it says."

First, you have to make magic possible inside your own head. Ravanna had repeated that instruction countless times over the last three days. *Only then can it be possible in the world.*

We flipped to the next page. And then the next. It seemed it was not an easy task to make a man turn into a bird. But it wasn't impossible. At least according to the Raven Queen's personal grimoire. The most important requirement was that the human must be absolutely willing. Any resistance and the process would end in failure.

So Crenshaw had been made into a raven. I had to believe that was true. But by who? Ravanna? Or Tyrn?

Later in the book, there were diary entries by Ravanna herself. They started when she was only Katrinka's age. Spells she'd tried and failed, additions and measurements, and the small changes it took for them to become successful.

I did not take time to read through everything, but the entries grew darker and crueler as I flipped the pages. Snippets like "She will not listen to me, no matter how many times I show her the way. I will be more persuasive next time I visit her."

Or "Mynot visited me again last night. He was drunk and incoherent. He's worried I'm poisoning him. He's such a fool. I hope the drink kills him."

Katrinka pointed at a later entry. "My brother suspects I'm the reason behind the latest attack in Elysia. The potion is nearly complete."

And even later. "The Bog is attempting another uprising. They are the vilest people with a hag for a queen. I will stomp them into dust before the end of this." It was dated three years ago.

She had not stomped them to complete dust, but I thought of how they scurried around out of sight. How they fled as soon as they heard birds take flight.

The birds. There were hundreds of them. Thousands maybe. Were they ravens? Or people?

Or both?

Since we arrived in Blackthorne, we had not seen nearly anyone besides the Bog Witch and Mrs. Blythe. But they couldn't all be . . . She couldn't have made them all . . .

The light moved in front of us again. "Do you see that, Kat?"

She looked up and nodded. "What is it?"

"A ghost?" The word sounded silly on my tongue, inappropriate for such a strange moment. "I don't know. I've seen them before. They're usually trying to tell me something. Or . . . show me something."

She processed my explanation without thinking I was mad. It was becoming one of my favorite things about her. She never thought ill of me as I struggled to make sense of this new world. She simply waited patiently for me to understand or explain.

"Then let's follow it. It must have something to show us."

So we did. It danced over the floor of the library and out to the balcony. The grave flowers were in full bloom by now, and the dark cemetery glowed with their luminescence. The light disappeared among them, and we hesitated near the staircase leading us to it.

"She hasn't forbidden us to leave," Katrinka said carefully. "We wouldn't be disobeying."

I nodded. "That's true. And I'm sure we will hear her return. Then we can come right back."

With the decision made, we hurried after the disembodied light, careful to stay on the path and not disturb the flowers or the graves.

"She told me our mother's name Finnick used to be Fenwick. And before the pagan war, we were the royal house."

"She told me the same thing," Katrinka agreed. "That the Fenwick power and dignity was taken as punishment for the war. And the curse." We had started to admire each gravestone and the flowers that bloomed. "Look, Tessa, they're all Fenwicks."

She was right. Ancient stones that had simple runes and singular names. And as we walked, and the stones became more elaborate, so did the runes.

"Do you know our grandparents' names?" she asked.

"No." But there was an urge within me to find it, to pay respect to our mother's parents. "Pressydias," I pointed out in an unadorned corner.

We walked over together and read the plain stones that bore no runes and had no glowing flowers to make them beautiful. In the farthest corner of the most distant section was the simplest stone. Mynot Pressydia. And nothing more.

"She did not love him," Katrinka said plainly. "Why did he marry her?"

"A love potion?" I had meant it to be a joke, but Katrinka's frown deepened.

"Do you think this is where the other witch meant the Crown of Light was hidden?" she asked instead, walking toward Mynot's stone and reaching out to rest her fingers on the top.

"What is the Crown of Light, Kat? What will happen if we find it?"

Katrinka turned back to me, her eyes wide with surprise. "Are you saying we leave it be?"

"I'm saying, I do not understand any of this. Ravanna being our aunt. Our uncle's madness. The magic we can suddenly wield. There are strange forces at work, and we have yet to know what any of them mean. Where any of them are from."

"Where they are pushing us to," she added thoughtfully.

At just that moment, the spectral beam of light began jumping in front of us and darting between where we stood and back the way we came. Katrinka and I shared a look of surprise and then raced for the balcony stairs.

Whatever the light meant, it did not intend to harm us. At least not this time. This was one small force I was beginning to believe we could trust.

We had just reached the balcony, out of breath and tight with panic, when my uncle's booming voice burst through the library.

"Where are they?" he shouted, stumbling over a pile of books in his way and sending them toppling in a spray of ancient pages and dust. "Tessana! Katrinka!"

He was wild with terror. So much so that my own fear flared to life and mimicked his. "We're here, Uncle," I said soothingly, stepping from the balcony. "We were admiring the flowers."

Tyrn swayed on his feet and had to catch himself on the table we had been working at. His unsteadiness knocked over the candles Katrinka and I had been lighting and unlighting with our new powers, but he did not seem to notice as they crashed to the floor. Or as we quickly extinguished any lingering flames before the entire library went up in flames.

"We're leaving," he growled. "Get your things together. We must go now."

"Leaving?" I did not know if Katrinka and I were safe here at Fenwick Keep, but there were so many mysteries to solve. And for the first time since my family had been murdered, I finally felt like I was on the right path to finding out what happened.

Why it happened.

"Now!" Tyrn screamed, his face turning purple from the force of it and spittle spraying the table. "Now, now *now*! We must go now! We must leave. We must. *We must!*"

Katrinka's hands pushed at my back, and I lurched into motion. Ravanna marched into the room and looked around at her upturned library. Her shoulders were rigid with tension, and her face a mottled red as though she'd been screaming. Whatever patience and grace she'd displayed the last couple of days was gone. The Cold Queen was back, and she was on a rampage.

"You are being foolish, brother," she snapped. "The girls have only just started their lessons—"

"I will not let you finish them," he snarled, sounding less mad and somehow more furious than ever. "I will not let you do to them what you did to Gwynnie." He took a lumbering stride toward her, wobbling and nearly tipping over but somehow managing to stay upright. "And I will not let you do to me what you did to Mynot." He looked back over his shoulder with the fiercest expression I had ever seen. "You cannot drive us all to madness just to get what you want, Vanna. Just to have what has never belonged to you." To us, he said, "We are leaving, girls. Get your arses in the carriage before I carry you there myself."

It was too low to be understood correctly, but I would have bet the Crown of Nine that Ravanna whispered, "It's too late for you," to Tyrn as he passed.

He seemed not to hear as he stalked out of the library, yelling obscenities the entire way.

Katrinka grasped my hand, and we stood frozen, unsure what to do.

"You better go with him," Ravanna finally coaxed. "He refuses to see reason when he's like this."

"Back to Elysia?" Katrinka asked, and I could tell she needed to be sure we were heading someplace safe.

"Yes, yes. Back to your home. I will join you there when I can."

She held my gaze. "Before your coronation. Keep practicing what I've taught you, but do not let Tyrn find out. He . . . he does not appreciate what we're able to do since he himself is not capable of it. Keep it secret. But stay persistent. You have much to learn before you wear the Crown of Nine, Tessana."

I nodded obediently. "Yes, of course."

"Should we tell our maids of our uncle's plans?" Katrinka asked.

"They're already packed and waiting. Tyrn began your departure procedures without telling me."

Katrinka and I shared a look. Had Tyrn really needed a break from the capital? Or was this his way of keeping us from Ravanna? Of collecting us after he'd been the one to send us with her?

Or had she been the one to orchestrate our company?

I was beginning to think Tyrn was more of her puppet than a freethinking man. Whether by potion or position, he seemed to struggle against her will.

Out in the hallway, our guards waited for us. I had not seen them since we arrived, yet here they were. I wanted to ask where they had been, but it seemed foolish to need them now when I had fought to be free of them for so long.

Ravanna walked us to the carriages. Clesta was there too to hand over Shiksa. We had never traveled at night before, but we had the safety of the Blessed Road at least until we were out of Blackthorne.

I took comfort in that. My ancestors might have been the ones to curse the land, but they'd also been the ones to fix their mistakes. At least in part. It wasn't just magic that we would be using to escape Blackthorne.

It was power from my bloodline. It made me surprisingly confident in our departure.

Finch was standing at the door of my uncle's carriage, holding a hand for me to take. I tried to smile at him, thinking I would warn him of the letter for Taelon I still carried in my pocket, hoping to find a better time to hand it over to him. But he would not look me in the eyes. He was obviously distraught, flexed from head to toe with tension. But his hand was gentle around mine as he helped me into the carriage. And I could have sworn he sighed audibly as I passed by him.

It wasn't until I was seated next to Katrinka inside the coach, across from my uncle, that I noticed the note he'd managed to slip me, tucked into the sleeve of my gown.

I let it be for far longer than I thought possible while the horses took off and we met our traveling speed. Soon enough, my uncle fell asleep, his legs curled against his chest and his cheek resting against the window. He looked like a tortured child like this. A toddler desperate to rest without the threat of nightmares.

When I was confident he was truly asleep, I pulled the note from my sleeve and held it to the window. It was not easy to read in the moonlight, but I struggled and shifted until I could see just enough to see the message. Then when I could finally make out the words, my mind refused to accept their truth.

Heprin has fallen.
The Ring of Shadows rules.
The Temple has been burned.
The Brotherhood of silence is dead.
Will come to you soon.
Trust no one.

CHAPTER
EIGHTEEN

The castle was in an uproar when we arrived back in Elysia. Preparations for my coronation had begun. The last celebration felt like it happened last week, although it was well over a month by now. But it was hard to reconcile that we were already preparing for a new one.

And that it would once again center around me.

When I left Heprin almost a year ago, I knew my destiny was to be queen. But for some foolish reason, I had not expected being the queen of the realm to require quite so much attention.

We'd left Elysia in the last days of spring and returned in the warmth of summer. Just as before when Taelon had smuggled me in. Only this time, I walked by Tyrn's side.

He had been nearly incoherent on the return trip to Sarasonet. His guards and footmen seemed familiar with his wide-swinging moods and gibberish. But Katrinka and I had only ever seen him composed. Surly and standoffish but composed.

His valet offered him medicine every few hours, which seemed to keep his mind held together, if only by thin strands of sanity. But it was clear that my uncle was growing sicker and sicker by the minute.

And all the while, I held a note in my hand that declared war.

I had tried to bring it up to Tyrn on the journey, tried to suggest that we might fight back and reclaim Heprin. But he didn't appear to understand what I was saying and turned away from me so he could sleep.

When he woke, he mumbled, "It is beginning," over and over and over until Katrinka and I begged his valet, Ofrin, to give him more medicine. By the time Ofrin had prepared another sleeping draft, Tyrn had started rocking back and forth in his seat, his hands pressed against his ears and his eyes shut tight. His mumbled words had become a shout of terror. "It is beginning! It is beginning! It is beginning!"

Ofrin was able to get him to sleep again, but Katrinka and I held hands until we stopped for supper, clutching each other in fear.

I wished we'd never left Blackthorne. I wished Ravanna were here to make sense of what was happening.

It was hard to reconcile the affection I felt for our secret aunt. And there were, of course, the signs that all might not be good with her. That maybe she was as nefarious as seemed obvious.

Yet, she was our mother's sister. More than that, she'd been kind to Katrinka and me. Not at first, maybe, but recently. There were mistakes in her past, but she cared about my future as queen. Which said something.

In a surprising way, she'd become a friend. And with the fall of Heprin and loss of the Brotherhood of Light I held so dear, I truly wished for my friend.

Taelon said he would ride straight back, but he did not date his letter, so I had no idea when that would be. I prayed to the Light he would bring Oliver with him. I did not know how we would survive the grief of losing the Temple, our childhood home, and the monks who raised us.

But we would do it together.

Just as I'd reached my bedroom, with Shiksa and Clesta at my side, a footman rushed down the hallway. "Your Highness." He started bowing and walking halfway down the corridor, so I resisted a travel-weary sigh and waited for him to get close enough to speak. "The Prince Caspian has requested an audience with you."

"Prince Caspian?" I gasped. I had forgotten to ask about him in all the news and chaos of our return.

"Yes, Mum, he's in the library awaiting your return."

"Thank you." I turned to Clesta and handed her Shiksa. "I will freshen up before supper. Thank you for all your help."

She frowned in a thoughtful way and stroked Shiksa's white mane. "Princess Tessana?"

Her use of my formal title instead of Lady caught my attention at once. Only my guards were in the hallway with us. The footman had disappeared back into the recesses of the castle.

"Yes?"

"Did you not find it strange at Fenwick Keep?"

Fenwick Keep had many, many strange things, but most of them had to do with magic. And I could not explain that to Clesta. "What do you mean?"

"Well, I've just noticed how relaxed Shiksa is here. At Blackthorne's castle, she would stalk the halls all night long. Of course, she never brought anything back to the room, but she'd be out all night hunting something, her hackles raised. And often, when I'd come to wake you in the morning, she'd be sat outside your door, almost as if she was guarding it."

I scratched Shiksa behind the ears affectionately. "That's because she loves me."

"And there weren't no people. Tabby, your sister's maid, and I had a hall to ourselves. There were no other maids or servants of any kind."

"I did notice that. Mrs. Blythe was about the only other soul I saw in the whole kingdom." Save for the Bog Witch, but Clesta didn't need to know about her.

"And the birds."

"The birds?" Unease trickled down my spine. "They'd follow

Tabby and me around the halls as if they were watching us. Their little claws clicked on the floor in a sort of warning. And they wouldn't let the guards near your rooms. Old Curtis nearly lost an eye when he tried to stand guard near your door."

I spun around, noticing Curtis's face for the first time. Had I been so wrapped up in my own problems that I'd ignored the troubles of the people around me? Sure enough, Curtis's face was scratched from temple to jaw. More down the length of his neck. Across his hands. The raw red marks were dried with blood. They'd been gouged deep enough that I knew they would scar.

"Is that true?" I stepped closer to both guards. Finch was the only one who seemed unharmed.

"It is, milady. It is not that we were afraid of them." He cleared his throat, indicating otherwise. "But we were instructed not to harm them by Queen Ravanna. And we could not reach you to ask you what to do."

I didn't know whether to laugh or cry. "She didn't want you to harm her birds, of course. But surely, you could have reached me at some point. The birds didn't fly away to eat or sleep?"

"There were so many," Dover explained. "And they were downright... vicious."

He was larger than Curtis and bulkier. But both men were strapped with muscles and weapons. How had birds kept them from guarding me? Why had Ravanna allowed any of this to happen?

I turned to Finch. "You seem unharmed."

He nodded, bowing his head. "I did not try to cross the threshold. I have seen this behavior before."

Magic was what he meant. I didn't need him to say it for me to understand. I noticed a necklace around his throat with a single charm—a horse and its rider. Was he Cavolia?

"We will discuss this later," I said meekly. But before I turned to meet Caspian, I said, "I'm sorry I did not check on you sooner, Curtis. Dover. I ... I truly did not expect you to be in trouble. But I will make this right to you. I promise you that."

Curtis bowed his head. "We were assured you were safe, milady. Had we thought otherwise, nothing would have stopped us from getting to you."

I knew that to be true, and I trusted him to be faithful to his word. But what a peculiar reason for dropping his duties. I would have to talk to my uncle later to see what he thought about the matter. Well, if he was in any state of mind to talk.

But I thought he might have some insight into the birds at Fenwick Keep. And what their behavior was like. If this was normal. If it could be stopped in the future. I wasn't sure of anyone else who would have knowledge of Ravanna's homeland.

Of course, I wanted to speak with Taelon about all of this. And I would. But I owed it to my guards to at least try to get to the bottom of this. And seek justice on their behalf if at all possible.

Caspian was waiting for me in the library. This was where Tyrn spent a great deal of his time, so it was more unfamiliar to me than I would have liked. Libraries were the singular place I felt most at home. I could not wait to make this one mine.

He stood as I entered the room, dipping into a short but respectful bow. He looked fully recovered in his Vorestran embroidered tunic, a dusky pale blue accentuating his tanned skin and dark hair. He looked so different than when I'd first met him weeks ago. When he'd surprised me in that hallway. He reminded me of the night sky, or just before the sky turned to night. When the moon had yet to appear but stars started blinking from the still blue twilight. All glittering light and earthy browns.

And those ghostly light eyes of him. Out of place with the rest of his shadowy corners.

I had grown fonder of him since he saved my life. Much fonder of him than I'd expected. And the sight of him now whole, healthy, *breathing*, made my spirit sigh with relief. I still did not fully trust him. But I was very happy to see him not dead on my account.

"Caspian," I greeted as he stood. "I did not know you stayed."

His wry smile made his pale eyes twinkle. "I have only just

been permitted by your healers to move around. While you were off on your tour of the countryside, I was here, fighting for my life."

I felt guilt wash over me, and I lunged forward, grasping his arm. "I'm so sorry, they told me you were all right, but my uncle wanted me to leave and—"

His smile widened. "I'm teasing, Tessana. I have been well this whole time. Merely immobile."

"You're well? Truly?"

"Truly."

"Thank the Light. Do you know what's happening in Heprin? Has news made it here?"

His brows furrowed. "Yes, I know, but how do you know? I was planning to tell you. A rider only just arrived, and I overheard—"

"It doesn't matter how I heard. I need to encourage my uncle to do something, but he doesn't seem fit to make decisions. Caspian, he's not well, and I—"

"There's more," he whispered, drawing me close. "Heprin fell, that's true. But the Ring of Shadows plans to take Tenovia next."

"They have enough of an army to occupy Heprin *and* Tenovia?" My heart dropped into my stomach and sloshed like a capsized ship while I tried not to lose my lunch.

"From what I've heard, there is not much left of Heprin to occupy."

I fell onto a nearby couch, my wobbly legs unable to hold my weight for a second more. "It cannot be."

Caspian sank next to me and reached for my hand. "I tried to speak to your uncle earlier. He did not seem, er, like you said, well . . . well."

I shook my head. How did I even begin to explain?

"And Queen Ravanna? How . . . was your time in Blackthorne?" His tone had turned toward conspiring. So many mysteries were at play that I wasn't sure where to start at first.

"Why do you ask?"

"There are rumors, Tessana. Rumors that she might be behind the Ring of Shadows."

I immediately wanted to deny his claims. I knew too well that it was easy to assume Ravanna was evil. But in my most recent experience, she wanted what I wanted for Elysia—peace and magic. Nothing so sinister as war. "No, I was with her. She did not . . . how could she have . . . there was no sign of a Heprin invasion. She did not seem to know of it herself."

"Carrigan sent me a message yesterday before the news of Heprin arrived. She's asked Vorestra to align with Blackthorne. She did not mention Heprin, but she made it clear he had to pick a side."

Pick a side? Pick a side for what? "What did he do?"

Caspian's mouth twisted into a grim frown. "He has not answered her yet. He wrote to me instead, encouraged me to propose."

"To what?"

"From my calculation, Elysia can count on support from Soravale, Tenovia if they still stand and whatever is left of Heprin—although it will not be much. And possibly Barstus, depending on their affection for your sister. Blackthorne has already aligned with Aramore and Kasha. A marriage to me would secure Vorestra for you. But if there is no reason for my brother to . . . he is an opportunistic man, much like my father. Give him a reason to join you, Tessana. One that is better than what Ravanna has already offered."

What had Ravanna offered? When had she done any of this? Was this, in fact, truth? Or a plan of Caspian's to trick me into a betrothal? "I—how can you ask me this now? When I have lost my home and the Brotherhood? When my uncle falls into madness. When my kingdom and the realm are only just on the brink of war?"

"I know you want a marriage of love, and maybe it can be that someday. But there are more important things than your happiness right now, Tessana. I'm trying to convince you to win this war before it begins."

He was right. If Vorestra joined Blackthorne, we would be too evenly matched to avoid fighting. But if Vorestra sided with the Seat of Power, there would be no reason to meet on the battlefield. The victory would be fully mine.

But still, marriage? Surely, there was time to negotiate. We didn't even know if Ravanna was behind this yet.

None of this mattered anyway. I still wasn't coronated. And it would be years before the Crown truly became mine. Coronation was merely a promise of future power, not the actuality of it.

Tyrn was who Caspian had to convince. And maybe Tyrn would see the advantage in an alliance with Vorestra or maybe not. He was not exactly at his best right now.

The door swung open, and my uncle teetered in unsteadily, much like he had in Blackthorne in Ravanna's library. My muscles and heart and soul seized up at the sight of him and the sickness that seemed to have stolen all reason and health from him in such a short time.

"We cannot wait," he slurred loudly, sounding drunk and off balance. "It must happen now, Tessana." For a second, I feared he meant Caspian's proposal, the marriage. But then over his shoulder, he shouted, "Bring the damnable Crown in here at once!"

"The crown? Uncle, what is this?"

He met my gaze, and his eyes temporarily cleared of the madness that seemed to have such a hold on him. "We must make it official. Before it's too late."

"Before what's too late?"

"Heprin has fallen, niece." He said the words as if I wasn't the one to have told him. "It is only a matter of time before she comes knocking on our door. The Crown must sit on top of your pretty head, or she will rip it away from you and take your head with her as a prize."

"You mean your sister? Ravanna?"

"I was just a boy," he began to murmur, losing the light of sanity. "I was just a boy, but I was foolish. I never should have let her use me. Gwynnie knew better. She tried to stop her. And me. And all of it.

But even she was deceived in the end." He sank to his knees suddenly, throwing his head into his hands and weeping. "I'm so sorry, dear sister. I'm so sorry!" He knelt there in front of us, keening and sobbing.

Caspian slid forward till he was also down on one knee, bowed his head, and put a comforting hand on Tyrn's shoulder. I was so surprised by his gesture of kindness that I forgot to move to my uncle's side. Instead, I sat there watching, wondering. Was this the man I knew Caspian to be?

"Uncle, how do you know it was your sister?" I asked when he settled some, calmed by Caspian's silent comfort.

Tyrn put a hand on Caspian's forearm and used it to push himself up to stand. Caspian returned to his seat by me, taking my hand in his once more. I couldn't help but glance over at him. Grief, pain, trauma . . . they were all hard things I'd experienced myself. But I hardly knew what to do when someone else felt them. I paced. I stared. I wrung my hands. I even asked practical questions in an effort to push those in pain beyond the worst of it.

I did nothing that Caspian did. Yet he intuitively knew how to do so much more than I ever had.

When I looked back at Tyrn, he was stalking toward the hallway. I jumped to my feet, ready to follow him, but he wasn't leaving. Merely retrieving something.

It was a bird cage. He swung it around with a flourish, sending the bird crashing against the cage bars. It squawked angrily and flapped its wings in a bird-like tirade, sending black feathers flying all over the floor.

A raven.

My uncle had trapped a raven in a gilded cage.

"Here is how I know," Tyrn raged. "Here is her spy, come to finish what he started." Tyrn threw the cage on the ground. It landed upright but skidded across the polished marble until it banged against the leg of the couch I had just occupied.

The bird screeched again, incensed and annoyed. Black feathers whirled around it as it waved its wings and hopped back and forth on its scaley feet.

"Don't you see?" Tyrn screamed, more at the bird than at me. He was losing his grasp on sanity again, slipping beneath the madness. "Don't you see what I see? Here is the leader of your assassins, Tessana. Here is the man who tried to kill you twice!"

I blinked at the bird, both knowing what he was saying was impossible and that he was right. But it couldn't be.

"They'd follow Tabby and me around the halls as if they were watching us. Their little claws clicked on the floor in a sort of warning. And they wouldn't let the guards near your rooms. Old Curtis nearly lost an eye when he tried to stand guard near your door."

"There were so many. And they were downright... vicious."

And then I thought about the spells Ravanna had. Her grimoire. *How to make an army... of ravens.*

The Bog Witch's accusation—The Raven Queen.

Caspian squatted in front of the bird, meeting its beady eyes. "I don't understand. You're saying that this creature tried to kill Tessana?"

"That is no creature," my uncle swore through heaving breaths. "That is a man who sold his soul to evil. He lied to me. Lied about his loyalty. And his origin. And she lied too. Spinning her web so I wouldn't see what was right in front of me. Feeding me poison, just like she did to her husband. Just like her sister. Just like our parents. All of it lies and lies and lies. All of it poison and murder and death."

Before we could calm my uncle down, he reached for the cage once more and tore open the door. The bird screamed shrieking protests and clawed and pecked at my uncle, turning his hand and arm bloody as he fought.

Caspian took to my side again, neither of us knowing what to expect next.

Then finally, Tyrn managed to wrap his hand around the bird's neck and yank it from the cage. The raven was much bigger up close than one would expect, and the muscles beneath its feathered exterior seemed particularly strong as it fought my uncle's punishing grasp.

"Do you know why we couldn't find the army of assassins that nearly killed you both? Or the guard who tried to murder you in your room, Tessana? Do you know why I have guards around the castle, ready with bows and arrows to shoot down anything that flies?"

"No, Uncle." My reply was a choked whisper.

He had both hands gripping the raven's throat now. It was struggling to breathe, and its fight was growing more desperate. "Because they're not birds at all." With a sudden, savage twist of his hands, Tyrn snapped the raven's neck, and it stopped flapping and clawing altogether. From one moment to the next, the room was feral with fight and then hushed and stagnant where a void of movement now silently echoed from wall to wall.

Tyrn dropped the dead bird to the ground at his feet. I gasped a startled breath and clung to Caspian's arm. He seemed as equally astonished as I was.

But then the impossible I could not wrap my mind around became possible in front of my eyes. For it was not a raven lying dead at my feet, but Crenshaw. He was wilder than I remembered him. Untamed and . . . more beastly looking. But there he was. Naked, and human, and dead.

"Dragon's blood," Caspian hissed as I gasped and fought to breathe again.

Tyrn looked from Crenshaw to me, his eyes as sober and intelligent as I had ever seen them. "I will coronate you tonight, Tessana. You will wear the Crown of Nine. And then you will get ready for war."

CHAPTER NINETEEN

An hour later, I met my uncle in the throne room. I'd half expected him to have forgotten how crazed he'd been. And even though he was here, and the Crown of Nine was in his grasp, he still did not convince me that he knew exactly what he was doing.

There was something ghostly about him . . . something fading. I couldn't put my finger on it, but I knew it was due to his sudden need to crown me before my birthday and the elaborate celebrations still in the works.

Caspian was here too, looking nervous for the first time since I'd met him. He hadn't seemed worried even when he'd saved my life on the balcony and taken arrows for me. He'd brazenly pushed his way through that just like he did everything else. But across the room, standing with armed men and wearing his kingdom's desert garb, he was pale and tight-lipped. The men with him stood protectively in a semicircle around him. They must be his guard detail.

What did he expect to happen? In the Elysian throne room of all places?

Katrinka was here too. I'd tried to explain what had happened in the library, leaving out the more gruesome details, but she'd been more interested in Caspian's practical marriage proposal to me than the coronation ceremony.

Nerves fluttered through me now that I was here, in this room. Something I had wanted for so long was finally becoming real. I should be thrilled, aflutter with excitement and possibilities. My eyes were fixed on the future and the change I could make happen. Instead, it felt as though I was waiting to be hanged. Death loomed in the corners of the room, and I couldn't figure out how. Or why. Or what was so dangerous about taking what was rightfully mine.

This was why I'd left the Temple of Eternal Light. Why I'd faced Conandra and fought to return to this castle. Why I'd left every possibility I could ever have with Taelon for a greater future, a necessary destiny.

So why did it feel as though all of the reasons I was here were slipping through my fingers?

Clesta had managed to dress me as a princess. A gown so white and diamond encrusted, it was an effort to stay upright in it. I felt as though I might blind anyone who looked directly at me, but this was the dress meant for this moment, and I didn't have it in me to break Clesta's heart. Or insult the master dressmaker who seemed to wield magic of her own.

We hadn't had time for my hair, though. So it remained loose around my shoulders, catching quite often on the diamonds. I was afraid I'd be bald by the time the Crown was set atop my head, but my hair was a minor detail in light of everything else.

"Finally," Tyrn gasped when he noticed me. He stood to his feet and staggered sideways before righting himself. Looking around the room, he said, "You should be escorted. By me, I suppose, but I cannot do both jobs."

There was a weighted silence while everyone looked around the throne room and tried to determine who held the highest rank. And who would make the most appropriate escort? Curtis was master of the guard but not nobility. My sister was nobility, but only a woman.

And younger than I was. Clesta was already beside me, but only my maid.

At long last, Caspian stepped forward. "I'll do it."

My breath trembled in my lungs. His proposal had been nothing romantic, but it resonated in some part of me that I didn't have time to examine. Here was a man willing to put duty before romance, before his own life, so that his kingdom and the realm could be secure.

Maybe that was heartless and foolish. But wasn't it the same thing I was doing?

Wasn't it the same trait I admired in Taelon? How I wished he was here alongside me. What would he think of all this? *Would he believe I'm doing the right thing?*

I jerked my head, repulsed at the idea of him witnessing this too-quick decision. He might not object. But how could I justify a marriage to anyone void of love in light of what he and I shared?

Caspian walked to my side and held out his elbow. His thoughts seemed to be the same as mine. "See how you like it," he murmured, low enough for only me to hear. "It might suit us."

I pressed my lips together and chose not to respond. In my dreams, I had imagined this moment with fanfare and celebration. There was music playing. Crowds of people cheering. And the room was resplendent with the best the castle had to offer. The best of Elysia. And the best of the realm I was set to rule.

Tonight, there were just a handful of people. No fanfare. No celebration. No music. My footsteps echoed off the cavernous ceiling, my heels clicking like the tolling bells of battle.

A guard rushed into the room as if I'd spoken my thoughts aloud to him. Caspian and I turned at the same time to watch him press himself back against the heavy door he'd just slammed and wince in apology.

"Your Majesty," he whimpered.

"Hurry, Tessana," Tyrn snapped, frantically waving me forward.

I only just realized I'd been dragging my feet, walking as slow as I could to prolong this procession and stay the fateful moments ahead. Caspian shot me a worried look, but we both picked up our pace and met my uncle at the dais.

"Kneel," Tyrn commanded.

I had to let go of Caspian's arm to do so, and it took nearly all my willpower to release him. I was thankful when he didn't move far.

Tyrn towered overhead, having both height and platform to cast his shadow over me. He pulled out his sword, and a chill ran through me at the vulnerable position I'd allowed myself to get into.

I knew Tyrn even less than I knew Ravanna, and he had always been cruel to me. Even before I left for Heprin.

So why was I here now? Why was I trusting him at all? Why had I allowed him to pull his sword on me and hold it directly next to my head? Only inches from my throat.

"Tessana..." he began but trailed off after only my name.

I was supposed to have lessons on the official ceremony, practice all the right things to say, and have a speech written for me to address the people. But everything had been pushed, ignored, or forgotten about.

So to my name, I simply said, "Yes?"

"Tessana..." my uncle began again.

"Yes?" Was I supposed to answer the call for every kingdom? Would Tyrn repeat my name until the Crown of Nine recognized me?

"Dragon's blood," he cursed. "What's your middle name, child? I can't remember."

So not some mystical part of the ceremony? Right. "Hadlyn," I supplied.

He cleared his throat. The silver sword quivered next to my cheek. "Tessana Hadlyn Allisand of the House of Extensia, are you the rightful heir to the Seat of Power? The one true wielder of the Crown of Nine?"

"Yes, I am Tessana Hadlyn Allisand of the House of Extensia, the rightful heir to the Seat of Power." I knew that was the correct answer this time. The word bubbled up out of me and burst forth with a kind of pride and power I didn't know I could deliver given the strange circumstances.

"And do you promise to rule the realm and your respective kingdom with justice and honor? Strength and grace? Fairness and mercy?"

"Yes," I said again, my voice stronger and truer.

The ground beneath me began to vibrate gently as if a large company of horses was galloping toward us all at once. Tyrn stumbled down a step, his sword just barely missing my ear.

Suddenly he was at my side, kneeling beside me. "There are things you need to know," he began quickly. "Lies I've told. Lies . . . lies that have been told to me."

I dared a glance at him. The Crown of Nine dangled from his fingers, but he no longer seemed interested in it. "What do you mean, Uncle? Should we finish the ceremony?"

"I killed her."

His words sent ice-cold dread spiraling through me. "Who?"

A ragged sob rattled out of him. "I didn't know what I was doing. She's had me under her control for so long that I didn't know to fight her. To stop her."

My trembling hand landed on his wrist, and I was surprised to find it gentle and comforting. Especially when my words were so steely. "Who did you kill, Tyrn? Tell me?"

He sobbed again, only this time there was blood mingled in the tear that slid down his cheek. And in his spittle. I wished I could feel sorry for him, call for help for him.

But the foreboding knowledge of what he was about to tell me had frozen me, and my good intentions, in place. I had been waiting to hear these words spoken for almost nine years. Had always known they would come from someone I knew. Someone my family had trusted. Had always known we had been betrayed for power and greed by someone we loved.

He started rocking back and forth again, cradling the crown

against his chest. "She loved me, and I killed her. I killed her for . . . for . . ."

"For *what*?" I raged, my touch no longer soft and soothing but punishing and fierce.

A whirring sound whooshed behind me, and I turned just in time to see another impossible thing become possible. A bird had flown into the throne room from one of the narrow vents near the top of the vaulted ceiling. A beady-eyed, black raven. Instinct beat against my breast and a memory exploded through my mind's eye. The day my parents were murdered, the day my family was taken from me. A raven, just as sleek and beautiful as this one, standing over their dead bodies with satisfaction gleaming through its onyx eyes.

But as this one swooped toward the ground, it transformed from something fowl to something human. Ravanna Pressydia shook off the last effects of the animal she'd been and stepped onto the marble floor as graceful as could be, fully human.

And fully dressed—unlike Crenshaw. I suspected that had something to do with her inherent magic. The watching crowd of maids and guards, advisors and nobles shrieked and stammered at the sight. Noblemen cried out in terror. Burly men retreated to the corners of the room, spooked by a bird turned witch. Fear gripped everyone who witnessed the spectacle. Except for my mad uncle, who did not even blink.

"Me," she said coolly, finishing Tyrn's sentence for him. Her dark eyes found his. "You don't look so good, brother. Not feeling well?"

The guards broke free from their terror and drew their swords at once. Metal clanged as steel was pulled from the scabbard. Seeming to have forgotten their training, they waved their weapons wildly back and forth while trying to make sense of how Ravanna Pressydia had been a bird just mere moments before. If they were also perplexed at her use of the word "brother" in reference to Tyrn, they still seemed to view her as a threat.

Caspian stepped toward me, but Ravanna suddenly had a sword in her own hand. She wasn't the aloof, docile queen now, but something terrible and brutal. She marched over and pressed the tip to the center of my back. "Second sons always have the luxury of being heroes, don't they?" Her sneer disappeared in a sober look of fury. "This time won't get you the girl, spare heir. I would reconsider your heroics before you do something rash and find yourself dead. My men won't miss this time."

Her gaze moved to the ceiling again, where square vents were built into the room's foundation all the way around the narrow rectangular point at the top of the tapered roof. In each space was a big, fat raven. And across their bodies, tiny bows and arrows that looked no more harmful than a child's toy wielded by wings.

At our looks of mingled astonishment and distrust, Ravanna snapped a finger. "Release."

The ravens obeyed, making quick work of the arrows as they effortlessly shot circles around Caspian. The arrows, which looked so small and unbothersome up above, pierced the marble floor with subsequent thwacks. And as they flew through the air, they grew to be long and large and dangerous enough to kill anything in their paths. Their steal tips dove straight through the hard floor, each point of entry displaying cracking spiderwebs of destroyed marble.

It made no logical sense.

Caspian slowly set his left foot down from where it had been held aloft, midstep, while arrows shot by birds rained down from the ceiling—without harming him. At least this time.

"How?" I asked the Cold Queen, desperate for answers. But even more so, desperate for a motive. Something to explain all of this. The birds. What was wrong with Tyrn? Who had killed my parents? I needed to answer these questions. No matter what the outcome might bring.

"Magic, foolish child." She laughed, the tip of the sword digging into the flesh at my back. "I told you all you had to do was get your mind to believe what your body could not. And it would be easy for you. But you're too much like your mother after all. Too uptight and practical to appreciate the gift that has been born to you."

For the first time since I'd discovered she was my aunt, I hated that she dared speak about my mother. Loathed that my mother's name had ever been in her mouth.

My hands were braced on the steps in front of me, my fingers curling into the edges. I wanted to fight back. Go sword to sword. Show her what it meant to taunt and deceive and lie. But first, I needed more answers. "What gift?"

She stepped forward, her sword digging deeper into the tender middle of my torso until I felt blood trickle down my spine. "You still don't understand? You kneel here, even now, waiting for the ultimate prize, and you still don't get it?" She laughed a cruel, dangerous sound. "The Crown, Tessana. *The Crown!* Don't you see? Your father's line might have controlled it for all this time, but we are the ones meant to wear it. The ones it chose. Your mother was too foolish to take it from your father. So I did it for her."

"You killed them. My parents." Tears had begun to fall from my eyes and drop onto the backs of my hands. But I forced the words out. Made the truth ring clear. There would be time for grief, but not yet.

Tyrn let out a keening sound at my accusation. Ravanna said, "Well, not me exactly."

"She loved me!" he screamed at his sister. "She loved me, and you made me kill her!"

My head was a hundred pounds, and I managed to only lift it high enough to meet Tyrn's wet, sorrowful gaze. "You," I hissed.

"She killed her husband," he said, sounding sane but barely. "Poisoned him. Mynot was in love with her, but she didn't care about him. She only wanted his throne."

Ravanna didn't argue with him. "He was in the way."

Tyrn reached out and clutched my wet hand. "She did the same to me. Poisoned my mind. Distorted the things I saw. The things I believed. When I found your mother and father, m-my sister . . . I didn't know it was me who had done those things. I didn't know it was me." He cried harder. "And now she's moved her poison to my body. She's killing me just like she did her husband, her sister"—he hiccupped a heavy sob—"our parents."

Ravanna leaned forward and pushed his shoulder with her free hand so he fell back on his arse. She grabbed the crown from his hands and clutched it to her side. "I haven't done anything they didn't warrant. Stop with this self-pity, Tyrn. They deserved it! All of them deserved what they got. Our parents didn't understand their three children's powers and raised them to expect less than they deserved. Mynot beat me when he was drunk and had no ambition for Blackthorne or the people who live there, who depend on the throne for their well-being. Our dearly beloved sister used us to marry a king and then turned her back on us. Of course, I killed them, brother. And I would kill them a thousand more times if I could. They didn't deserve the power they were given. Or the thrones they ruled from. They were weak, Tyrn." She straightened, finding some of her poise again and releasing some of the sharp pressure on my back. "And it seems as though you've decided to follow their path."

"You killed me," he accused, his voice ragged and wet. "Long before you deemed me weak."

She stepped back, pulling her sword to her side and addressing us both. "I will admit, the magic had a harsher impact on you than I had planned. But, if it consoles you any, I did not intend to kill you at first."

"Just bend me to your will," he screeched. "Just turn me into your willing soldier. Your puppet king."

"Well," she hissed. "If we're being perfectly frank, you wanted the same thing. To rule without having to lead. To have power without having to work for it. To sit on a throne you did not deserve and will not keep."

"He's truly dying then?" I gasped, seeing the life go out of him even as we watched. His skin was a sickly grayish color, and his eyes were more sunken than even minutes before. I reached for his hand. "Is there no way to reverse this? To fix whatever you've done?"

"You want to save him?" Ravanna barked, laughing once more. "The man who hunted the realm for you with the intention to kill you? Even as a child?"

"At your bequest," he rasped, his breath turning shallow in his caved chest. He struggled to lean back against the stairs and look up at his sister. "You wanted them all dead. But I saved two of them. Even when you had me so firmly in your control."

Had he known I was in Heprin? Had he been the one to command Brahm Havish to send Katrinka to Barstus?

Mind control or elixir or whatever Ravanna had put him under, and he'd still managed to hide us away? He might not have magic, but I knew that had taken much willpower.

"And look where it got us!" she screamed at him, her voice shrill with rage. "You sold the Crown to a cheap substitute. Your sister's death means nothing now. And you will rot, brother. Oh, how you will rot for it."

I took the opportunity to roll away from both of them. My feet tangled in my dress, and it was hardly graceful, but I managed to make it to standing. I rushed toward Caspian, willing the ravens not to shoot us dead. Our guards immediately surrounded us, swords outstretched, bodies ready for battle. Or to cover us should arrows start to fall.

He stepped out of the ring of arrows and lifted his sword toward Ravanna. "You can have the Crown, but let her go. She hasn't done anything to you."

Ravanna's smile was merciless. "I'm not going to kill, Tessana. I'll let her watch as I kill everyone she loves." Her cruel gaze found mine. "I'm sure you've heard about poor Heprin by now. Those peaceful monks never saw it coming, unfortunately. But I suppose Soravale won't either. Poor dears."

I cried out, emotion overcoming me. "I trusted you! I trusted you, and you lied to me!" I hadn't always trusted her, but I had bonded with her recently. She'd shown me how to use magic. She'd seemed to want a relationship with me. With Katrinka.

"Darling girl, this is a kingdom built on lies." She nodded toward the throne. "A thousand lies to make the Seat of Power. A thousand more to fashion the magical crown. And a thousand more with each generation of Allisand trying to bleed the land dry of magic and money." There was suddenly violent pounding on the door. The Elysian army had arrived. She flicked an annoyed glance toward it, then back at us. "It's too bad, though. We could have built a beautiful alliance. An unbreakable one. Had you not tried to steal the Crown from me."

"I will never build an alliance with you. I will never let your evil rule this realm."

She smiled wider. "Ah, maybe not. But his brother will. And then it will be you and some ruined kingdoms against me, the Crown of Nine, and all the power in the world." She sheathed her sword and slipped the Crown into a pouch at her hip. "See you on the battlefield, niece. Come ready for bloodshed."

And then she was a bird again, lifting into the sky with more grace than any natural thing should possess. Her company of ravens took flight with her, circling the room at first, cawing and swooping so that all of us had to duck and cover our heads. Then they flew out through the vents and into the sky.

The army broke through the heavy throne room doors as soon as they were gone, ready for a battle that would not happen. At least not today.

I rushed to my uncle's side, grasping his hand in mine. "Tyrn," I croaked. "What can I do?"

He looked up at me with glassy eyes and a faraway look. "Kill her," he whispered, his voice graveled and choked. "Before she kills everyone else."

And then he was gone. Dead from the poison Ravanna had been feeding him for years. And from the guilt that had taken his family.

I turned to Caspian, not knowing what else to do. "Okay."

He raised an eyebrow. "Okay, what?"

"Okay, I'll marry you. If it gets me Vorestra, I'll do it."

We stood together, neither of us knowing what else to say. When I turned to face the army and guards, Curtis yelled, "All hail the Queen of Elysia! All hail the Queen of the Realm!"

And then the guards who had not protected the Crown of Nine and the army that had been too late to stop the Blackthorne queen, my maid, my sister, and even Caspian, dropped to one knee in reverence.

I was a queen without a crown.

A witch without much power.

A woman who had no idea what to do next.

CHAPTER TWENTY

"Do you have a way to get word to your brother?" I asked Caspian as we marched toward the war room. The castle was upended with servants and guards and my uncle's advisors running everywhere. Curtis had ordered my uncle's body be prepared for burial. Maids had jumped in to the melee to tidy the throne room.

In a few minutes, it would be as though nothing had happened in that room. As though my uncle hadn't died suddenly, thrusting the Seat of Power onto my very unprepared shoulders. As though my aunt had not just declared war and threatened to make me watch as she killed everyone I loved. As though I had not yet agreed to marry Caspian.

Everyone that had something to say or suggest had assaulted me as soon as Ravanna's army was out of sight. But I had demanded thirty minutes of privacy to wrap my mind around all that happened. I knew it would not be enough time to accept what had happened and plan what to do next. But I couldn't . . . couldn't jump into war plans and battle strategy just yet. My uncle had died. I'd agreed to marry Caspian. After only just learning that Ravanna Pressydia was my aunt, she'd sieged the castle, stolen my crown, and threatened war. And I'd finally learned who had killed my family. Who had actually been the one to slit their throats. And who had orchestrated the whole gruesome affair. I wanted to curl up in a tight ball on my bed and cry until no tears were left.

Instead, I'd asked for a half hour and planned to use it to remember how to breathe properly. This was what it meant to be queen. And I planned to embrace this destiny as fully and stalwartly as possible.

Katrinka trailed behind us, looking unnaturally pale and utterly overwhelmed. I wanted to take her hand and promise her everything would be all right, but Elysia needed to prepare our borders for an attack. I had to find a way to warn Soravale and Barstus, assess the damage in Heprin, and send word to the remaining kingdoms—whether they had sided with Ravanna or not, nothing official had been delivered to me—and somehow stop a war before it began. Oh, and marry the prince of Vorestra.

My agenda was a little full.

"Yes," Caspian agreed. "I'll send a rider and a bird."

Our steps faltered at the same time, and we shared a look. Birds could no longer be trusted.

"A falcon," he assured me. "Non-magical in nature."

"How can you be certain?" I asked, hating that my entire outlook on the natural world had been altered.

His lips twitched as if holding back a smile. "She laid eggs not long ago. She's been my personal courier for a couple years."

A grin tickled the corners of my mouth. "Okay. I think it's safe to assume birds laying eggs are not secretly humans."

"I would hope so."

"Then do it. Send whatever message you need to in order to keep Vorestra allied with the Seat of Power."

"Of course." He shot a sidelong glance my way. "At some point, not this moment, I suppose I don't need it exactly this moment . . . but I'm hoping you can offer a better explanation of what happened.

Of what I saw. The birds with weapons . . . the Blackthorne queen . . . how is any of this possible?"

"You're right to say now is not the time." I swallowed the rising bile back down. "But you are also right in that you deserve an explanation. And I promise to give it to you. Just as soon as I . . ." I gestured at the flurry of movement around us, knowing I didn't need to finish the sentence. He understood. We would communicate with those we needed to count on. Plan for what was ahead. Get married. And then . . . Well, there would be time to discuss birds and evil queens later. I swallowed again, only this time it was a ball of complicated nerves. "Caspian, we will marry tonight."

He paused mid step, reaching for my hand to collect his balance. "My brother will answer the call, Princess. There is no need to doubt him. And no need to, er, to rush, uh, this."

I let him clasp my hand, taking strength from his confidence in his brother, in his kingdom. "I do doubt your brother. But . . . somehow I trust you, Caspian. And that is enough for me."

He held my gaze and smiled softly for just a moment. But it was enough to steady my racing heart and free my lungs from the invisible constraints that had increasingly tightened over the last, oh, eight hours or so. But then he let go and walked in the opposite direction I was headed and all the nerves and fears and nightmares returned.

"I will be back," he promised. "With news. And a ring."

I shouldn't have smiled. Now was not the time for a smile. But the irony of Caspian running off to find a ring so I could marry him so I could save the realm was . . . totally ridiculous. And somehow funny.

Or maybe I was already slipping into the magical madness.

Katrinka filled his place, and we continued on our path to the war room. I had never been to this part of the castle before. It had been for grown-ups when I was a child, and since I'd been back, until today, it had been Tyrn's domain. And it showed.

The halls were draped in dark cloths, covering windows. Lit

sconces dotted the corridors, but it was like walking through a forest at night. Or a network of tunnels beneath the earth. It was meant to be black as an abyss. Black as the hopeless hole Tyrn had fallen into.

When at long last, Curtis led us into the war room, I heaved a sigh at the large paned window letting moonlight flood the space. But the room revealed more of Tyrn's madness. It was decorated with equal parts fierce masculinity and crazed lunatic.

There were weapons displayed on every surface. On three of the walls, they were hung as decorations. On the fourth, someone had drawn a bull's-eye on the paneled wood with paint, and Tyrn seemed to have used it for target practice. Axes and daggers and swords were plunged into the splintered wood at varying places on the large set of circles. In other places were gaping holes exposing the stone foundation of the castle.

Piles of books were scattered around the room, reminding me of Ravanna's library but even more chaotic. On a desk in the corner were a set of open books. I perused the pages, hoping they would tell me about warfare and what to do next. But only found titles on poisons and paragraphs on their effects. Tyrn had made notes in the margins and circled words that he seemed to identify as part of his illness.

On one very old book, a word was circled in black ink on its thin, yellowed pages: The Slow Death. I quickly scanned the text and found a rare plant used to make a paste that would kill a person so slowly they did not even suspect they were ill until the very last days. Depending on how little or much of the paste was used would depend on how quickly the victim succumbed. From a year to several decades, it seemed.

Mynot had died the same way, but perhaps quicker than Tyrn, I realized. Ravanna had been using poisons on those closest to her for decades.

Symptoms of the poison included controlled delusions, walking nightmares, and extreme paranoia. Many recipients of the poison had been known to kill themselves when the madness grew too extreme.

Others wasted away until their bodies finally gave out.

What kind of sister poisoned her own brother?

What kind of sister used her brother's madness to make him kill her other sister?

"I love you," I told Katrinka rather out of the blue. She blinked at me, looking as though she was struggling to understand. "I don't think I've said it to you since you've been back. But I do, Katrinka. I love you. I'm so glad you're here. I don't know how I would handle any of this without you by my side."

Tears formed in the corners of her eyes. "I l-love you too, Tessa."

"Are you okay?"

She collapsed into a fur-lined chair that was covered in scrolls and maps. Most of them scattered on the floor as her body displaced them, but she hardly noticed. "No." Her fearful gaze met mine. "Are you?"

I shook my head. "No."

"What are you going to do?" Her voice was so small, but her question loomed large.

"Get the Crown back. Kill Ravanna. Unite the kingdoms again. Avenge our family. Avenge Heprin. Maybe bring magic back to the realm. I have not fully decided on that yet. And marry Caspian. Tonight." I cleared my throat, trying not to keel over from apoplexy at the task list ahead of me. "Oh, and learn to be queen."

Her lips tilted in a crooked smile, and she pushed her spectacles farther up her nose. "Is that it?"

I shrugged. "Well, it's a start, at least."

We were silent for a few minutes, and then she suddenly giggled. "Are you really marrying Caspian tonight?"

The affirmation stuck in my throat. More terrifying than the war ahead of me was the idea of marriage. Specifically marriage to Caspian, who was as ruthless as he was somehow thoughtful. And as dangerous as he was apparently loyal.

The war room doors swung open, and Curtis, Dover, and Finch walked inside. It was like watching stone stand and move. They were as formidable as I'd ever seen them. As I'd ever needed them to be.

Curtis immediately dropped to his knee, and the other two followed suit. "Your Majesty, I must apologize for our lack of action. Your life was in danger, and we did nothing to save you. We accept your punishment however you—"

"Please." I laughed, although the sound was bitter . . . brittle. "Spare me your apologies and penance. I don't think anyone in the realm could have guessed we would go to war with an army of birds. Least of all me. We were caught by surprise, and that is not your fault. We have one enemy today, and you would do better to blame her than heap guilt upon yourselves. Now, please stand. I have a real need of protection, and I would prefer it if it was you doing the protecting."

They stood at once. I held Curtis's eyes, showing him the seriousness of my word. He nodded humbly. But took his place at the door. Dover mimicked his moves exactly.

"Finch," I called before he could leave. "I need to get a message to Taelon."

His chin jerked, a sign that he could do this for me. "Aye, Your Highness."

I weighed the silence around his words but could not hold back my curiosity. "I need it to be immediate. Are you capable of this?"

His chin jerked again. "Aye."

"Do you mind telling me how? Shapeshifting? Are you also a bird?"

His lips tilted in a half smile. "I'm Cavolia," he said by way of explanation.

"Not a bird then."

"The spirit of a stallion, milady."

The spirit of a stallion. What did that mean? A memory played through my head of Taelon telling me that the Cavolia allowed horses to sleep in their beds. Maybe it wasn't horses sleeping in their masters' beds. But horses sleeping in their own beds.

"Oh," I managed to say.

"But I will use the Cavolia way today. It would take me days to find him otherwise."

"So it can be immediate?"

"As long as he is still with Gunter, aye."

"Good. Then tell him to go straight to Soravale. Tell him Blackthorne is marching on his kingdom even now. Ravanna Pressydia has the Crown and Kasha and Aramore. They will not stop until the realm is theirs. His people will need him to lead. I will send him another message as soon as I'm able. And tell him . . ." *I love him. I miss him. I need him. I'm . . . I'm sorry.* "Tell him I'm okay. That I am unharmed."

Soravale would need their Crown Prince to put up a strong fight. Of course, Hugo was still their king. But Taelon was their future and leader of the army. Besides, his family would need his quiet courage and indomitable strength to see them through this dark time. I would support them in any way I could. But for now, I could at least give them their son.

Finch nodded and left the room. In his place, ten advisors, generals, and politicians filled the space, shouting their orders and strategies at me. I looked around my uncle's room and wished he was here. Which surprised me. Even more, I wished my father was here.

Ignoring the voices of old men screaming at me, I walked over to the textured map of the realm in the center of the room. It was a lot like the one Taelon's father, Hugo, kept in his own war room. Detailed images of the kingdoms were all laid out in a smaller version of reality. Elysia with her Diamond Mountains glittering between the glossy boundaries of the Marble Wall. Barstus with her rolling moors and jagged Ice Mountains. Vorestra with her golden dunes and lush oasis gardens. And Soravale with her back to the Crystal Sea and her cliffs deep with sleeping dragons.

Could Ravanna really take Soravale? Could she conquer the capital, Desmondin? Could she occupy the country and make it her own?

My eyes flicked to Heprin. It was a small kingdom comparatively. Three of its sides bordered the sea. It had been so peaceful. So . . . free of struggle.

What did it look like now? Did the sum of it burn? Had it been razed? What happened to the royal family?

What would happen if I did not squash this rebellious sickness and take back the Crown that belonged to me?

Something hot and harsh swept through me, setting my blood on fire with purpose. This was more than a war of men and weapons and advancement. This was a war of magic and history and two queens who would decide the realm's fate.

"Enough!" I shouted at the men, who were all trying to talk over each other. "I cannot understand you when you're all yelling at the same time!"

One exceptionally pompous middle-aged man pushed to the front. "Your Highness, I am General Leffenmore. You may remember me. I am the general of the Royal Army."

"I remember you," I told him coolly. He'd been at the first supper Tyrn had invited me to. I had yet to face Conandra then. The meal had been meant to humiliate and belittle me. Leffenmore had been happy to do his part.

To his credit, he didn't flinch at the mention of that night. "We must pull our men away from the Wall and bring them back to Extensia. The marble will hold. Our defenses must be used to protect the castle."

I held his gaze, wondering how someone who was not yet eighteen could possibly win a war. Worse, how anyone could win a war with that kind of foolish advice. "If the walls will hold, why do we need to use all our resources to defend the castle?"

He opened his mouth, shut it quickly, then opened it once more.

"What's more, General, what good are walls when our enemies can simply fly over them?"

At this, his face turned a sickly yellow, and I thought he might have stopped breathing. With great effort, he seemed to compose himself barely, but before he could explain his reasoning or suggest something different, there was a commotion at the door.

I could hear Curtis arguing with someone. Stepping to the side of the group of men who looked like a gaggle of geese bobbing their heads around, I moved to see what was going on.

"You cannot go in there," Curtis was saying to someone. "The queen is in a meeting!"

The confrontation was getting physical. I could hear someone arguing with Curtis, but his voice was muffled beneath Curtis's strict commands.

Finally, a lanky arm poked into the room. I caught sight of a shock of blond hair. And then that sweet, familiar voice. "She is not a queen to me. She is my friend. And I need to see her." Then louder and more desperate, he yelled, "Tess! Let me in! Tess!"

"Let him in," I echoed, taking my first real breath since maybe he left more than a month ago. A sob trembled through me at the promise of his presence, but I bit him back and shouted my command. "Let him through! Dragon's blood, Curtis, he is always allowed through."

Oliver appeared in the doorway, bedraggled and beat up as one would expect after his travels. His hair was singed on the ends, and he was covered in dirt and grime. His lips were cut, bloody in the corners, and he sported a black eye that seemed to be just on this side of healing.

Tears pushed at my eyes, hot and desperate. I had not known how much I needed him until this moment. Until he was standing in front of me as familiar and Oliver-like as ever.

I pushed past the men who thought they knew everything and leaped into his arms. "How is this possible?" I cried against his shoulder.

"I've been riding nonstop for days. The Temple, Tess . . ." His voice broke at the mention of it. "The brothers."

We clung tighter, only now just letting the full weight of what had happened hit us. "Father Garius?" I sobbed.

"I do not know. I . . . I did not find his body. But many had been —" His voice cracked again, and he took several deep breaths to compose himself. "But several had been burned. The whole kingdom was just as bad. They flattened it all."

"Was Taelon with you?"

"He's all right, if that's what you're worried about. He has the demons of Denamon in him, I'll tell you that. He's ready to go to war today."

"We're already at war," I told him boldly, realizing how much he'd missed if he'd been riding nonstop.

I looked around the room at the men who were supposed to lead my kingdom into battle, the old, ostentatious men who were to protect and defend this realm. I did not know them. I did not know their intentions or plans or families. I did not know their loyalties.

But I knew this man's. I had already decided to make him my advisor long ago. He was the only advice I trusted. He was the only voice I truly listened to. The only heart I fully believed.

"Out," I told the room of career counselors and politicians. "Get out."

"But Your Majesty," they all protested.

"Your Highness, you can't be serious."

Leffenmore shouted, "We have a war to wage!"

"And we will," I answered him specifically. "We will go to war. We will fight back. We will defend not just this kingdom or even this castle but the whole of the realm. From Blackthorne and her army. And from the very nature of this rotting rebellion. We will do something before it's too late. But I will not take advice from any of you. You are dismissed. You may wait for my orders elsewhere." I looked around the group of men once more, at their sneers of disapproval and their haughty glares of superiority. "Or your dismissal," I finished, making it clear that not all of them would have the inflated positions they had enjoyed under my uncle for much longer.

When they opened their mouths to start squawking again, Curtis made a grand gesture of opening the war room doors. "The queen has spoken," he boomed.

Which shut them up. Who would have thought?

I would have smiled had our circumstances been less dire.

They filed out, grumbling the whole way. And when they were finally out of the room, I let go of Oliver and walked back to the map. Sweeping a hand over the vastness it represented, I said, "I wasn't kidding, Sir Oliver. What should we do first?"

Oliver's mouth dropped open. "You cannot be serious. Tess, I don't know the first thing about warfare."

I shared a glance with Katrinka. Her eyes were growing sharper, more in-tuned. She was slowly shaking off the shock of the bedlam that had only just happened and fully joining us once more.

"Now, that's not entirely true. Father Garius prepared us for this, Oliver. How many battles did we read about in the Temple? How many strategies by generals? Both failed and successful? How many countless hours in the ring, learning to fight and defend? He knew this day was coming. He prepared us for it. We just need to figure out where to start."

Curtis stepped back into the room and shut the doors behind him. Dover stepped in front of them after locking them.

"Might I suggest you start with this?" Curtis said, walking over to where a large stone fireplace was set into the wall between towering bookshelves. I had not noticed before now that it was identical to the one in my parents' rooms. The one where I found the grimoire.

Curtis's fingers followed a similar path to how I'd found the secret drawer. He pressed on gemstones and worked his way down.

Diamond for power. Ruby for love. Emerald for magic . . . Then suddenly, a hidden compartment popped out.

I could not see what he was doing, but my breath had stalled in my throat. Instinct swirled through me, nerves and hope and . . . something entirely indefinable.

"Your uncle was . . . focused after you returned. Well, more focused than he had been prior. And also more crazed, if you don't mind me saying." He stood, holding a black pillow covered with a black velvet cloth. "He was also obsessed with the idea of protecting the Crown of Nine. He would stay up all hours of the night working in here in secret except when Queen Ravanna was in residence. Then he would act as though he'd never heard or seen this room before. This morning, he showed me why." Curtis carefully picked up the cloth and pulled it away. A gleaming, golden crown rested on the pillow, an exact replica of the Crown of Nine.

"He fashioned a replica?" I gasped, amazed at his craftmanship, at the way it even seemed to look aged and weathered. At the way it seemed to ring with power and whisper the magic that had been stolen from it, just like the original.

"Yes," Curtis confirmed.

I walked over to the crown and ran my fingers over the inset gemstones. "It looks exactly like the original."

"It does," Curtis agreed. "Which is why Queen Ravanna did not notice she had the fake."

I took a step back. And then two steps forward. "You're not—" I looked closer at the Crown. "You can't be serious."

"I don't know how he knew. Or why he didn't go to greater lengths to stop Queen Ravanna. But somehow, your uncle knew the Blackthorne queen was coming for the Crown of Nine. So he made sure she got it."

Carefully reaching for the Crown that had caused so much destruction, I lifted it from the pillow and held it up to the moonlight. Katrinka had stood to her feet and walked over to marvel at it as well.

"You need to put it on," she said in a low, somber voice. "You need to finish the coronation."

I didn't know what it mattered at this point. I was queen one way or another now that Tyrn was dead. The Crown was just a formality now.

Still, her encouragement resonated in some deep, secret chamber inside my heart. I wanted to wear the Crown of Nine. I wanted to claim it as mine.

I wanted to finish what had been started when Father Garius pulled me from the river. Or maybe what had been started before even that—when my family had been murdered, and I'd been the oldest survivor to a royal, ancient bloodline with magic in her veins and power in her heart.

Purpose and destiny and something potent whispered through me as I placed it on my head. My hair was loose around my shoulders, tangled in the diamonds sewed to my gown. And so there was nothing to get in the way of sliding it into place.

I sucked in a sharp breath at the burst of sensation that exploded through me. At the weight of it—not just in gold, but in the calling of it. In the fate of it.

Just like the time I'd tried it on back in Heprin, I felt the magic and power of this ancient diadem connect with the magic and power inside me—although I could not name what it was back then.

The crown seemed to call to the thing inside me and sing to it. They entwined together in something beautiful and harmonious.

I had never felt more like myself, more like the self I was supposed to be. I had never felt more alive. More powerful. More . . . full of magic.

The Crown of Nine was part of my family's legacy. And part of my destiny. And I would do whatever it took to end the threat to my realm. Even if it meant killing Ravanna Pressydia myself.

"Thank you," I whispered to Curtis, tears pricking the corners of my eyes once more.

"Thank you, Your Majesty. For what you have done." He paused, letting the burden of his words settle around us. "And what you are going to do."

To the room at large, I said, "Now, let's figure out how to win this war."

Katrinka held up a finger, pushing her spectacles up her nose with her other hand. "Shouldn't you get married first?"

I cringed as Oliver screeched out a question. "Married to whom?"

But then he was there. Dover let Caspian in the room. He looked as though he had something to say but stopped short at the sight of me wearing the true Crown of Nine.

"Where did that come from?" he gasped.

I smiled a true, real, genuine smile. "My uncle had more tricks up his sleeves than we gave him credit for."

"It is truly the Crown then?" he asked. I nodded. "And the one Ravanna has?"

"A replica."

"Then the war will be won," Caspian murmured reverently. "Because who could ever prevail against Tessana Allisand wearing the Crown of Nine and the second son of Vorestra at her side?"

My smile widened as purpose and promise, and some very serious nerves swept through me once more. Who indeed?

THANK YOU

Thank you for reading Throne of a Thousand Lies! The final book in the Nine Kingdoms Trilogy is coming Summer of 2023. While you wait, be on the lookout for Rachel's newest Young Adult Dystopian Romance, The City of Never, coming December 6th, 2022.

And keep reading for an excerpt from her new NA Paranormal Romance, House of Dusk and Dawn, releasing exclusively on Substack.com

City of Never

I was there the day the wall fell from the sky. The day they gunned down my mother and permanently separated the rich from the poor. I was there the day my father decided he could force utopia on a certain half of the population and leave the rest to rot.

Pragmapax was once a great city, the only remaining outpost of civilization in our part of the world. But now, divided by an impossible wall, we've become two cities. Two peoples that despise each other. Two different ways of life—one idyllic and peaceful, the other savage and lawless. Civil war seethes in the air, breathing down our necks.

The only thing I know is that if war finally breaks out, I'm trapped on the wrong side.

Acknowledgments

In a season of life where I feel pulled every single direction and my attention is always needed everywhere but in writing. . .I feel especially grateful to the God who gives so abundantly. And Who sees me in my small life and small problems and small suffering and pours out great big rescues just because He loves me. To my husband too, who puts up with laundry chaos and takeout suppers and a hundred forgotten things. Zach, you are the best man I have ever known. And I'm so grateful you're not just my life partner, but my business partner too. And after 17 years together, that's saying something. And, of course, to my children, who still believe "maybe" might mean yes. And who don't mind wearing shorts a couple days in a row or making themselves ramen at 10pm when I forgot to even think about dinner.

To the people who made this book possible. Zach, my cover designer. My patient editors, Marion and Jenny, who put up with half finished manuscripts, and late turn-ins, and confusing emails. You ladies make me a better writer and a better human. And I'm so grateful for you. And to Karen, who slides in last, but who always fixes my elipses, and all the other last minute mistakes, and who is hands down one of the best fact checkers ever. You are a joy to work with.

To the bloggers too. Who sacrifice so much time and energy to get early reviews posted and beautiful pictures made and so much more. You all are the best part about this job. Thank you for all that you do.

And to the readers, who took a chance on this story, and on me. Thank you for reading. I hope you fell in love with Elysia and Tessana and maybe even Caspian. I mean, Taelon. Ahem, who I really mean...is Oliver. Haha! The story continues next year and I hope you are as ready to continue this adventure as I am.

About the Author

Rachel Higginson was born and raised in Nebraska and spent her college years traveling the world. She fell in love with Eastern Europe, Paris, Indian Food and the beautiful beaches of Sri Lanka, but came back home to marry her high school sweetheart. Now she spends her days raising their five kids, wrangling their giant dogs and reading whenever she can. She is obsessed with reruns of *Top Chef* and all things coffee.

Book #3 in The Nine Kingdoms Trilogy is coming Summer 2023!

Other Books Out Now by Rachel Higginson:

Love and Decay, Season One
Volume One
Volume Two
Love and Decay, Season Two
Volume Three
Volume Four
Volume Five
Love and Decay, Season Three
Volume Six
Volume Seven
Volume Eight
Love and Decay: Revolution, Season One
Volume One

Volume Two

The Star-Crossed Series
Reckless Magic (The Star-Crossed Series, Book 1)
Hopeless Magic (The Star-Crossed Series, Book 2)
Fearless Magic (The Star-Crossed Series, Book 3)
Endless Magic (The Star-Crossed Series, Book 4)
The Reluctant King (The Star-Crossed Series, Book 5)
The Relentless Warrior (The Star-Crossed Series, Book 6)
Breathless Magic (The Star-Crossed Series, Book 6.5)
Fateful Magic (The Star-Crossed Series, Book 6.75)
The Redeemable Prince (The Star-Crossed Series, Book 7)

The Starbright Series
Heir of Skies (The Starbright Series, Book 1)
Heir of Darkness (The Starbright Series, Book 2)
Heir of Secrets (The Starbright Series, Book 3)

The Siren Series
The Rush (The Siren Series, Book 1)
The Fall (The Siren Series, Book 2)
The Heart (The Siren Series, Book 3)

Bet on Love Series
Bet on Us (An NA Contemporary Romance)
Bet on Me (An NA Contemporary Romance)

Every Wrong Reason

The Five Stages of Falling in Love

Trailer Park Heart
Never Fall in Love with a Rockstar

The Opposite of You (Opposites Attract Series)
The Difference between Us (Opposites Attract Series)
The Problem with Him (Opposites Attract Series)
The Something about Her (Opposites Attract Series)

Decisions We Make After Midnight (Decisions in Durham Series)
Secrets We Whisper in the Moonlight (Decisions in Durham Series)

Constant (The Confidence Game Duet)
Consequence (The Confidence Game Duet)

Connect with Rachel on her website at:
www.authorrachelhigginson.com

Or on Twitter:
@mywritesdntbite

Or on her Facebook page:
Rachel Higginson

Keep reading for an excerpt from House and Dusk and Dawn, a story about a clueless witch you is accidentally and magically bonded with her college professor.
This book is released exclusively on Substack.com.

TEASER

"Well, you look smokin' hot." Spinning around, I grinned at my roommate, Valeria, who had just stepped into our dorm room and paid me just the compliment I was hoping to hear. "Is it too much?"

Her dark brown eyes narrowed. "Depends. Are you preemptively trying to get out of Statistics midterms? Because if so, then no, it's perfect. Professor Pervert will love it." She drew a deep breath, finding her transition from slides to slippers much more interesting. "But if it's for Adrian, then yes. You're trying way too hard for him. You're going to make that fool fall in love with you."

"Come on." I waved her off and turned back to the vanity mirror above the built-in desk in our shared space. My high-waisted red cigarette pants were a new diamond-in-the-rough thrift store find and they fit perfectly. Paired with a set of black wedges and a slinky black tube top, I was at the top of my going-out game. "It's not like that with Adrian."

"Mm-hmm."

I spun around again, plopping one hand on my hip. "He's hot, Val. And he can get into places I can't." Her raised eyebrow called out my bullshit. "He's taking me to a house party tonight. Some super rich guy that lives up the mountain. He promised all kinds of epicness."

Her other eyebrow jumped to meet the first. "I bet he did."

"It's okay for me to have a little fun." Now that I felt sufficiently insecure, I grabbed for my black boyfriend cardigan and slipped it over my shoulders. It turned me from sexpot to frumpy in a matter of seconds, but maybe Adrian would think I was going for that slutty librarian thing if my shoulders were covered.

My stunning roommate, who had never felt insecure a day in her life, hopped on her bed and tucked her hands beneath her thighs—officially repentant. "I know. I'm not saying I don't want you to have fun. But, you just got out of a serious relationship with Matty. I don't want you to get your heart broken again so soon."

The reminder of my high school boyfriend dug deep at whatever confidence I had left. I didn't want my heart broken again either. Or ever. It had been rough enough the first time. I didn't think I would survive another shattering like that one.

But I wasn't in love with Adrian, like I thought I had been with Matty. I knew better. Adrian wasn't the kind of guy you fell in love with. Adrian was the kind of guy you had fun with until the rebound stage wore off and dating seriously again felt possible.

He was just paying for my meals and giving me an excuse to look good until my chest stopped feeling like someone had punched a hole through it.

"Adrian is not going to break my heart," I promised her. "He's just *fun*." But now that I'd repeated the word so many times, I started to worry about who I was trying to convince. "Besides, he's not the kind of guy that wants to settle down ever. He's all smarmy playboy and mysterious emotional baggage. And I want none of that. *But* this party sounds really cool." Resisting the urge to nibble my bottom lip and ruin lipstick that had taken way too long to apply perfectly, I faced her again and waggled my eyebrows. "You should come with us."

She wrinkled her nose. "To a house party?"

"A house party *in the hills*. Adrian's driving."

She glanced at her backpack slumped against the footboard. "I should get a head start on my comp paper."

"Bah. That's boring. And it's Friday night. Come on, you can be my Jiminy Cricket and make sure I don't do anything stupid."

The corner of her mouth twitched. "Adrian won't mind?"

"Who cares?" I rolled my eyes, feeling that truth to my toes. "I'm not trying to impress him. I'm using him for his hot body and good party connections. Oh, and because he takes me out to dinner. A girl on my budget cannot turn down a free meal."

"True."

I could see the wheels turning in her head. Her big brown eyes were windows into her every thought and emotion. She could hide nothing. Valeria and I had been matched together our freshman year at Piney State University and two years later, we'd decided we couldn't live without each other. Seriously, it was going to get awkward if either of us ever got married and we had to break it to our future spouse that we were a package deal.

"It will be fun..." I sing-songed, hoping to lure her into a night of debauchery and drunkenness. "I know you want to." A strange feeling burned at the tips of my fingers, like I'd pressed them against a hot stove burner. The feeling quickly sizzled up my forearms, tensing my biceps and triceps and all the little muscles in my heart. I sucked in a deep breath while my insides contracted in discomfort. I glanced at my hands, expecting them to be fully on fire, but nothing on the outside was amiss. This was a strictly internal inferno. My heart stuttered and tripped and failed for just two short seconds as I pushed the burning sensation back. It wasn't the first time I'd fought the fire. And it wouldn't be the last.

Just when I thought I would explode into a million burning embers, the feeling was gone. Suddenly sucked beneath an invisible doorway like a treacherous backdraft.

Valeria lifted her head, her dark eyes showing concern, worry, surprise. "Are you okay?"

I tried to speak, but my throat had been charred, the hot coals were gone, but their wounds and scars remained. It didn't exactly hurt, but it didn't feel wonderful either. I shook my head, damning my wild imagination for the millionth time. There hadn't been a fire. There hadn't been a burning sensation. There hadn't even been a reason to worry. I had social anxiety. That was all. It was a battle I'd fought my entire life. Crippling moments of insecurity and awkward unsurety always left me reeling. And while I'd learned to push past the worst of my "condition," it was harder to fight the fictional narrative that played along with the physical effects. There was a bottle of Zoloft in my medicine cabinet, but I wanted to have fun tonight. I wanted to drink and forget I had papers due, and bills to pay and that Matty wasn't coming up to visit me this weekend like we'd planned months ago. "Fine," I croaked. "I'm fine."

Her eyes narrowed again. "Are you sure?"

Gulping down a steadying breath, the last remnants of heat gradually dissipated. Embarrassment replaced anxiety and a humiliated lump traded the burning-coal-feeling in my throat. "I swallowed funny. You know when you choke on your own spit?"

She released an easy laugh. "Are you serious?"

"See? I need you to come with us tonight, so I don't accidentally kill myself during beer pong."

"You're sure Adrian won't mind?"

"Why would he mind? You're gorgeous. You're fun. You're my friend."

Her lips twisted into a frown. "But you're forgetting the other side of the argument."

"Which is?"

"He's a total douche!"

I couldn't help but laugh. She wasn't wrong. Adrian and I had met a couple weeks ago at my job—a bar called Pigley's. It was a favorite among the local college crowd. But Adrian was definitely not a fellow student at Pinewood University. He'd come into the bar all by himself, seeming frustrated and pissed and totally not in the mood to be wooed by his bartender.

But I'd worn him down eventually. Not that I cared about all my customer's moods. But I could tell he had money. It was the cut of his unrumpled suit and the flashy gold ring he wore on his pointer finger, inlaid with a sparkling emerald. He wore matching diamond studs in his ears and a flashy gold watch on his wrist. He had a nose ring too, a hoop that seemed totally out of place with the mobster-esque rest of him. He'd sat down with a scowl and a wad of cash and I knew, *I just knew*, if I could turn his night around, he would tip well just so he could have the opportunity to show off his wealth.

So, I'd smiled and flirted and remained totally unruffled by his surely snark. Eventually, he'd relaxed. I made sure his drink was always refilled and listened to him complain about the small college town like it was dog shit beneath his expensive shoes without rolling my eyes once. I deserved some kind of award for my patience, but at the very least I earned a fat tip.

Tips were currently my biggest goal in life. Sure, good grades and a healthy education were up there too. But I couldn't get either of those things without the tips. Hence the pretty smiles and perfectly doe-eyed listening look.

Unfortunately, my customers were usually college kids with as much extra cash as I had. But Adrian was different. He'd left his number on a napkin with a fifty-dollar bill. I'd been flattered by his attention and ecstatic about the extra money. And proud of myself. All that work had paid off. Honestly though, I never intended to call him. Fifty dollars was nice, but it hadn't erased my mounting student loan debt or anything.

I'd moved on and hadn't thought about him at all after that. I had other grouchy customers to woo, drinks to sling, cash to earn. He'd been a bright spot in endless reruns of the same night, but that was all. Until he showed up again a few days later.

This time he hadn't been sulky or judgmental. He'd been sweet, charming, funny even. And somehow, after a night of laughing over whiskey sours and another fifty-dollar tip, he got me to give him my number too.

Now we were loosely seeing each other. He was fun for the most part, if not stuck-up. And I was in the mood to forget Matty, so honestly, I would have dated a horse if he promised to pay the check at the end of the night.

Adrian was not the first guy to hit on me at Pigley's. But he was the first guy I said yes to. And so far, he hadn't made me regret my decision. But he hadn't even kissed me yet. And I got the impression both of us knew this wasn't going anywhere.

Thirty minutes later, Valeria was just finishing her "going out" makeup, which was all smokey eyes and crimson lips, when I got a text that Adrian was downstairs. "He's here," I told her.

Her reflection blinked at me from the mirror. "He doesn't come up to get you?"

I leaned forward, unable to resist the chance to blow her mind. "He doesn't even open the car door for me."

Her expression crumpled with disgust. "See? This guy is a total sleezebag."

It was impossible not to laugh at her old-fashioned ways. Valeria came from a gigantic family. She had something like five brothers and two sisters. Her parents were high school sweethearts and still in love with each other. Her dad had taken her out on her first "date" to show her how a man should treat her and after that her brothers had promised to beat up any guy that didn't follow suit. I totally understood where she was coming from. While my parents weren't exactly doting, they did genuinely love each other. I knew what a healthy relationship looked like.

But I wasn't looking for a healthy relationship. I had that with Matty and look how that had ended. Adrian was all the things he was supposed to be. Aloof, uninterested in the finer details of my life and yeah, a little bit sleezy. I didn't want a relationship.

I wanted a good time.

We grabbed our purses and headed for the door. Our hall on Harder Four was all girls, but boys were allowed in our rooms and on the hall before curfew. "I don't know if you remember, but I dated a gentleman for three years, Val. He opened car doors for me and walked four flights of stairs to pick me up at my door, he sent chocolates on Valentine's Day without fail and regularly surprised me with flowers." I hit her with a look. "And then he dumped me for Stacia Fairway and her expensive new boobs."

"What a hooker," Valeria murmured supportively.

"She was always after him in high school. And it never made sense to me why he didn't dump me for her back then. She was popular and a cheerleader and..."

"Easy."

"Yes! So easy!" Val didn't know Stacia personally. All her information came through me, but I liked to think, even though I hated Stacia more than any other person on the planet right now, this was an accurate, unbiased account. Mostly, I wanted someone to tell me that I hadn't totally succumbed to bitter jealousy.

Valeria put her hand on my shoulder as we landed on the ground floor. "He didn't deserve you, babe. Any idiot can see you're a catch. It's his loss."

Her words soothed the jagged edges of my broken heart, but it was a temporary, fleeting feeling. I had been planning my happily ever after with Matty for years. He was the only boyfriend I'd ever had, the only man I'd said "I love you" to, the only guy I'd ever been with. The only guy I had ever imagined being with.

Not that I didn't have my doubts too. And to be fair, I'd started to worry that maybe we weren't as compatible as we had been after a couple years of college under our belts. We didn't even go to school in the same state. While I'd stayed close to home, Matty had picked a college near Denver, three hours away.

But I really hadn't seen the breakup coming. Or at least I hadn't wanted to acknowledge the clues that Matty had been dropping more and more often lately.

We stepped out into the breezy fall night, dusk turning the sky soft pinks and purples. The sun hid somewhere behind the mountains and the moon had started to rise in all its full, glossy glory.

Electricity danced over my skin as the fresh mountain scent filled my lungs. I loved the night. I was a classic night owl to my core. But it wasn't just that I hated mornings and focused better once the sun set. It was like I came alive after dark. Like my brain finally turned on and all my senses awoke. The buzz of anxiety slipped behind an invisible wall and I could finally, effortlessly, feel totally myself.

When I was a little girl, my parents would find me outside our small Crested Butte lodge, dancing under the moonlight. My dad had always called me his Little Star because I preferred to be out underneath them. The dark was where I was my best. And tonight especially, I felt the fervor of possibility waiting for me just beyond sunset.

Adrian leaned against his fancy sports car, his arms folded across his chest in that devil-may-care way I couldn't get enough of. He was classic bad boy tonight in dark washed jeans, a pristine white t-shirt and a faded leather jacket.

Butterflies took flight low in my belly. He was inhumanly beautiful, like he'd been chiseled from stone. His dirty blonde hair was full of waves that he pushed artfully back with product. His cheekbones were high, his jaw was cut, and his entire body rippled with muscle. I wanted to throw myself at him whenever I saw him.

He tipped his chin in acknowledgment. I may have sighed. Val made a sound in the back of her throat, not at all amused with Adrian's post-chivalrous ways.

"Hey." I felt kind of stupid being the first one to speak, but that was just another one of his traits. He was so cool, he made everyone else feel less than. "Do you care if Val tags along?"

Even though they'd met before, Adrian's eyes narrowed in confusion. "Val?"

I jerked my thumb toward my friend. "This is Val." When the

silence stretched on and my skin prickled with the painfully awkward tension, I added, "Val this is Adrian."

"We've met," she said clearly.

Adrian finally turned his attention on her, taking in her curvy figure with an expression that was just north of bored. "Does she talk a lot?"

Okay, even I found that question to be outrageously rude. My breathy nervousness turned into flat irritation. "She talks the normal amount."

His gaze tracked over her tight jumpsuit in a way I did not like. Or appreciate. Or try to excuse. But I also couldn't blame him. I hadn't exactly claimed Adrian as mine. And Val was drop dead gorgeous with her perfect brown skin, pouty lips and long, thick black hair.

His expression hardened and he eyed both of us with a look that was decidedly less sexy and more on the side of angry dad. "Stick with me," he ordered. "This isn't the kind of place you want to get lost at, yeah?"

Val and I shared a look, and I knew she felt as uncertain about the night as I did now. "Uh, okay." He pushed off the car and headed for the driver's seat. "We could do something else," I threw out, nervous energy buzzing through me, anxiety flaring like a kindled flame. He'd sold the party tonight in his typical way. "You want to hit up a house party with me in the hills Sunday night? It'll be cool." How could I say no to that invitation, right? Actually, I'd told him no first. Sunday night was one of the few nights I didn't work, but I also had my heaviest class load on Mondays. And since fall semester had just started last Thursday, tomorrow was the first Monday I would have class. I was in the mood for fun, but I also didn't want to get dragged to a seedy frat house and not have a ride home. "We could go see a movie?"

I followed his "Nah," into the car as he climbed behind the steering wheel. "I have to make an appearance. It'll be fun." The way he said "fun" sounded stilted, forced. He smiled to take the edge off. "Just don't wander off."

Val's what-did-you-get-me-into glare burned the side of my face, but before I could turn around and reassure her, Adrian pushed the ignition button and the engine roared to life with a deafening growl. Dark, thumping music blared from the speakers and any would-be conversation was drowned beneath the rumble of the muscle car and manic music. Adrian settled his hand on my knee for a beat, his thumb rubbing possessively along my thigh. I tried to shake off some of my irritation and settle into the excitement and anticipation I'd had earlier tonight, but I couldn't manage to ignore the dread curling around my thumping heart.

I'd forgiven Adrian's surliness prior to tonight because he was so different than Matty. I'd naively enjoyed his brusque way of speaking as endearing, chalking it up to that mysterious side of him that I found so alluring.

Now, exposed in front of Val, I realized it wasn't endearing at all. It was asshole-ish and rude. Maybe Valeria had seen what I should have a long time ago, but that didn't mean we couldn't still have fun at the party. We'd just have to figure out a way to ditch Adrian and do our own thing.

Despite his warnings to stay close to him.

Adrian didn't turn on his GPS, so I relaxed a little, assuming this party was at a friend's house. Twilight turned to night as we wound our way higher up the mountain, passing million-dollar ski lodge after million-dollar ski lodge.

This part of Colorado was absolutely breathtaking. It was only the beginning of September, but the deciduous trees had already started to turn pretty shades of orange and yellow. In a couple more weeks the temperature would drop too, and we would start praying the snow would hold off until November. Knowing our prayers were futile.

Forty minutes later, Adrian pulled up in front of a stunning, well-lit mansion that resembled more of a castle than a house. We'd seen the lights from a long way away as the house sat on top of a hill. The mountain road felt especially dark in light of the stunning sight in front of us. Even the moon hid behind a blanket of milky clouds.

The house was all stone façade and big glass windows perched at the edge of a cliff. The warm glow of light from inside spilled out on the circular drive, revealing a manicured lawn that ended at just beyond the house where towering pine trees clustered together in dense forest. Elegantly dressed partygoers with drinks and appetizers in hand were clearly seen through the arching windows. They laughed and chatted animatedly, while snatching bite-size food from passing waiters.

The corner of a matching stone balcony was visible around the side of the house. I knew houses like this, the balcony would wrap all the way around and offer stunning views of the mountains and valleys below. The house was three stories tall and classically mountain chic. One of the several million-dollar homes that belonged on the front of magazines that dotted this section of Colorado. I felt my eyes go big and stay that way as I tried to take in all the details. Last summer I'd helped Val at her catering job and worked several of the other big homes, but I had never seen this one, let alone been inside —even as a waitress.

No wonder Adrian wanted us to stay close. He was obviously afraid we'd wander off and break something expensive and irreplaceable.

Adrian came to a stop beneath a covered portico made of natural timbers. A valet opened my door, startling me from my wide-eyed wonder. Without speaking, he held out a hand for me to take.

Adrian had already jumped out of his still-running car and was in the process of handing his keys over to a different attendant. Accepting help, I let the formally dressed valet support my weight as I stepped from the vehicle onto a crimson carpet that led to the front door.

I suddenly felt very underdressed. Glancing helplessly at the valet, I found his eyes darting from Adrian to me, a question lingering in their dark depths that I didn't understand. Adrian waited for us under an arched entryway that led to an open breezeway, lit torches illuminating the way to the house.

"Am I dressed up enough?" I whispered to the valet, hoping he would give it to me straight.

His eyes moved over my face, my blonde hair piled on top of my head in a loose knot of curled strands. His gaze darted to my tight tube top and worn cardigan. "Are you invited?" he whispered back.

I licked my lipsticked lips and lost the ability to answer. Was I invited? Would it be a problem if I wasn't? "My date was," I told him quietly.

He shot a horrified look at Adrian. "He was?"

"Let's go, Willow." Adrian's harsh tone jostled both of us. The valet took a quick step back and I took a quick step forward.

Val slipped her arm through mine and tugged me along. "Is this what you were expecting?"

All I could do was shake my head. Obviously not. At least she was kind enough not to gloat. We moved quickly to keep up with Adrian's pace. "Should I take my cardigan off?"

Valeria snickered, as uncomfortable as me. "Probably a good idea."

We stepped into the breezeway and I marveled at the details of such a seemingly unnecessary part of the house. Large-bulbed lights were strung back and forth in crisscross patterns across the open ceiling. Torches, real, working torches, lined the walls, hanging over heavy, crowded white peony bushes that were still in bloom. A butler in full coat and tails stood at the door to the house.

Since Valeria and I were a few steps behind Adrian, I didn't hear the conversation exchanged, but when we joined Adrian in the doorway, it appeared to be tense.

"I am only following orders," the butler was saying.

"This is some serious bullshit, you know that, right?" Adrian snapped back.

The butler seemed extraordinarily frazzled. "Mr. Lazotti, this is out of my hands. He will be down shortly. If you would just wait here."

Adrian growled another curse word. "I'm not going to wait here. I'm going inside, Jensen. He can find me later."

The butler moved to block the door and for a second I thought Adrian was going to hit him. I lurched away from Valeria, intending to intervene. What I could have done to stop two grown men from fisticuffs was something I hadn't entirely thought through, but I felt the instinct to at least try to stop them from bloodying each other unnecessarily.

Now that we were inside the breezeway, I found that I didn't want to leave this place. I had to at least explore the inside. Count how many bathrooms there were. Check out the wine cellar. This place had to have a wine cellar. All places like this had a wine cellar. I moved next to Adrian, settling my hand on his shoulder. "Is there a problem?"

His gaze moved to my face for the first time and I could have sworn I heard him audibly curse at the sight of me. Which was rude. I wasn't awful to look at, but I wasn't a total knock-out like Valeria.

However, remembering the well-worn cardigan still frumpifying my outfit, I quickly slid it off and tied it around my waist. Not the smoothest of moves, but it was done. And now it was important to just act cool. The butler was also staring at me. Clearly, he wasn't fooled by my coolness. "We won't be any trouble," I promised him, flashing a smile. "Promise, we'll be on our best behavior."

Another voice answered my plea from inside the house. A man's voice and with it, came a man. Somewhere in his thirties, I would have guessed, dressed even sharper than Adrian. A crisp white button up shirt, open at the collar, tailored gray pants, a silver watch on his wrist and a silver ring on his pointer finger, like how Adrian wore his gold one. I noticed because he was tugging at his opposite cuff in a frustrated kind of way and the torchlight glinted off it, catching my eye.

There was something more than this man's appearance that set me on edge though. His dark hair was longer than it should have been, tucked behind his ears, brushing the crisp collar of his shirt. There was a boyish look to his very manly physique, and I was unnerved so suddenly I didn't know what to do with my hands. A shiver rolled down my spine at his indifferent laugh. "That's unlikely," he said in response to my claim that we wouldn't be any trouble.

The butler snapped to attention, stepping out of the way, and mumbling a repentant, "Sir," under his breath.

"Thank you, Jensen. Stalwart as usual."

Adrian's shoulder, where my hand rested, felt wrong, off somehow now that the stranger stood so close. I quickly pulled my hand away, tucking it into my pocket.

I tried to tear my eyes away from this new man and his alluring face, but I couldn't seem to do it. Black hair so dark it seemed to repel light. Tanned, olive skin and long, slender fingers, a sprinkling of hair where his shirt opened to reveal his throat and rough sandpaper along his jaw like he'd forgotten to shave this morning. He was all man, the manliest man I had ever encountered. I didn't know why I felt that way, only that I did. And in comparison, Adrian was nothing but a boy. Matty an infant. All men were now babies comparatively.

He was unlike anyone I had ever met before. Unlike anyone I had ever seen period. That same strange heat lit inside me again. Only this time it started at my toes and curled its way upward, lighting my bones on fire as it went.

"Adrian, I thought I was clear. We'll finish our business in the morning—"

"Professor Dessai?" Valeria whispered next to me.

This was Professor Dessai? This was the gorgeous professor no one could stop talking about at Pinewood? Even Valeria?

My heart fluttered in my chest, a girlish response that felt totally immature compared to the intensity standing in front of me.

Professor Dessai's gaze moved to Val, widening in surprise before alighting on me. That was when the world screeched to a halt, like an explosive car crash. Tires burning rubber, metal crunching against metal, the reality in front of me that I had fixated on for so long spinning, spinning, spinning...

Our gazes met and the fire inside me grew hotter, singeing my bones, burning them to ash. A buzzing began in my ears and dove into crescendo with the roaring flatness of a hornet's nest. It grew louder and louder and louder until it seemed to scream inside my head.

The fire inside me exploded into an inferno, as if someone had doused my insides with an accelerant. I felt it inside and outside. It consumed me from the center of my bones to the tips of my hair. It wasn't just uncomfortable now, it was painful. My hands burned against my thighs, tucked inside my pockets. The pain moved beyond internal imagination. It became a crushing, torturous external reality. The smell of seared hair settled in the air, stinking and pushing my panicked thoughts deeper down a rabbit hole of fear and paranoia. Could everyone smell the hair? Did everyone know that it was because I was on fire? I tore my gaze from the professor's light brown eyes, almost golden in their color. I had to look away. Shame and surprise burned through me. I knew my cheeks and chest would be the color of a ripe strawberry.

Leaning into Adrian, I rested my chin on his shoulder. It felt cool against my warmed skin. I gasped for breath and hoped no one noticed how unsettled I was. Out from beneath the professor's scrutiny, the fire was able to recede once again, sucked behind the invisible curtain of restraint for now. "What's the problem, Adrian?" I asked in a voice made raspy by the charred feeling of my throat.

Adrian slipped his arm around my waist, pulling me to his side. "No problem, babe. We're here to have a good time."

Professor Dessai's gaze never moved off me. I could feel it burning the side of my face, stoking the fire I knew waited to ignite again.

"Who are your guests, Adrian?" His voice was cultured, bored, annoyed. He sounded exactly like I imagined a man from a house like this would sound. "I should know before I let them in my house, don't you think?"

Adrian smiled smugly, an expression of victory sparkling in his eyes. "Valeria," he said, motioning behind him. "And this is my girl, Willow."

Professor Dessai held out his hand. "Willow?"

"W-Willow Burke." I avoided his gaze, but allowed the handshake. So what? He was beautiful. Adrian was beautiful too. The point was that I had been around good-looking people before. I had been around wealthy people too. Our part of Colorado was brimming with money. Prime ski resorts and perfect mountain powder, not to mention it was a summer vacation hot spot.

"And how do you know Adrian Lazzoti, Willow Burke?" The way he said my name caused another tremble to roll down my spine. The feeling was exactly contrary to the fire still simmering inside my blood. I couldn't help but jerk from the sensation, plastering myself against Adrian in the process. It wasn't a pleasant feeling. More like animal instinct. I couldn't shake the need to hide from this man, to avoid him at all costs.

"We met at work," I said vaguely.

Dessai didn't let me get away with it though. "I know what Adrian does. What do you do?"

I realized I didn't know what Adrian did. We had only been out a handful of times, but there hadn't been many personal details exchanged. He sometimes asked questions about me. But usually, our conversation revolved around the place we were at, the food we were having, the weather... Thinking about it now, I knew nothing about Adrian. Shame washed over me. Was I so desperate to forget Matty that I'd become some kind of vapid party girl? "I'm a bartender," I finally admitted. "We met at the bar I work at."

Professor Dessai made a disagreeable sound in the back of his throat. "Of course, you are."

His tone was clearly haughty, clearly condescending. I wanted to crawl beneath a rock or run back home or do anything but stand here beneath his snobby judgment. But I refused to let this teacher look down on my job just because he was on the other end of school. Like he'd never worked a poorly paying scrub job just to make ends meet? "What do you do?" I demanded.

Dessai's gaze flicked back to Valeria, who was uncharacteristically quiet behind me. "I'm a professor," he said evenly. "At the college your friend attends."

I let my gaze flatten while I took in the charming entryway to his magnificent home. With all the boredom I could muster, I repeated, "Of course, you are."

His head cocked to the side, he hadn't expected me to fire back. Not that making a bazillion dollars as a tenured college professor was a bad gig. But, honestly, at this point it was a little much. The clothes. The look. The house. God, he was like a recipe for pretentious.

As if he'd had enough of me, he turned back to Adrian. "Why are you here, Lazotti?"

Adrian flashed a slimy grin. "We both know why I'm here, Eli. The board would like answers. You had until tonight to produce proof of… union."

Eli. Eli Dessai.

His name stuck in my head, settled there like it belonged. "Eli," I heard myself whisper. His gaze snapped to mine again, and he took a step forward wearing a dangerous scowl. Fear doused the fire within me, turning my insides cold with dread. Something was about to happen. But I didn't know what that something was, and it terrified me. Adrian tucked me closer to his side, half stepping in front of me and I knew my instincts were right.

I shouldn't have said his name out loud.

"We won't stay long!" I blurted. "Adrian promised to have us home early tonight." I forced my lips into an innocent smile. "School night and all."

"You're a student?"

I nodded.

"At Pinewood?"

I nodded again. Slower this time. Reluctantly.

"Have you taken one of my classes?"

This time I shook my head. "N-no."

"We're both sophomores," Valeria explained. "Willow just declared her major."

He raised an eyebrow, waiting. "Journalism," I told him.

Valeria's shoulder pressed into mine and she added, "With a minor in creative writing."

I expected him to say something rude again, but he looked curious instead. "I'm surprised I haven't seen you then. For one of my classes."

"I have poetry this semester. And intro to nonfiction writing with Holken," I explained. "He worked better with my schedule." At his cold stare, I quickly added, "Even though I've heard you're the best."

"This is sweet," Adrian put in, clearly annoyed. "The school reunion and all. But we have business, Dessai."

Eli opened his mouth to speak, but a man stepped up behind him and whispered something to Jensen, who then relayed the message to Eli. His expression revealed his disappointment. When he finally spoke again, it was to Adrian, not to me. "Enjoy the party then." His gaze flicked to mine for just a moment, so brief I wouldn't have noticed if I hadn't been staring at him so intently. Then he vanished inside the massive house.

And I was left to catch my breath and thank the scheduling powers at be that Dessai's class had interfered with my one required math credit.

Made in the USA
Coppell, TX
12 November 2022